JULIUS ZEBRA

JOKE BOOK JAMBOREE!

by

GARY NORTHFIELD

WALKER BOOKS

For my mum, whose jokes
were worse than mine.

This is a work of fiction. Names, characters, places and incidents are either the product of the author's imagination or, if real, used fictitiously. All statements, activities, stunts, descriptions, information and material of any other kind contained herein are included for entertainment purposes only and should not be relied on for accuracy or replicated as they may result in injury.

First published in Great Britain 2019 by Walker Books Ltd
87 Vauxhall Walk, London SE11 5HJ

2 4 6 8 10 9 7 5 3 1

This book has been typeset in Stempel Schneidler

Printed and bound in Great Britain by CPI Group (UK) Ltd, Croydon CR0 4YY

British Library Cataloguing in Publication Data:
a catalogue record for this book is available from the British Library

ISBN 978-1-4063-8827-5

www.walker.co.uk

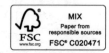

MIX
Paper from responsible sources
FSC® C020471

JULIUS ZEBRA
JOKE BOOK
JAMBOREE!

What do you call a royal giraffe?

Your royal high-ness!

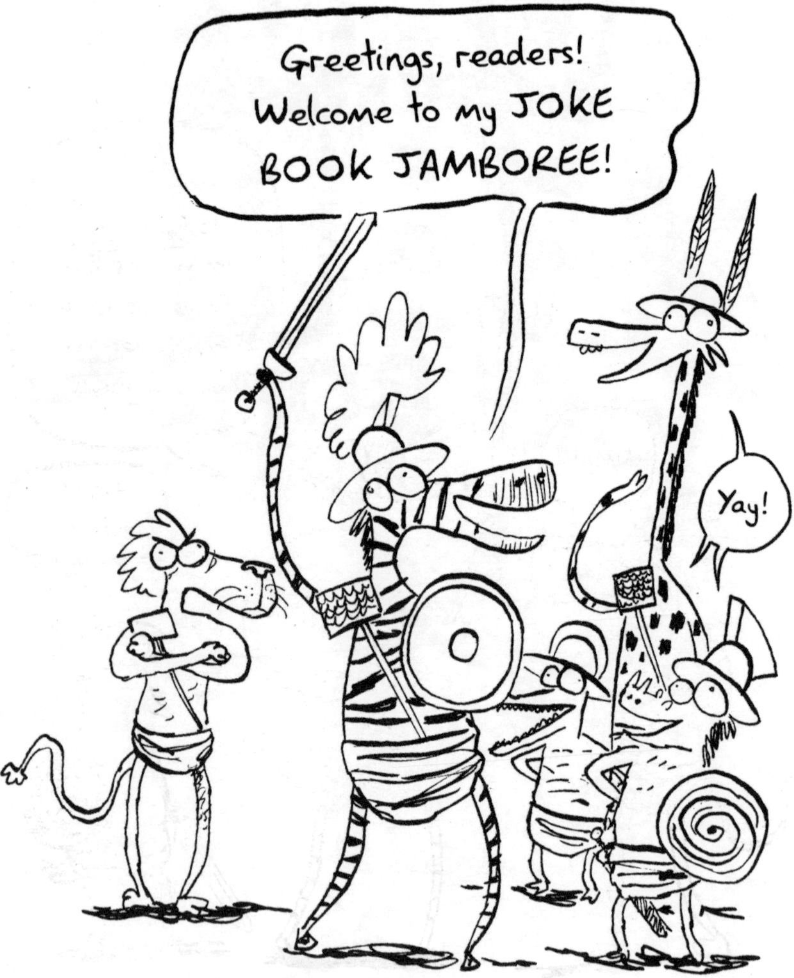
Greetings, readers! Welcome to my JOKE BOOK JAMBOREE!
Yay!

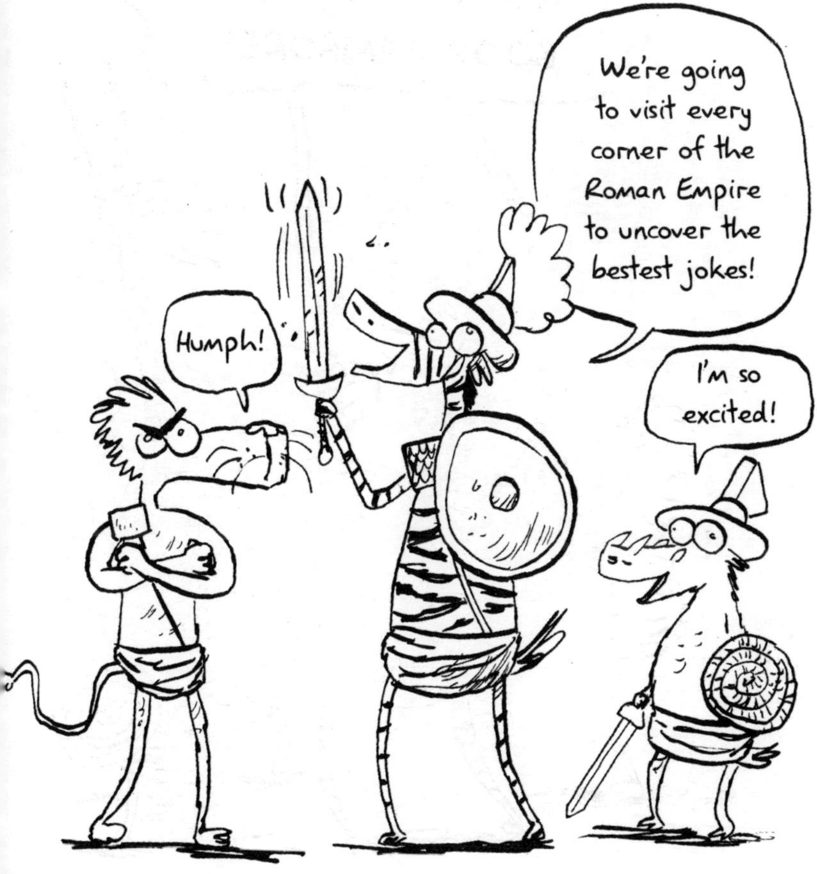
We're going to visit every corner of the Roman Empire to uncover the bestest jokes!
Humph!
I'm so excited!

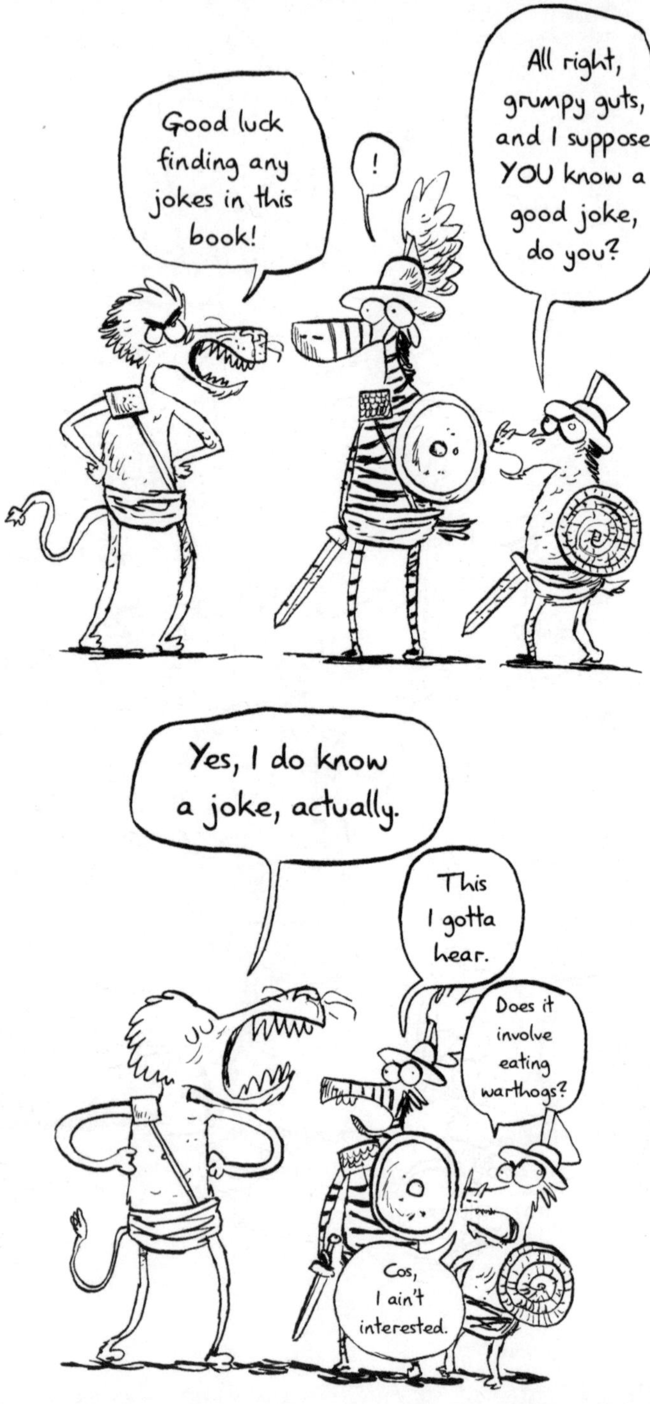
Good luck finding any jokes in this book!
!
All right, grumpy guts, and I suppose YOU know a good joke, do you?
Yes, I do know a joke, actually.
This I gotta hear.
Does it involve eating warthogs?
Cos, I ain't interested.

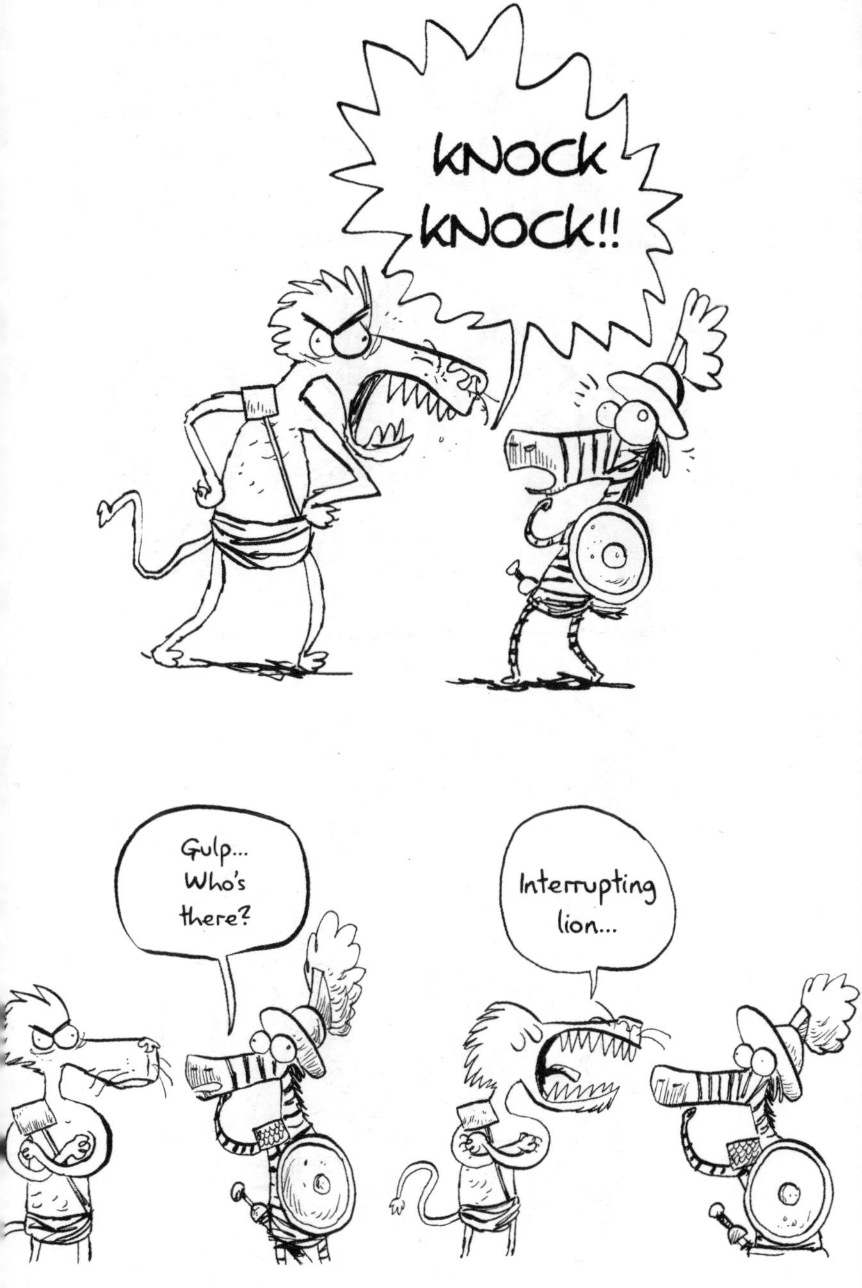
KNOCK KNOCK!!
Gulp... Who's there?
Interrupting lion...

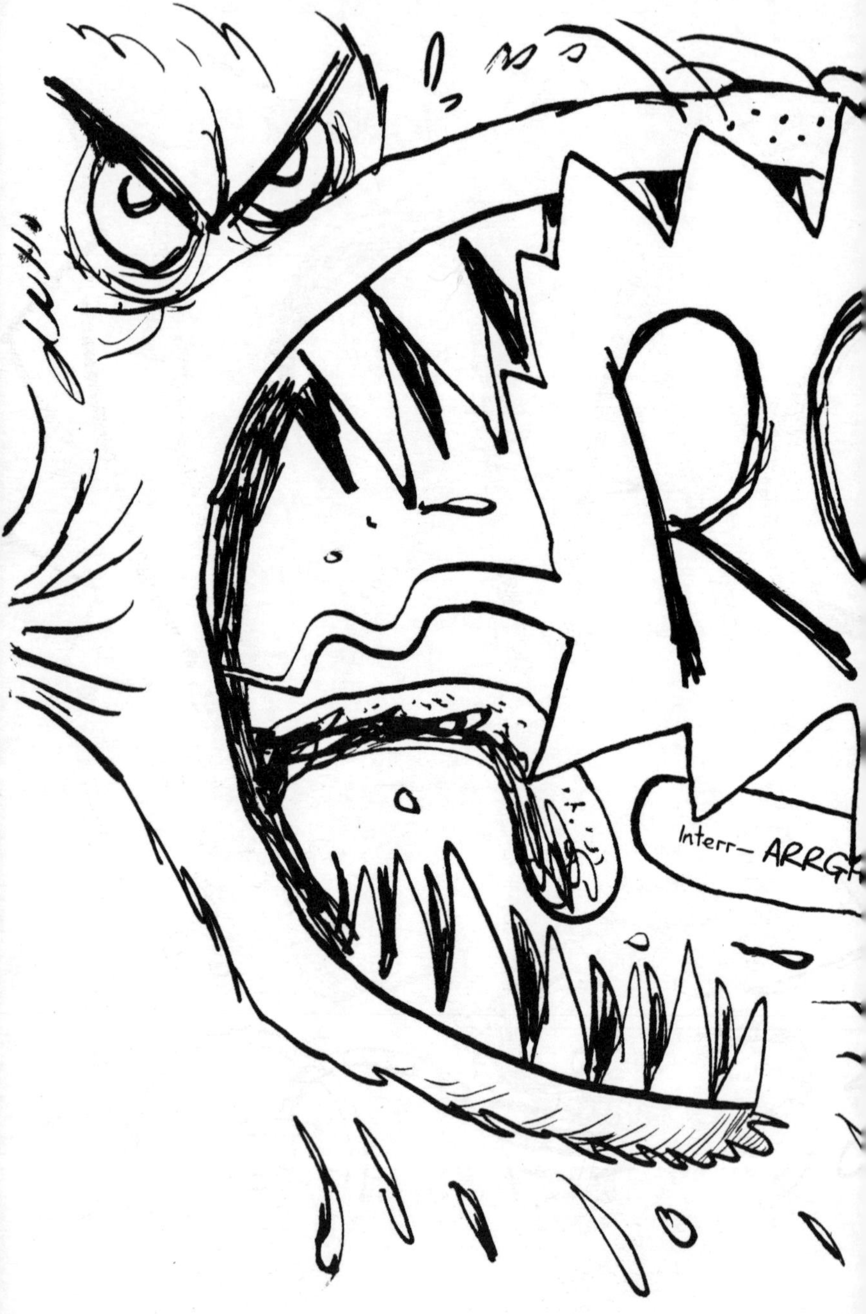
Interr– ARRG

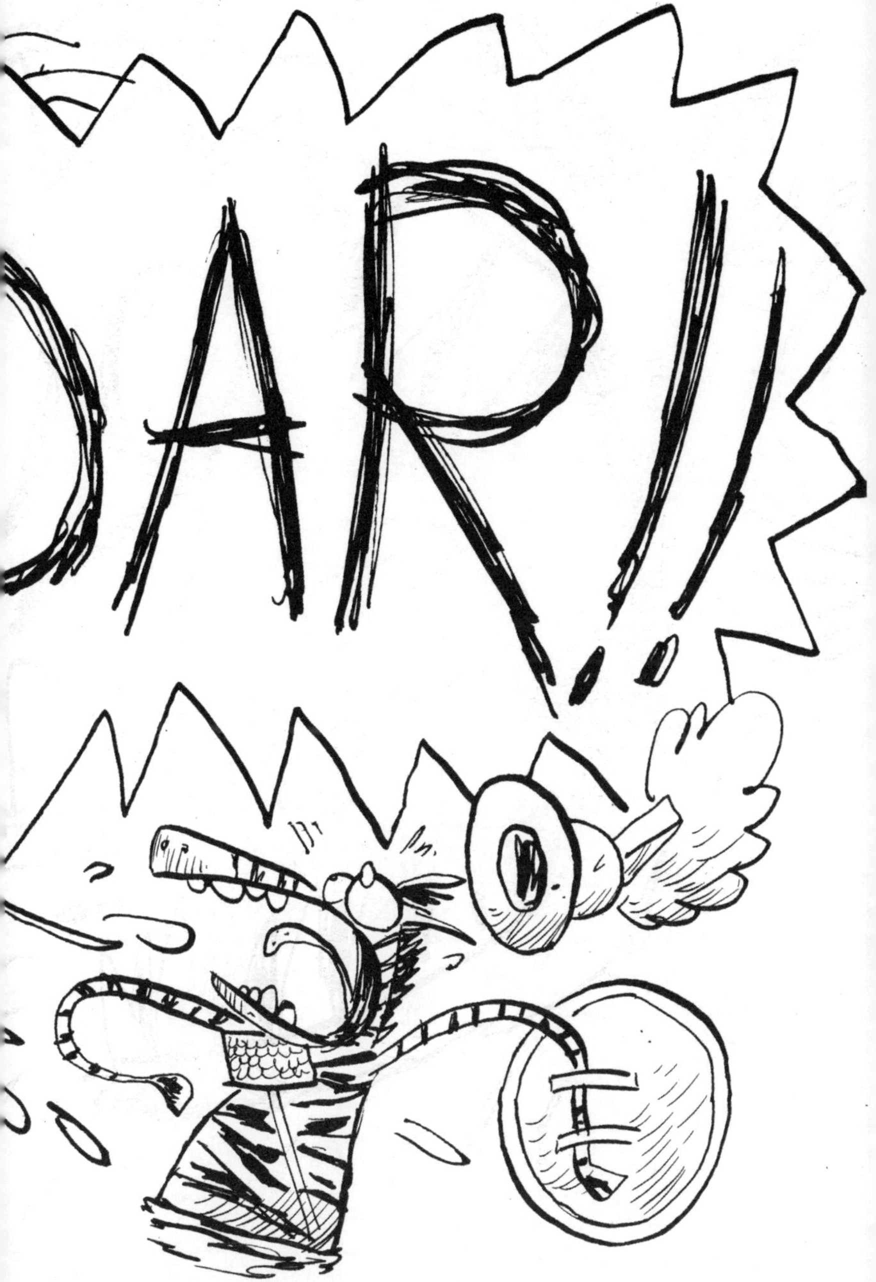

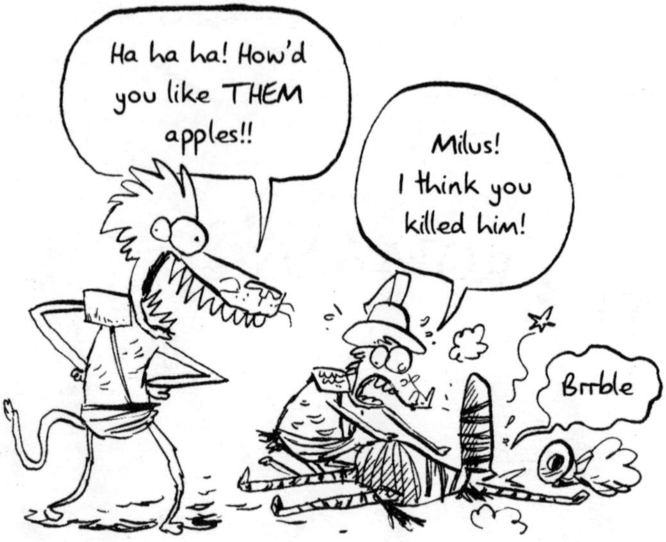
Ha ha ha! How'd you like THEM apples!!
Milus! I think you killed him!
Brrble

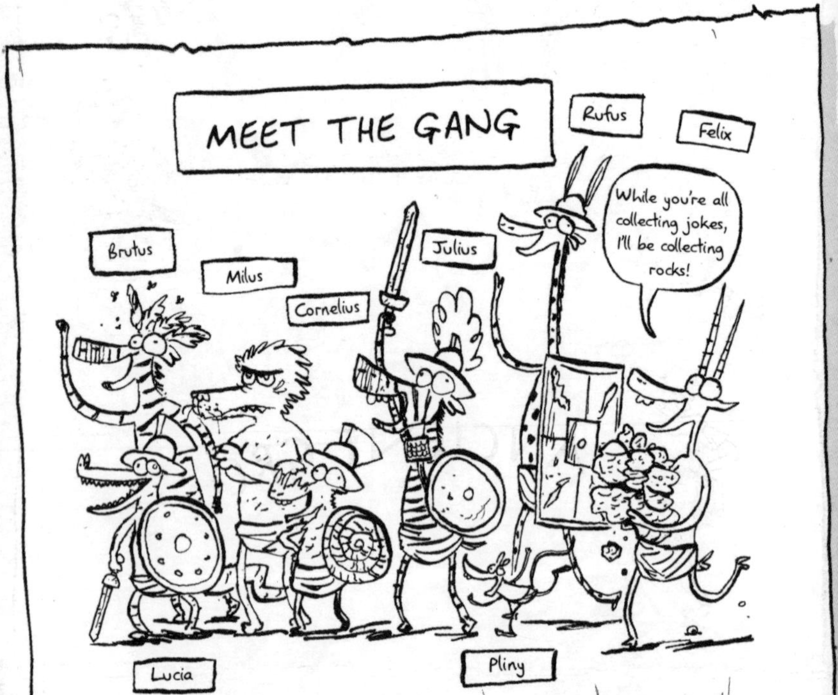
MEET THE GANG
Rufus
Felix
While you're all collecting jokes, I'll be collecting rocks!
Brutus
Milus
Julius
Cornelius
Lucia
Pliny

CONTENTS

PART I
THE ROMANS

PART II
ANCIENT BRITONS

SLURP!

PART III
ANCIENT EGYPTIANS

PART IV
ANCIENT GREEKS

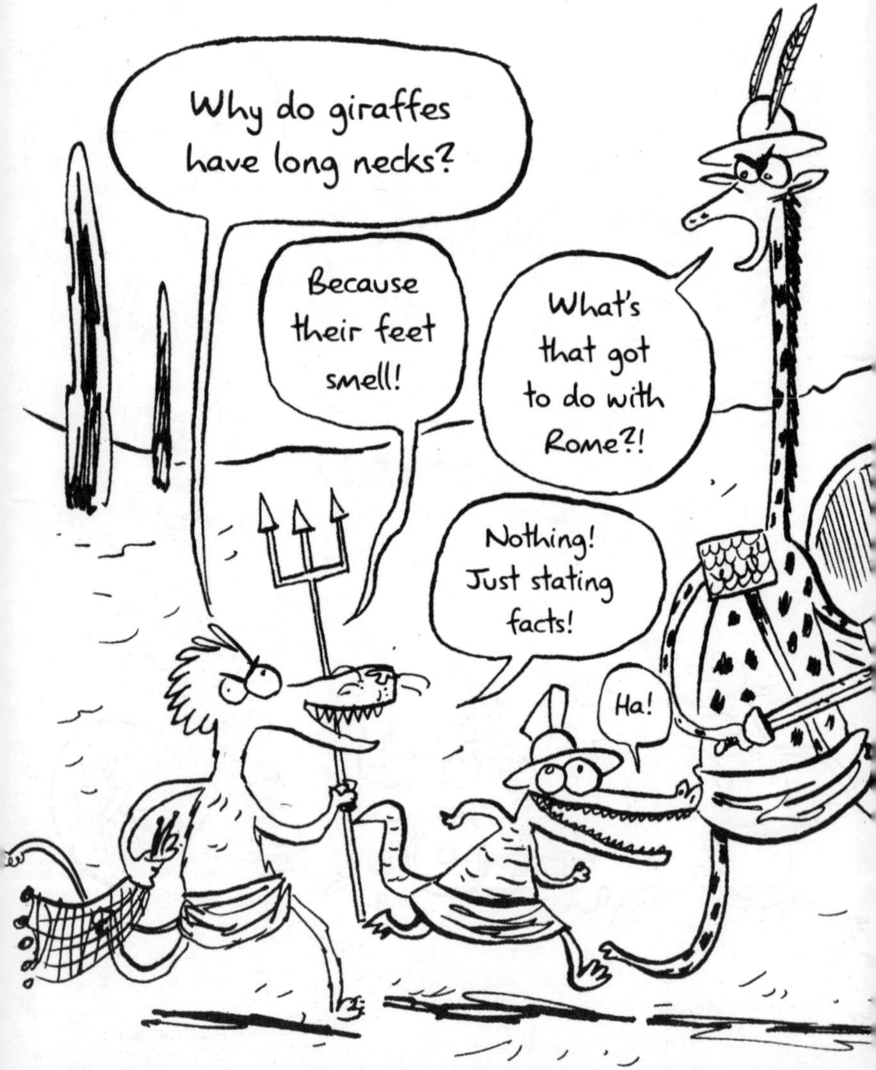
Why do giraffes have long necks?
Because their feet smell!
What's that got to do with Rome?!
Nothing! Just stating facts!
Ha!

PART I
THE ROMANS

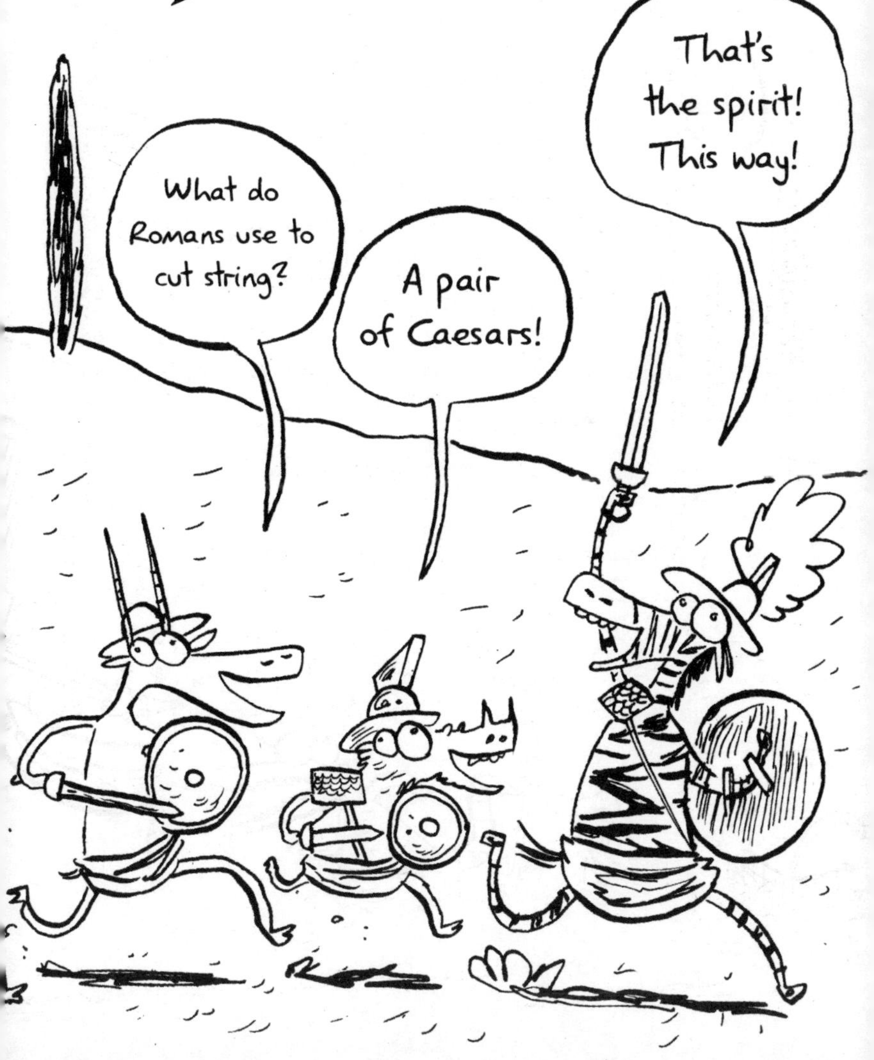
What do Romans use to cut string?
A pair of Caesars!
That's the spirit! This way!

MEET THE ROMANS

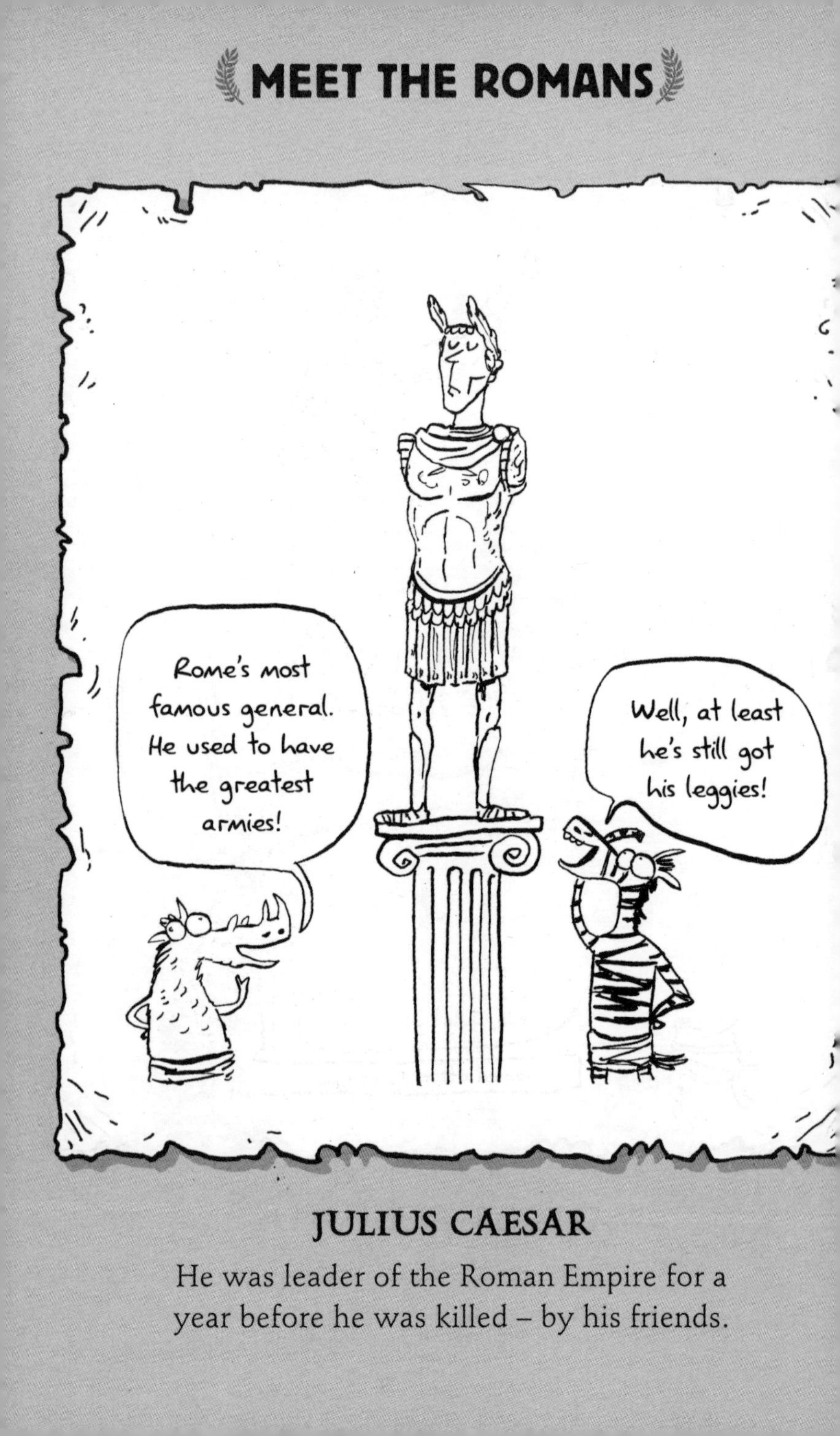
Rome's most famous general. He used to have the greatest armies!
Well, at least he's still got his leggies!

JULIUS CAESAR

He was leader of the Roman Empire for a year before he was killed – by his friends.

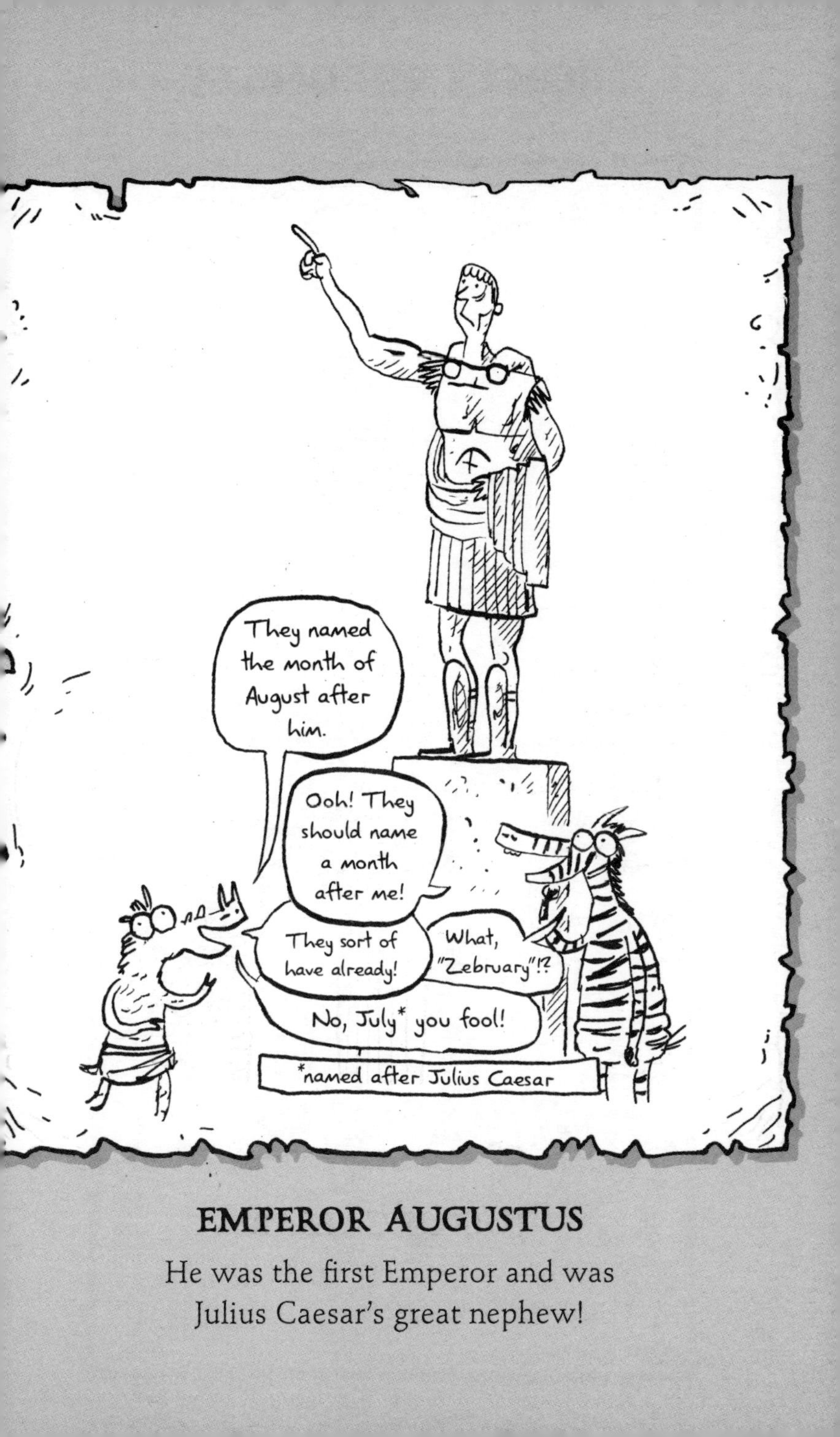
They named the month of August after him.
Ooh! They should name a month after me!
They sort of have already!
What, "Zebruary"!?
No, July* you fool!
*named after Julius Caesar

EMPEROR AUGUSTUS

He was the first Emperor and was Julius Caesar's great nephew!

ROMAN RIB TICKLER

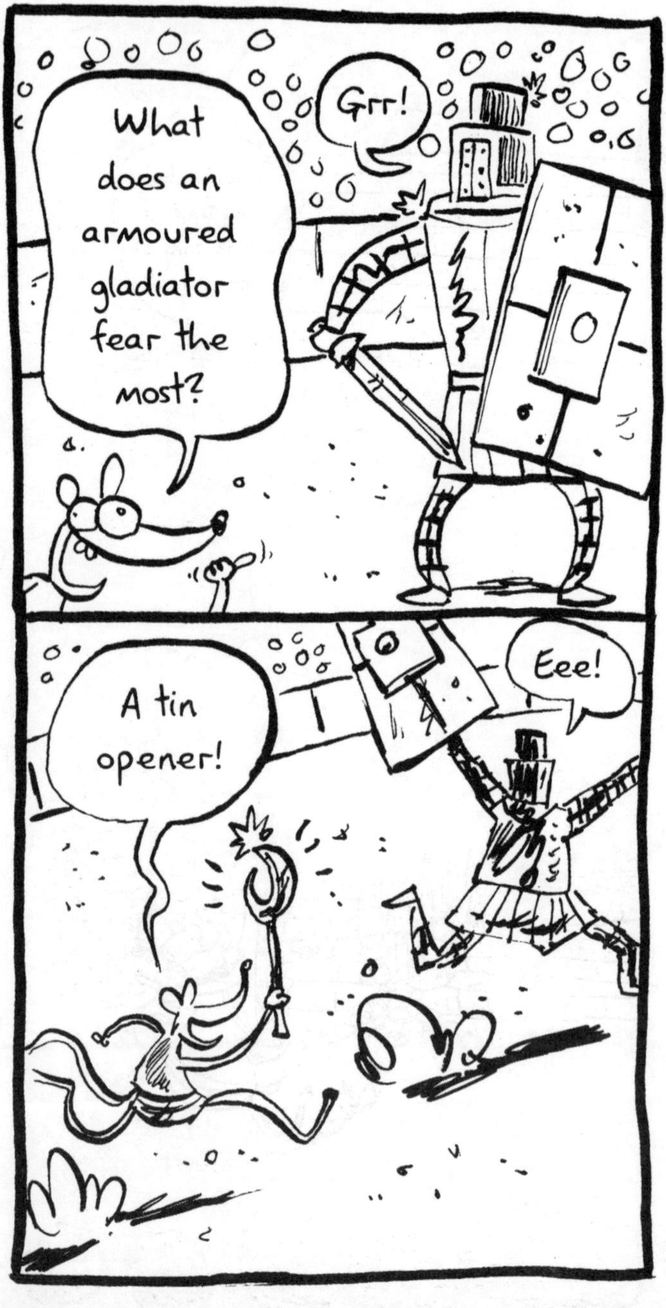

What does an armoured gladiator fear the most?
Grr!
A tin opener!
Eee!

FELIX'S ROCK COLLECTION

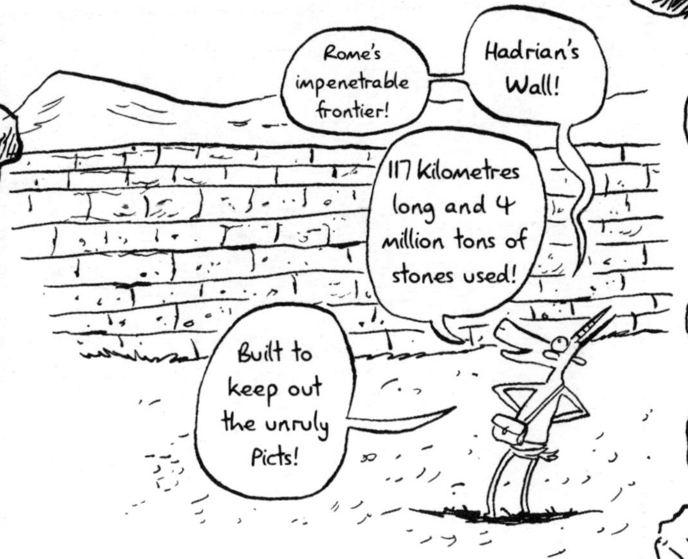
Hadrian's Wall!
Rome's impenetrable frontier!
117 Kilometres long and 4 million tons of stones used!
Built to keep out the unruly Picts!

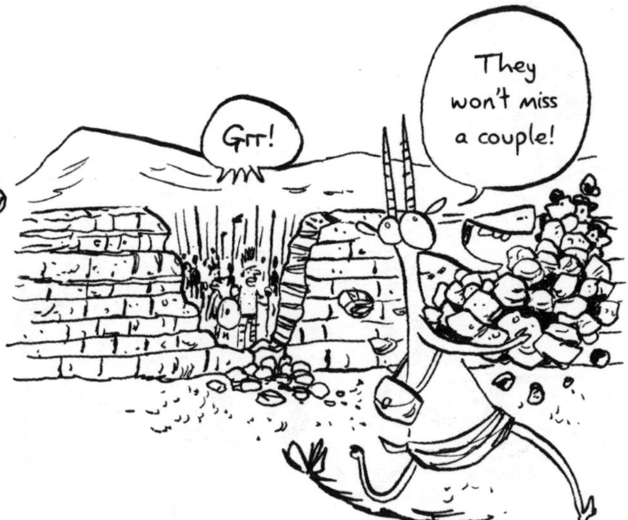
Grr!
They won't miss a couple!

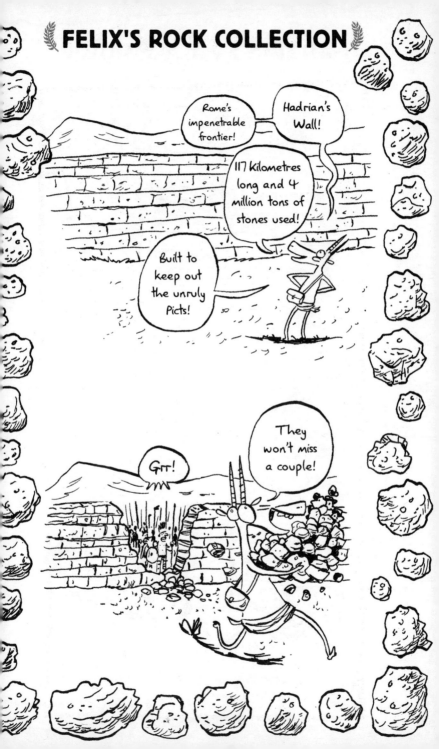

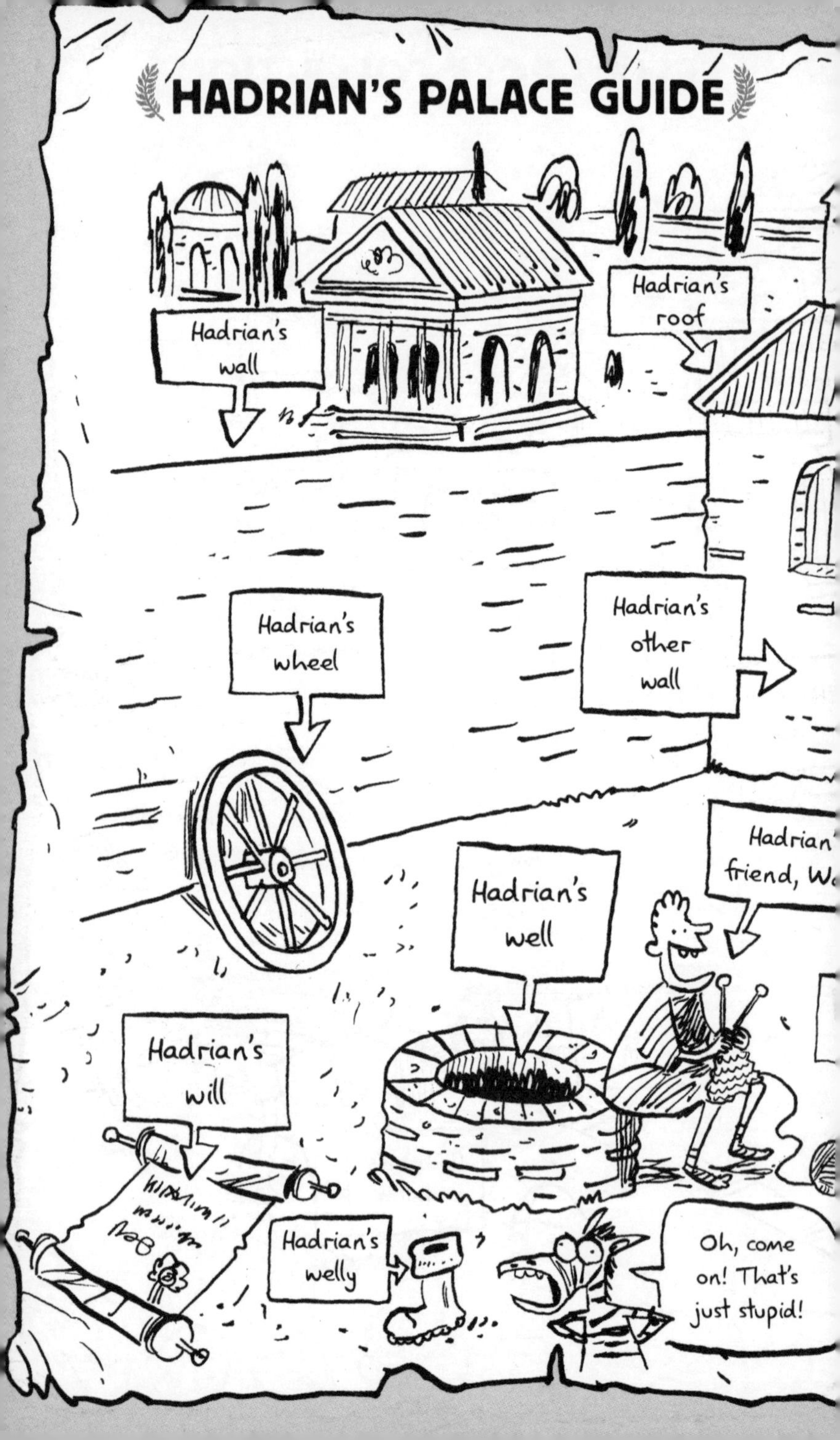
HADRIAN'S PALACE GUIDE
Hadrian's wall
Hadrian's roof
Hadrian's wheel
Hadrian's other wall
Hadrian's well
Hadrian's will
Hadrian's welly
Oh, come on! That's just stupid!

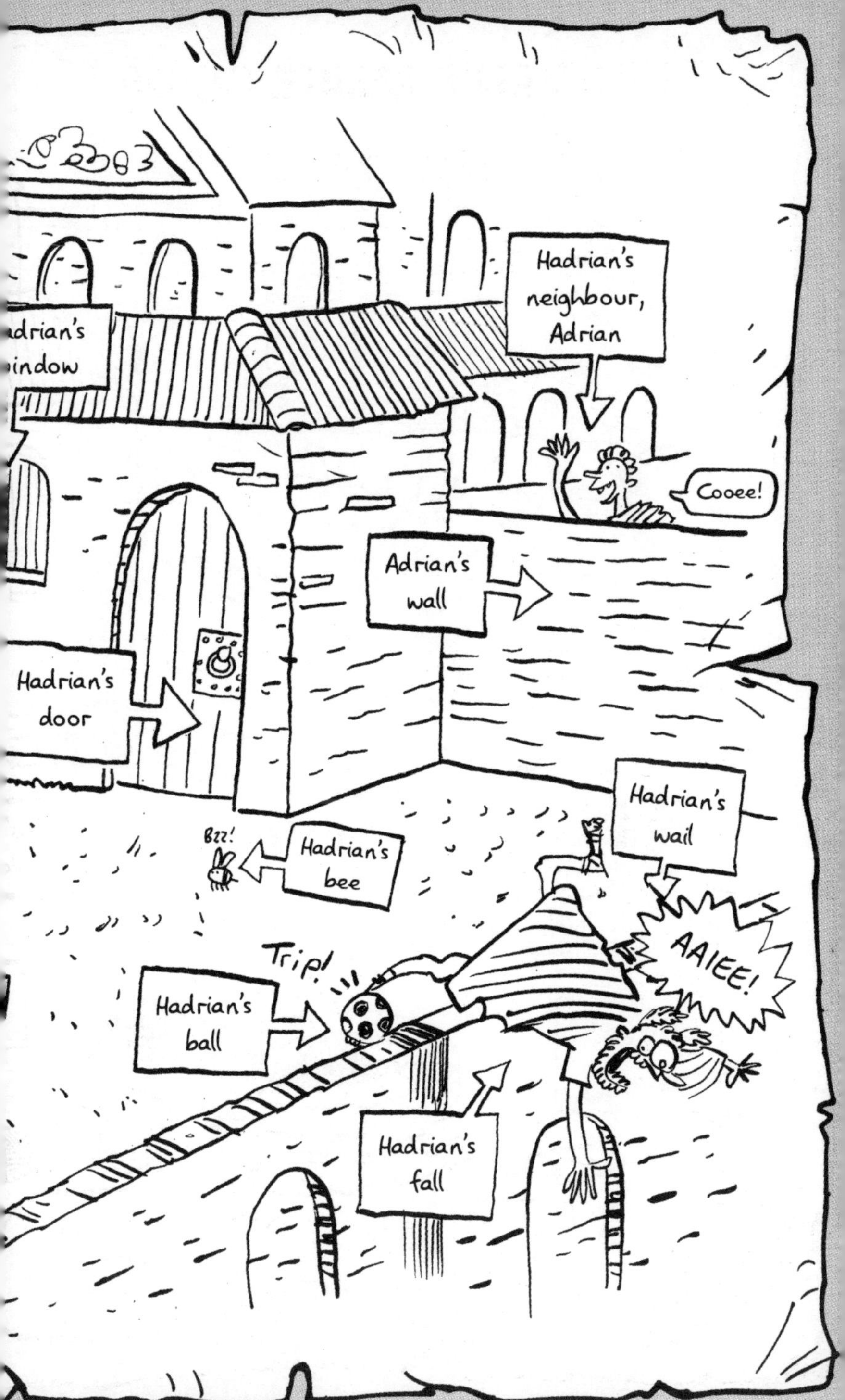

adrian's
window
Hadrian's
neighbour,
Adrian
Cooee!
Adrian's
wall
Hadrian's
door
Hadrian's
wail
Bzz!
Hadrian's
bee
AAIEE!
Trip!
Hadrian's
ball
Hadrian's
fall

LAVA LAUGHS

DID YOU KNOW THAT POMPEII IS FAMOUS FOR ITS GRAFFITI? CHECK OUT THESE RECENTLY UNCOVERED SCRIBBLES.

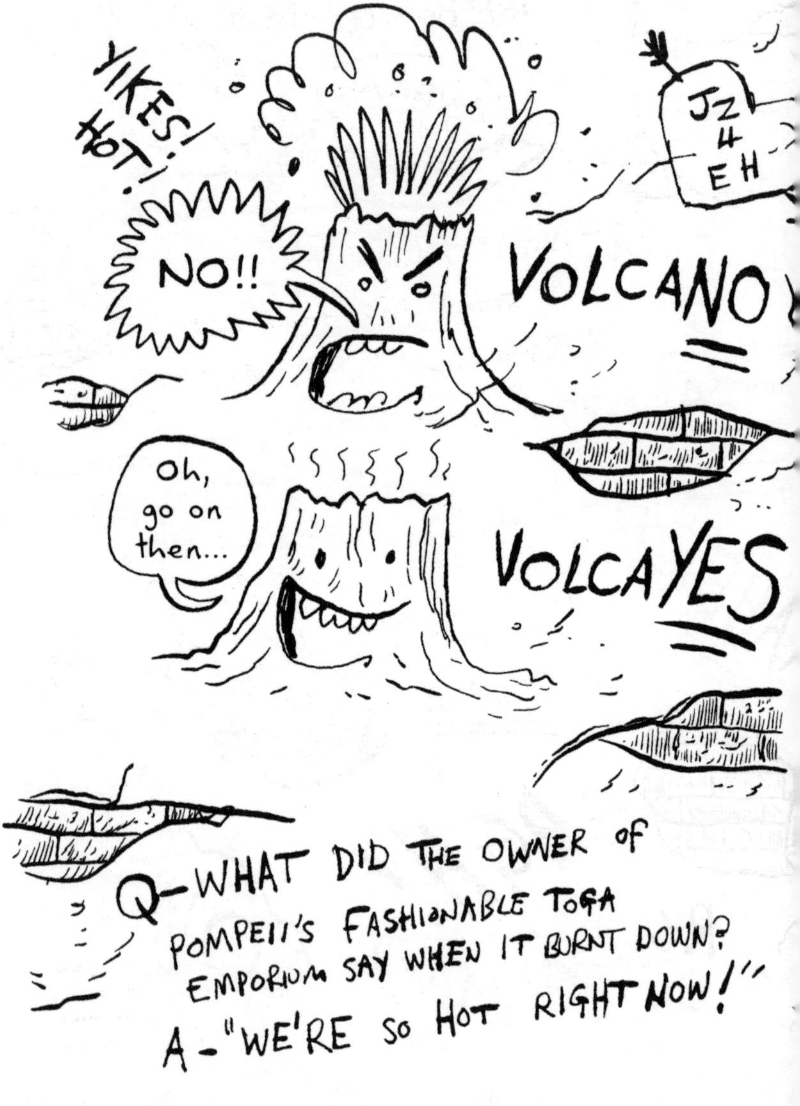

YIKES! HOT!
JZ 4 EH
NO!!
VOLCANO
Oh, go on then...
VOLCAYES
Q-WHAT DID THE OWNER OF POMPEII'S FASHIONABLE TOGA EMPORIUM SAY WHEN IT BURNT DOWN?
A-"WE'RE SO HOT RIGHT NOW!"

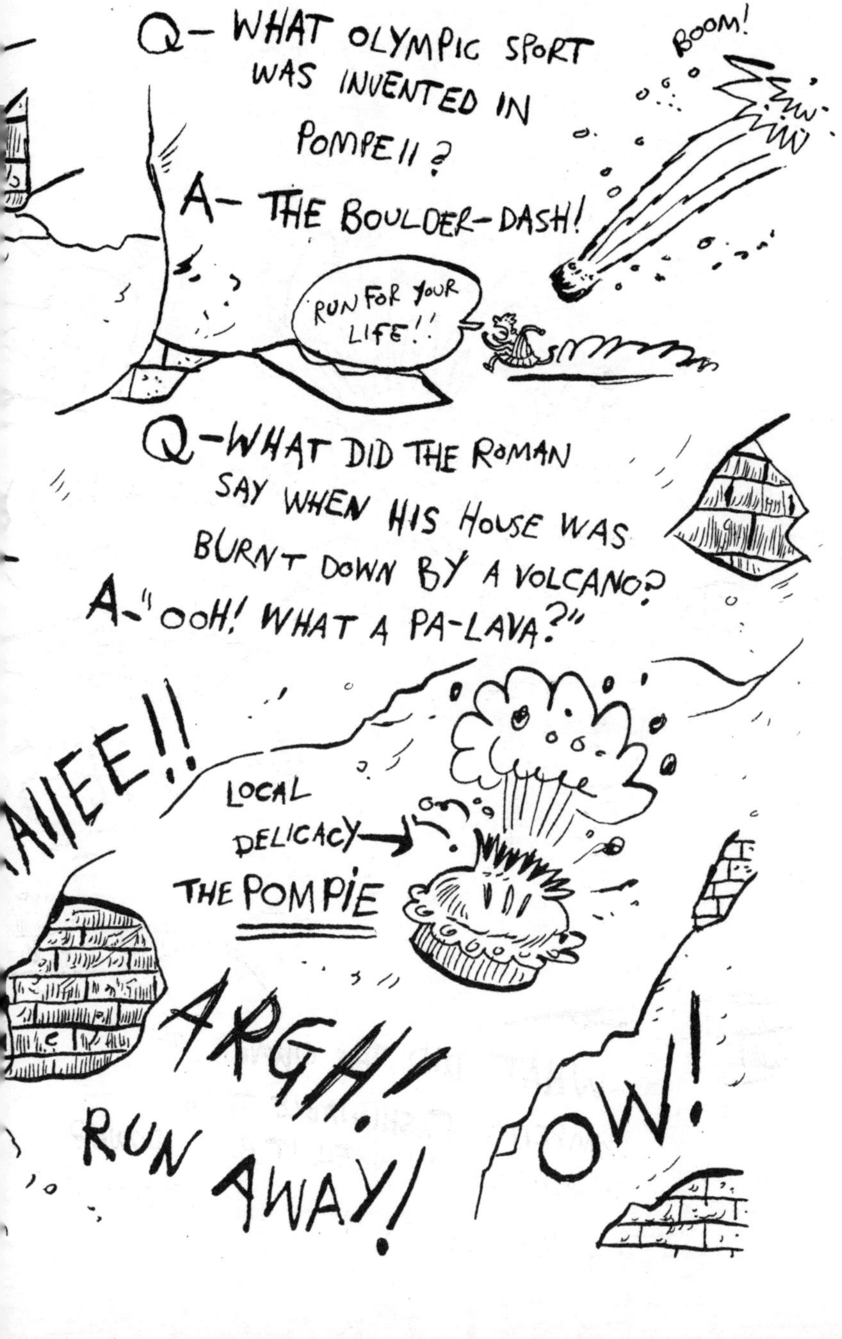
Q- WHAT OLYMPIC SPORT WAS INVENTED IN POMPEII?
A- THE BOULDER-DASH!
BOOM!
RUN FOR YOUR LIFE!!
Q-WHAT DID THE ROMAN SAY WHEN HIS HOUSE WAS BURNT DOWN BY A VOLCANO?
A- "OOH! WHAT A PA-LAVA?"
AIIEE!!
LOCAL DELICACY
THE POMPIE
ARGH!
RUN AWAY!
OW!

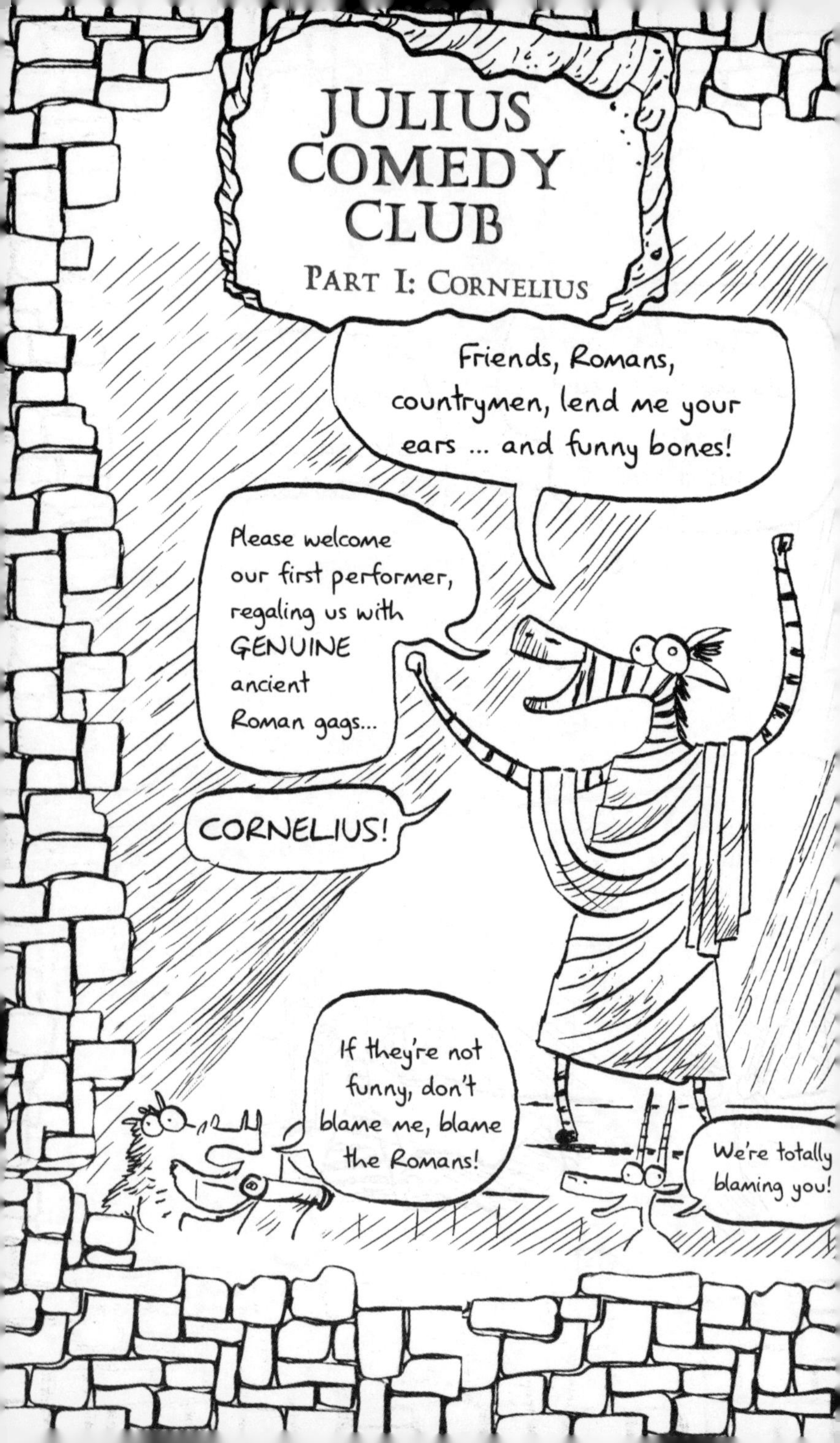
JULIUS COMEDY CLUB
PART I: CORNELIUS
Friends, Romans, countrymen, lend me your ears ... and funny bones!
Please welcome our first performer, regaling us with GENUINE ancient Roman gags...
CORNELIUS!
If they're not funny, don't blame me, blame the Romans!
We're totally blaming you!

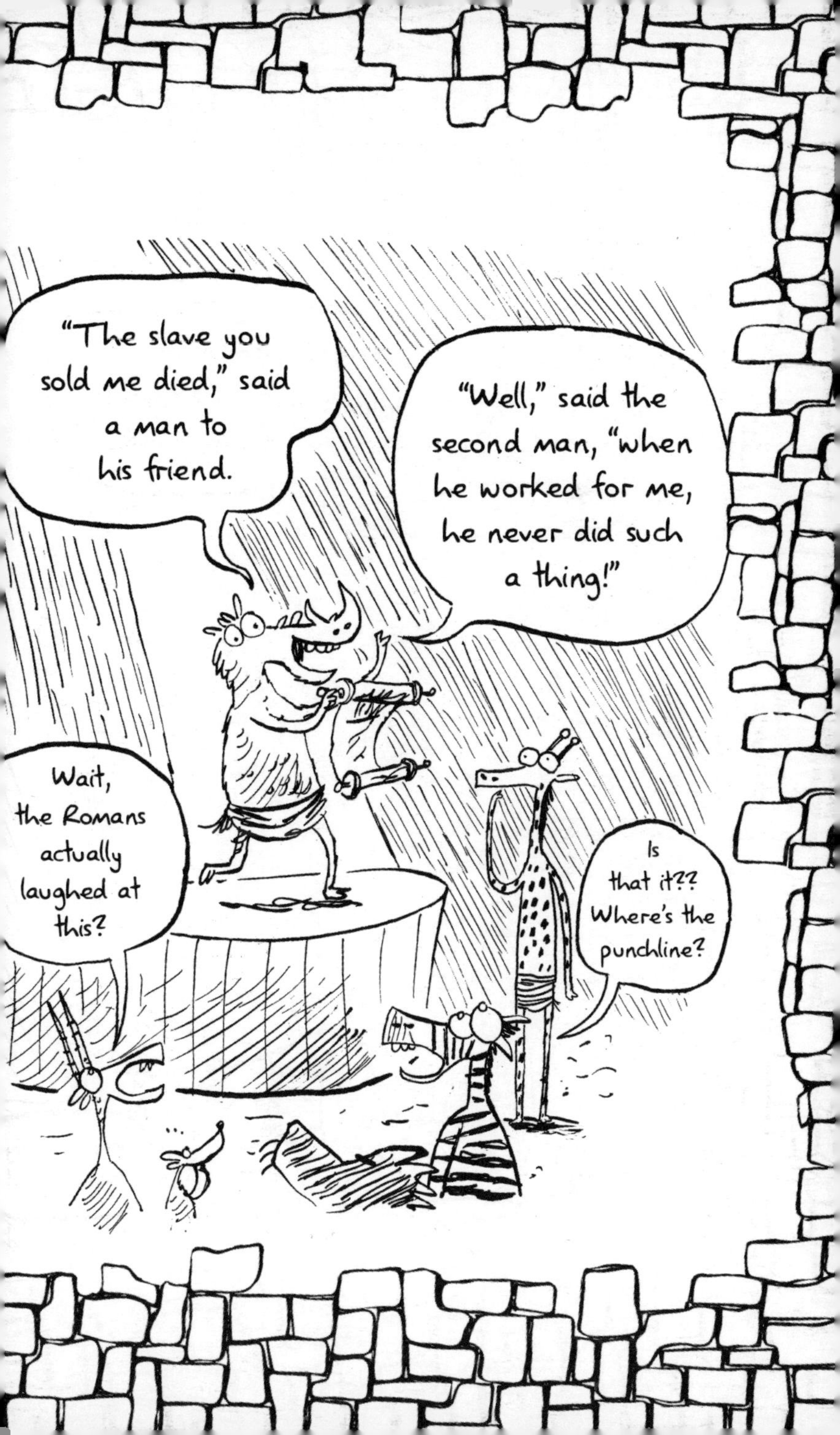
"The slave you sold me died," said a man to his friend.
"Well," said the second man, "when he worked for me, he never did such a thing!"
Wait, the Romans actually laughed at this?
Is that it?? Where's the punchline?

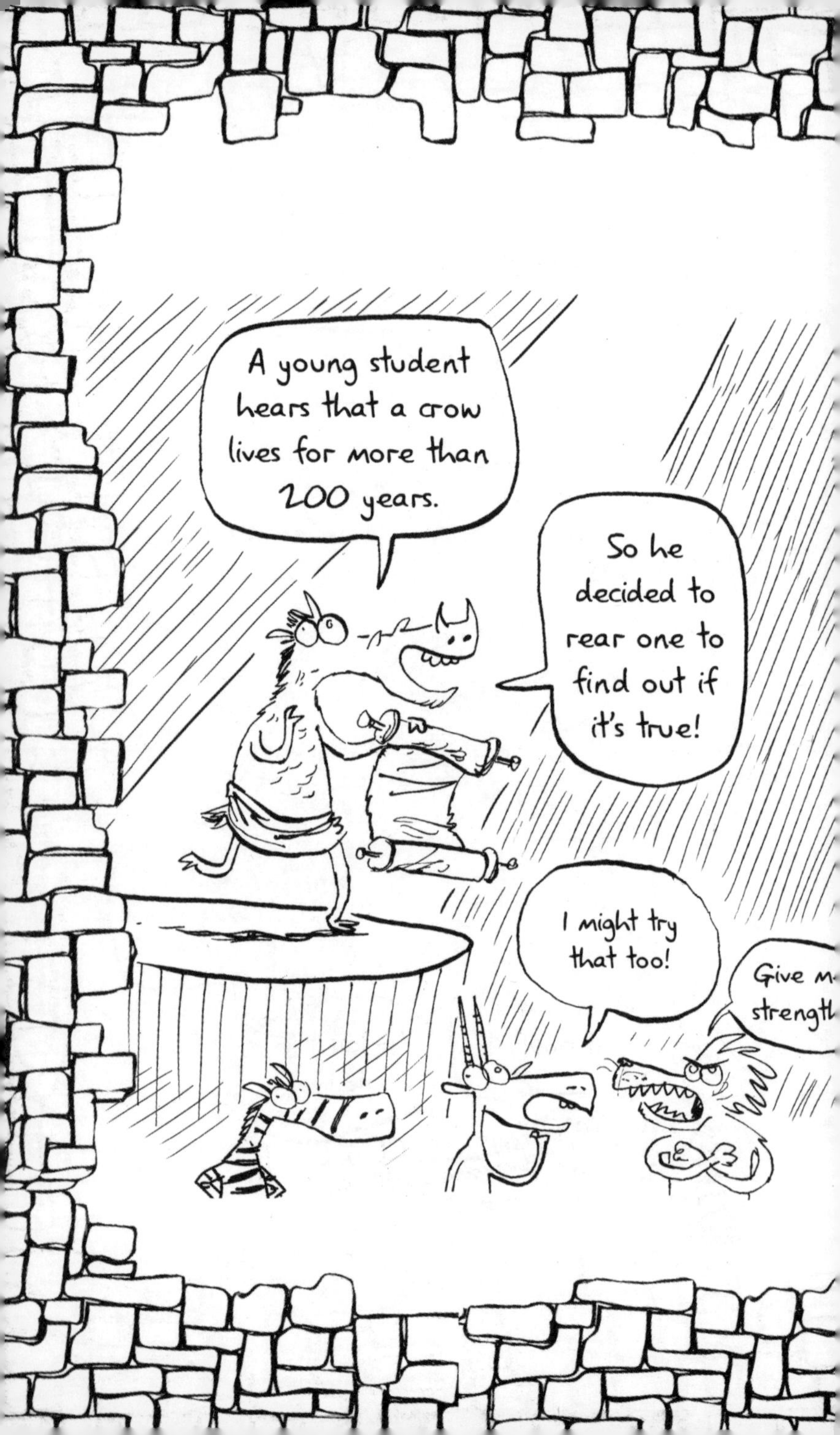
A young student hears that a crow lives for more than 200 years.
So he decided to rear one to find out if it's true!
I might try that too!
Give m
strength

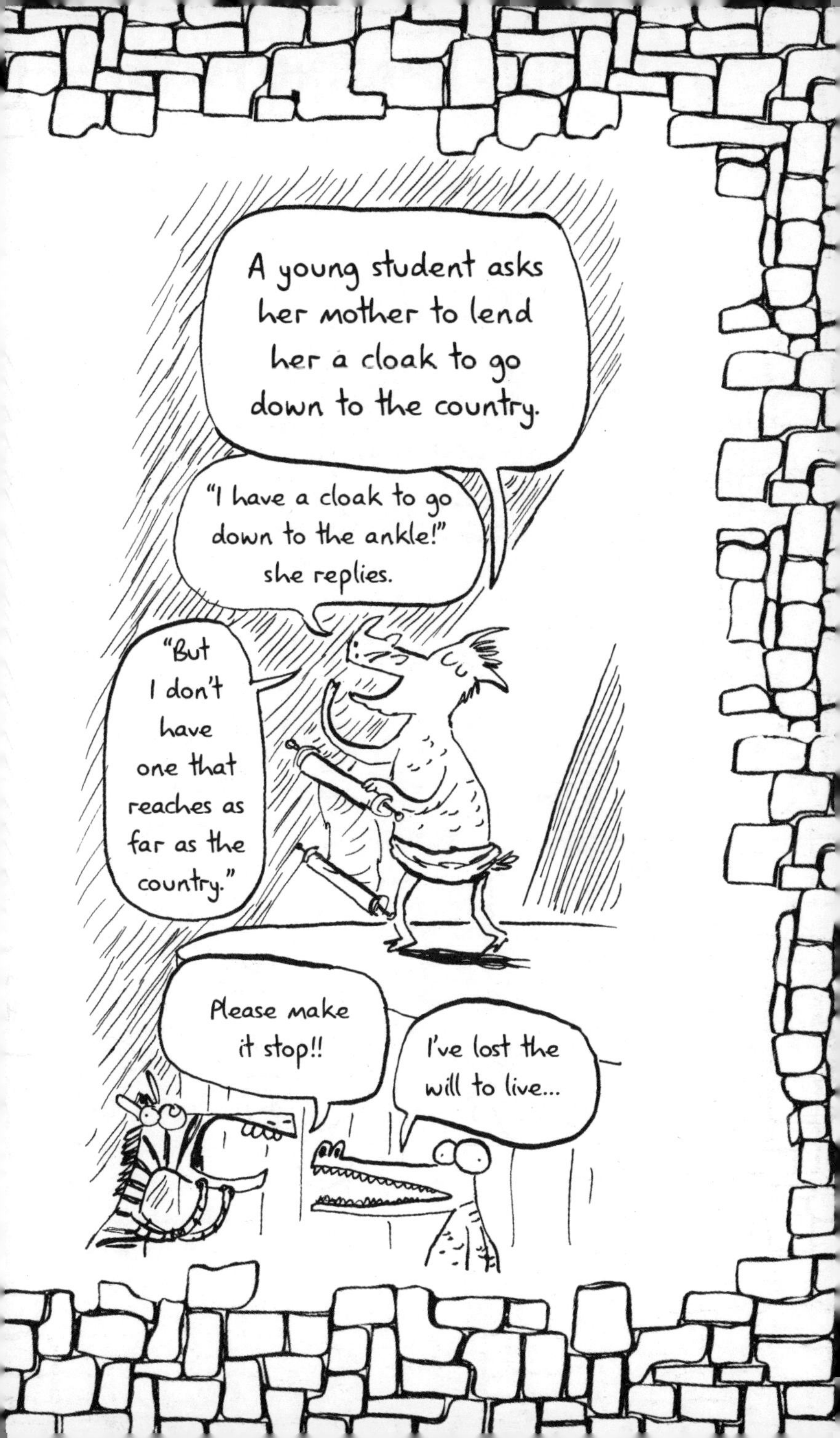
A young student asks her mother to lend her a cloak to go down to the country.
"I have a cloak to go down to the ankle!" she replies.
"But I don't have one that reaches as far as the country."
Please make it stop!!
I've lost the will to live...

JULIUS'S AMAZING FACTS

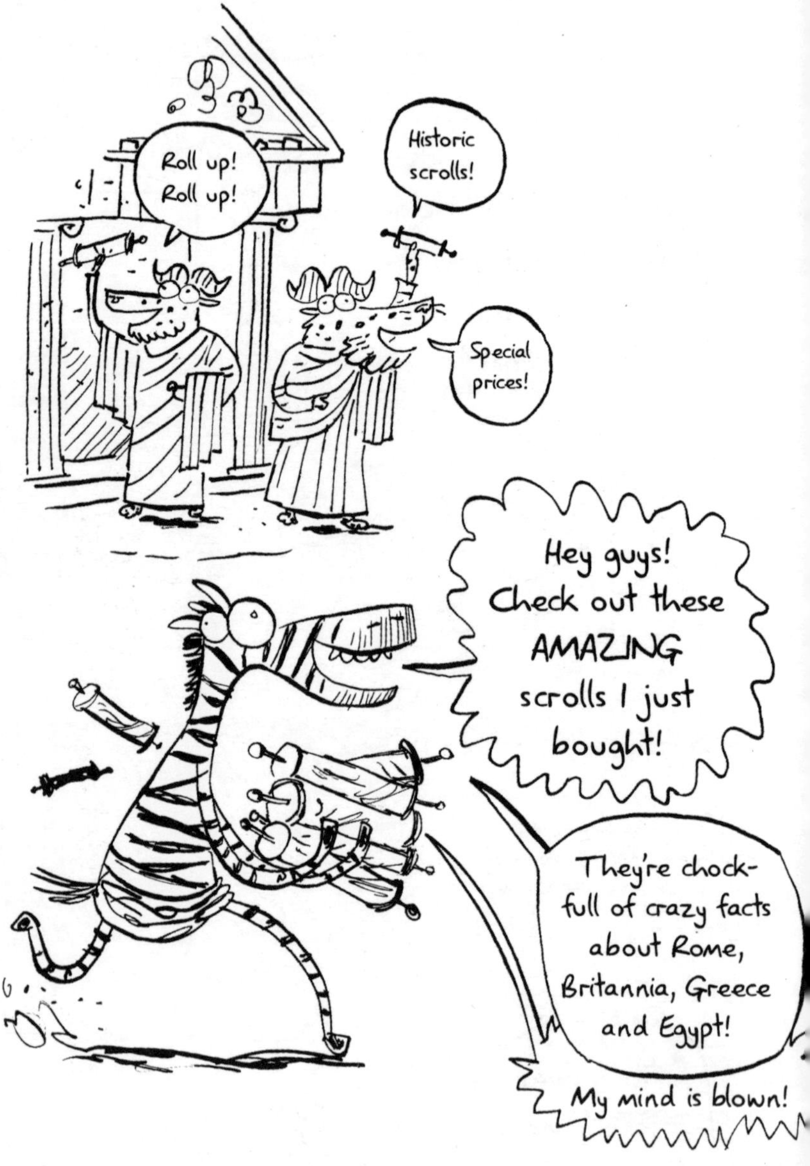
Roll up!
Roll up!
Historic scrolls!
Special prices!
Hey guys! Check out these AMAZING scrolls I just bought!
They're chock-full of crazy facts about Rome, Britannia, Greece and Egypt!
My mind is blown!

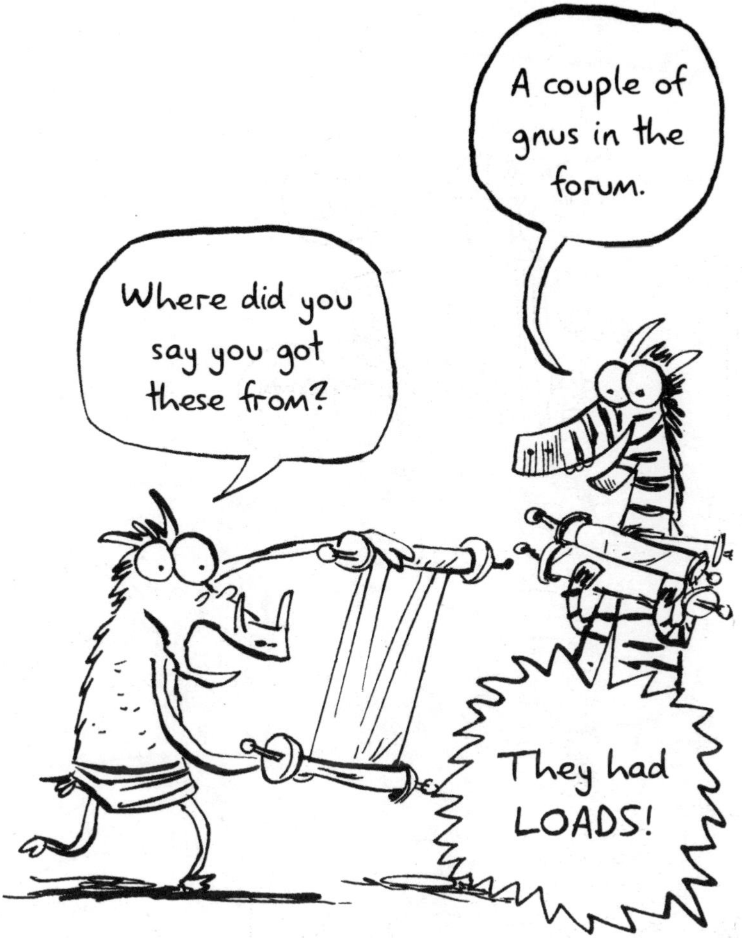
Where did you say you got these from?
A couple of gnus in the forum.
They had LOADS!

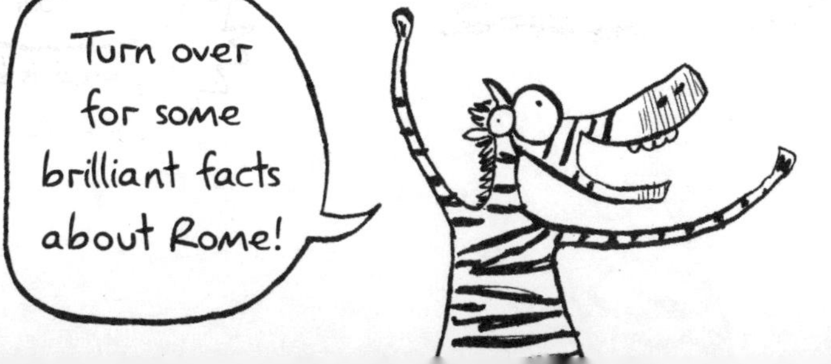
Turn over for some brilliant facts about Rome!

JULIUS'S AMAZING FACTS

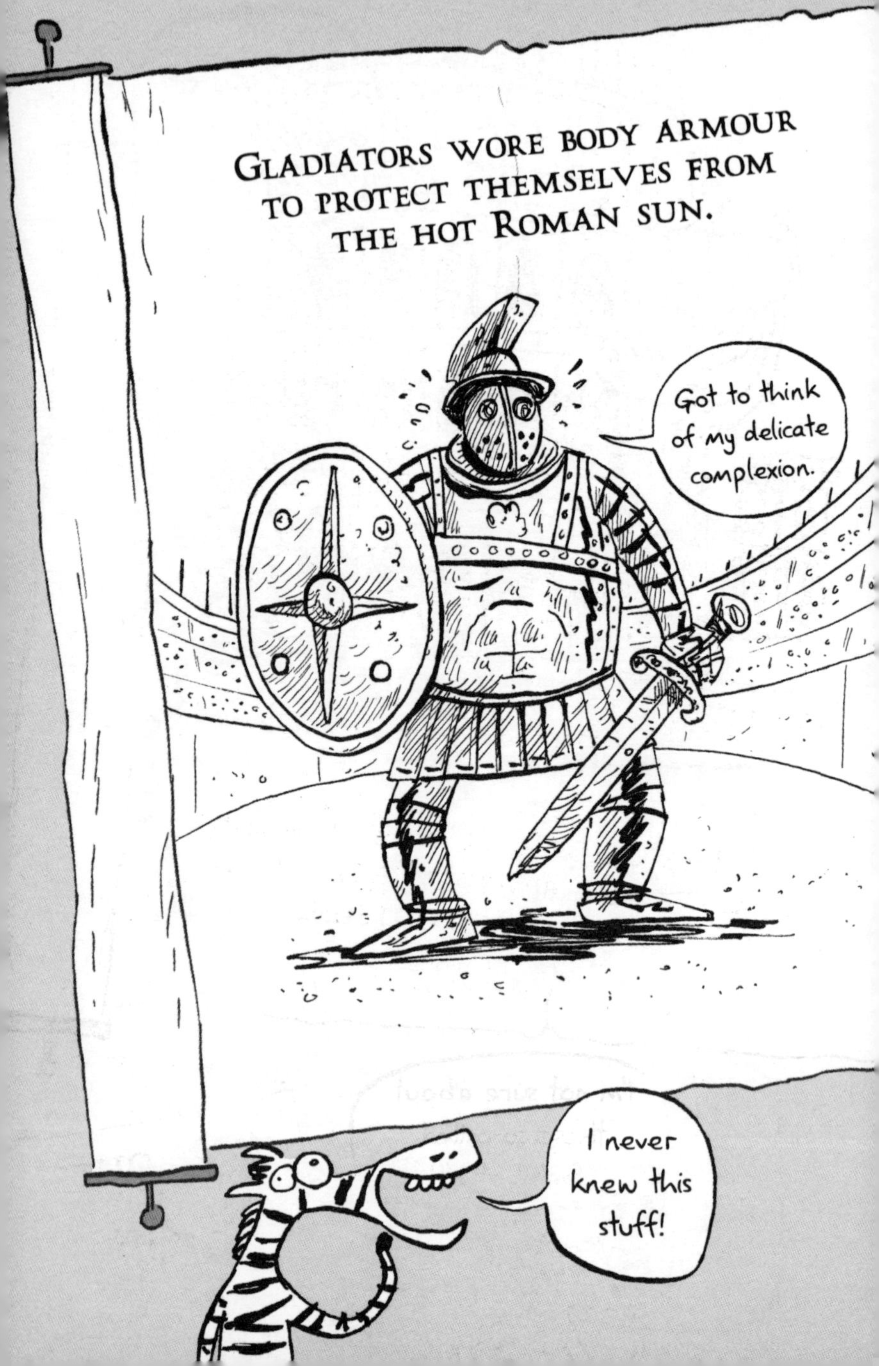
GLADIATORS WORE BODY ARMOUR TO PROTECT THEMSELVES FROM THE HOT ROMAN SUN.
Got to think of my delicate complexion.
I never knew this stuff!

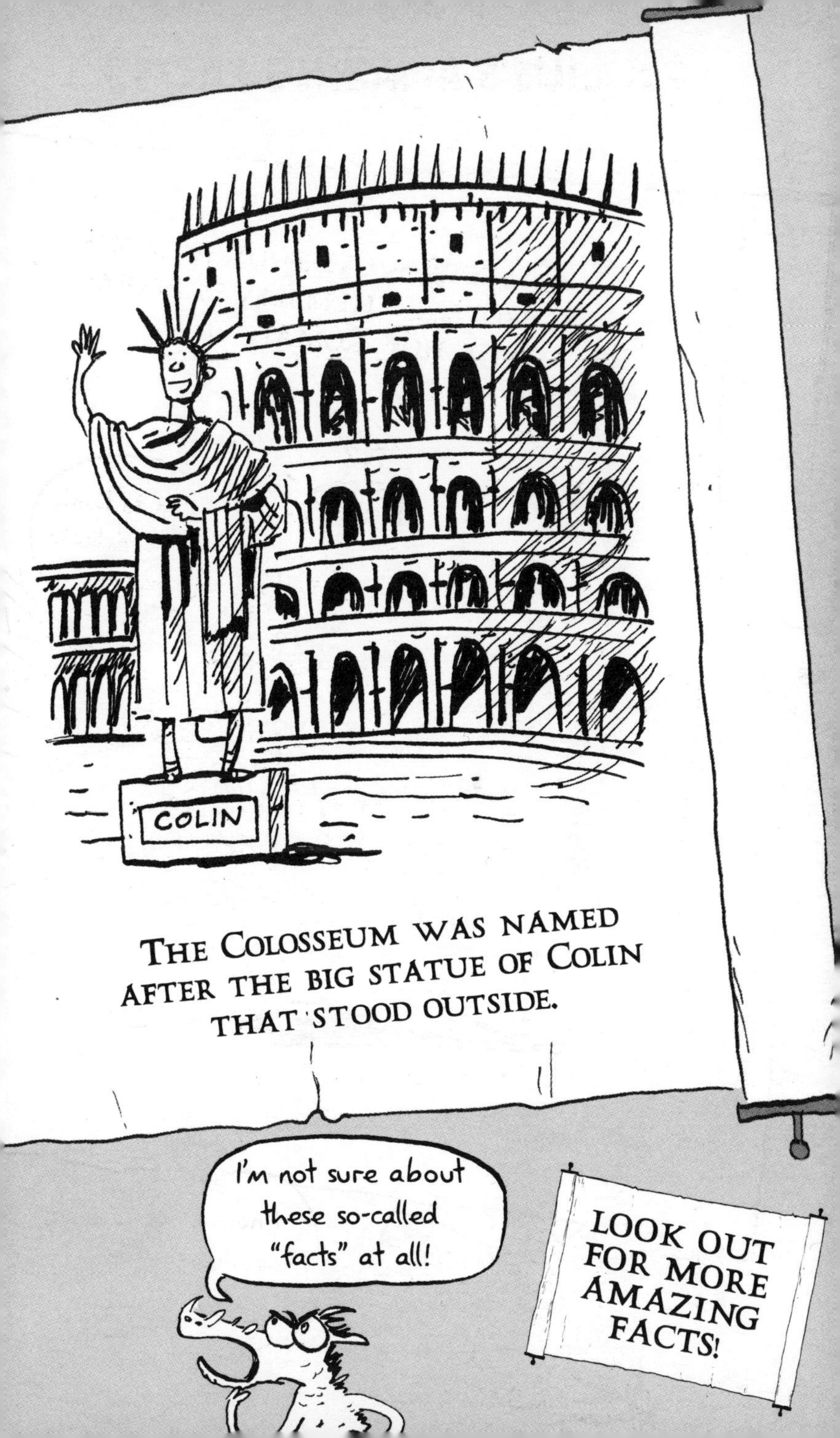
COLIN
THE COLOSSEUM WAS NAMED AFTER THE BIG STATUE OF COLIN THAT STOOD OUTSIDE.
I'm not sure about these so-called "facts" at all!
LOOK OUT FOR MORE AMAZING FACTS!

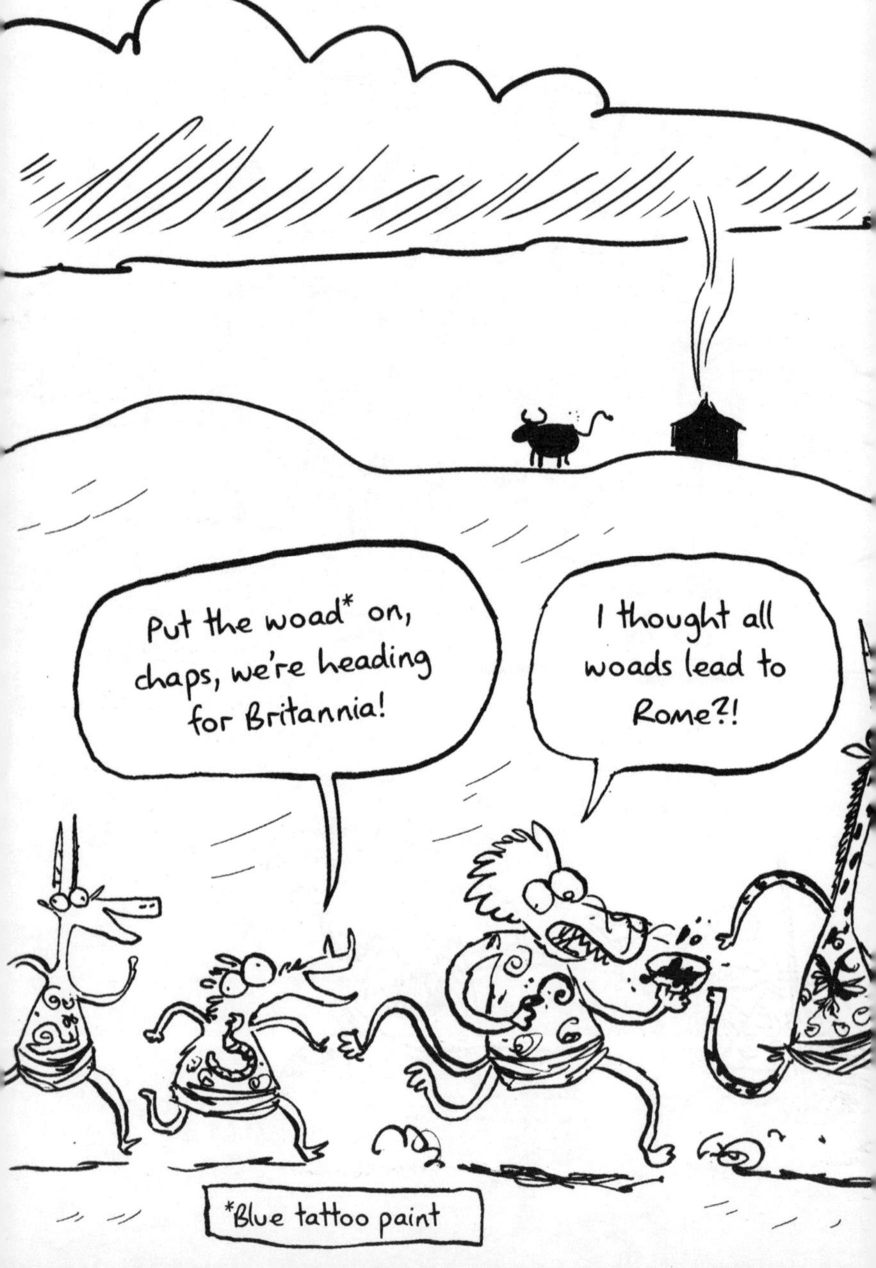
Put the woad* on, chaps, we're heading for Britannia!
I thought all woads lead to Rome?!
*Blue tattoo paint

PART II
ANCIENT BRITONS

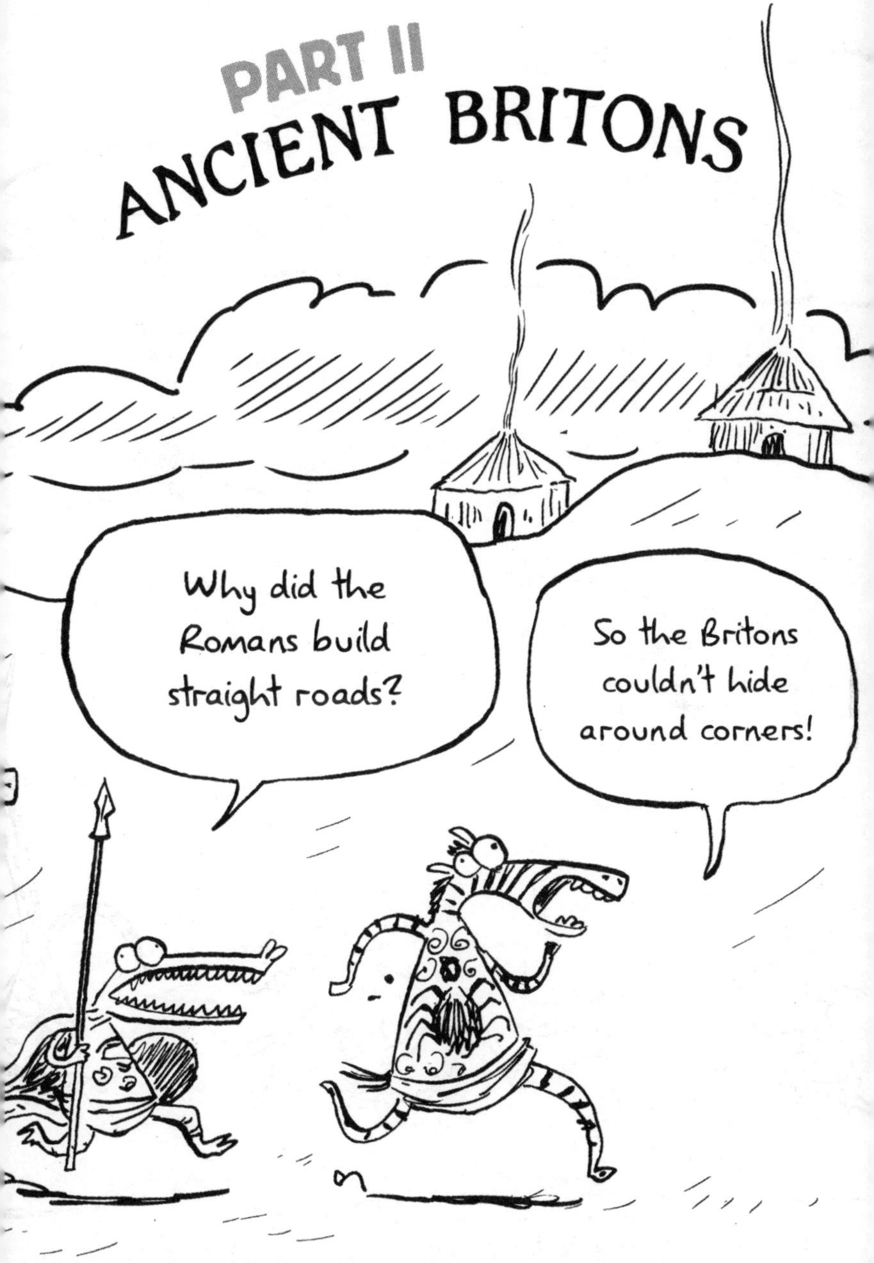
Why did the Romans build straight roads?
So the Britons couldn't hide around corners!

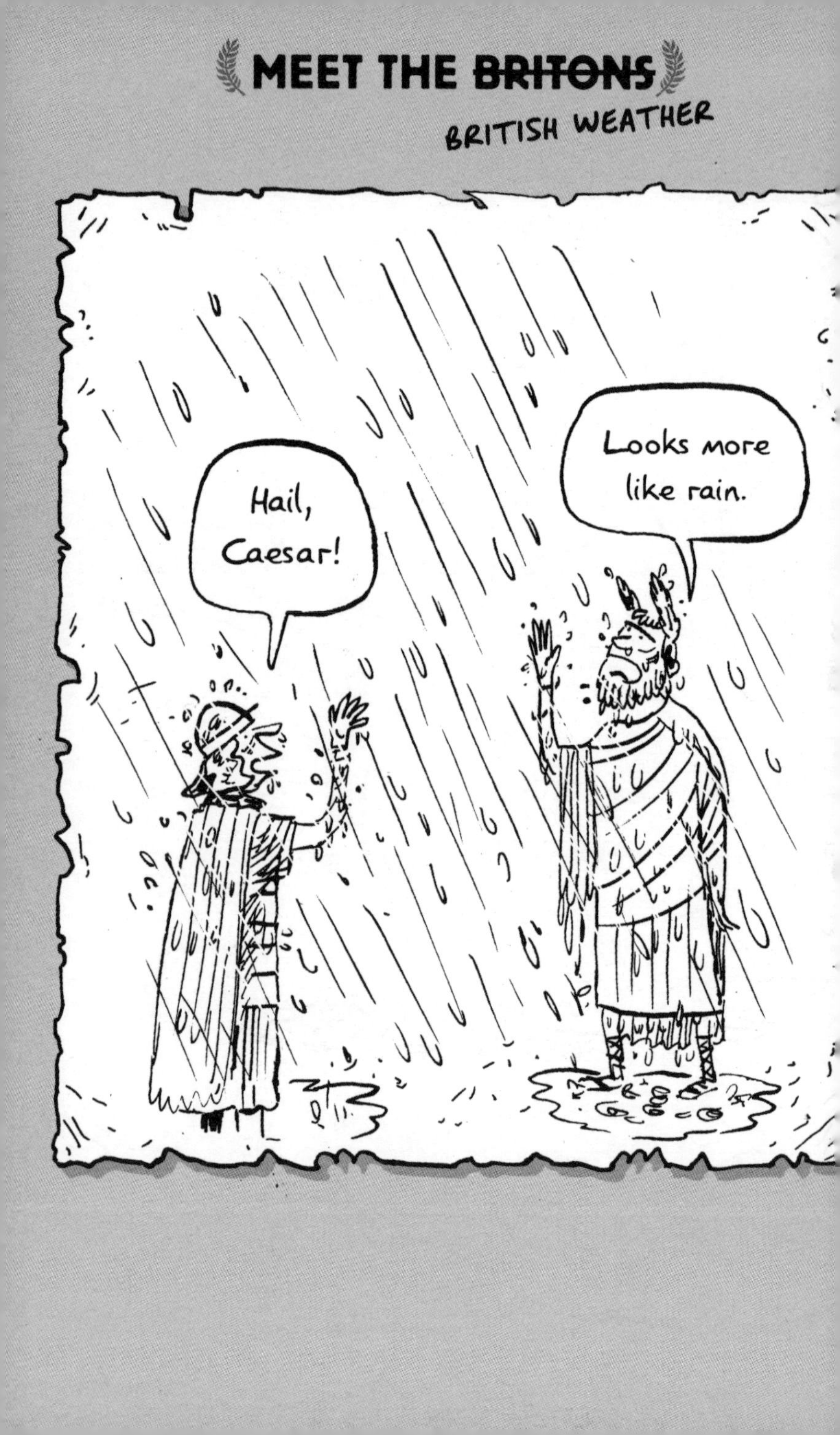
Hail, Caesar!
Looks more like rain.

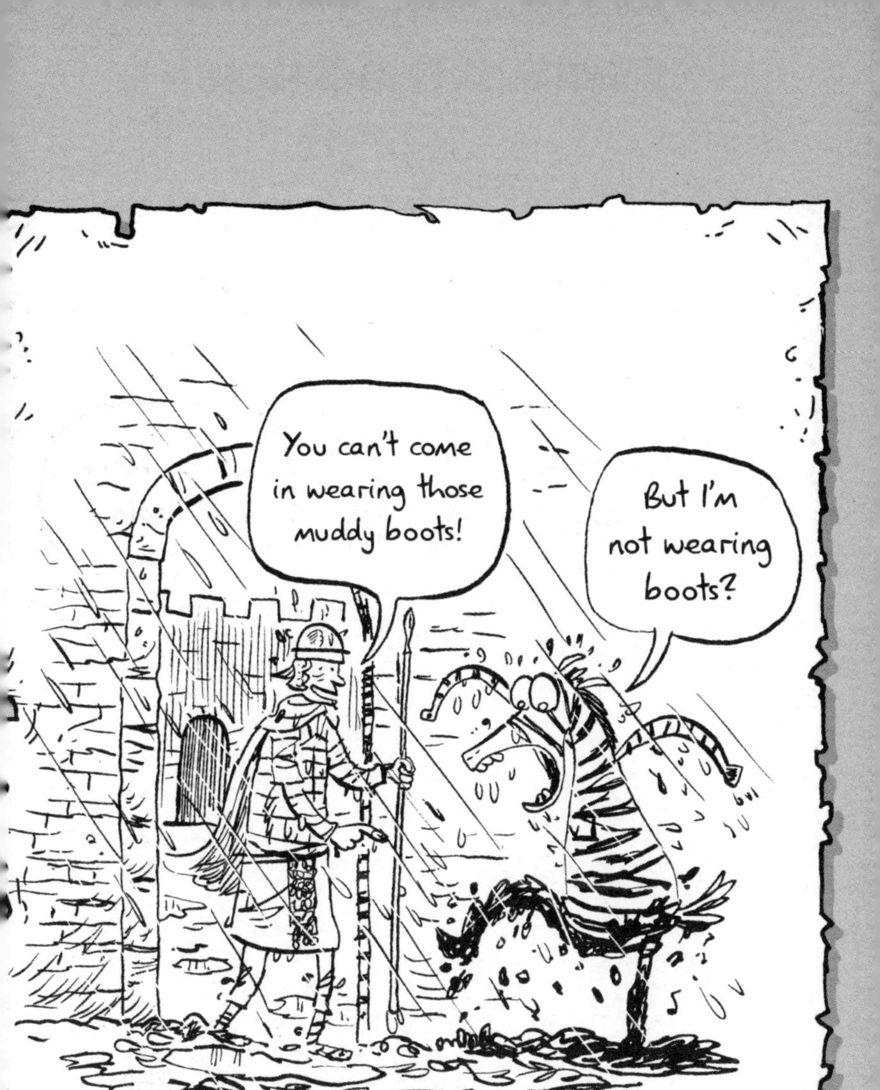
You can't come in wearing those muddy boots!
But I'm not wearing boots?

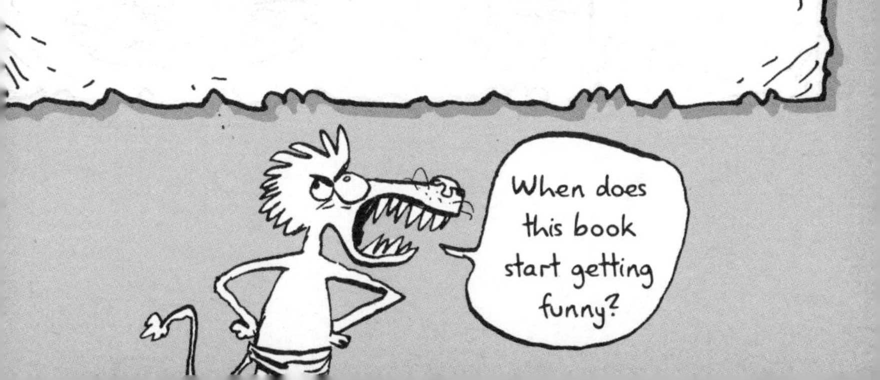
When does this book start getting funny?

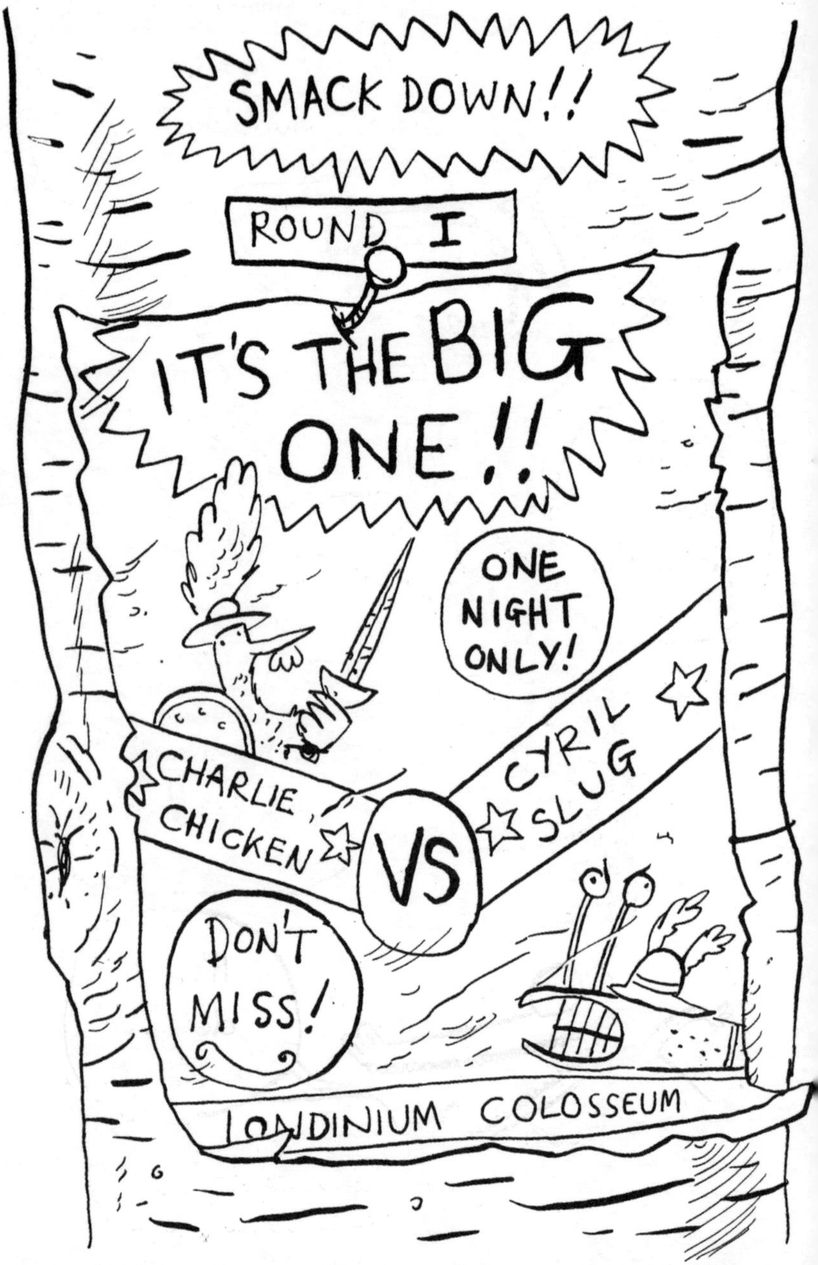

SMACK DOWN!!
ROUND I
IT'S THE BIG ONE!!
ONE NIGHT ONLY!
CHARLIE CHICKEN
VS
CYRIL SLUG
DON'T MISS!
LONDINIUM COLOSSEUM

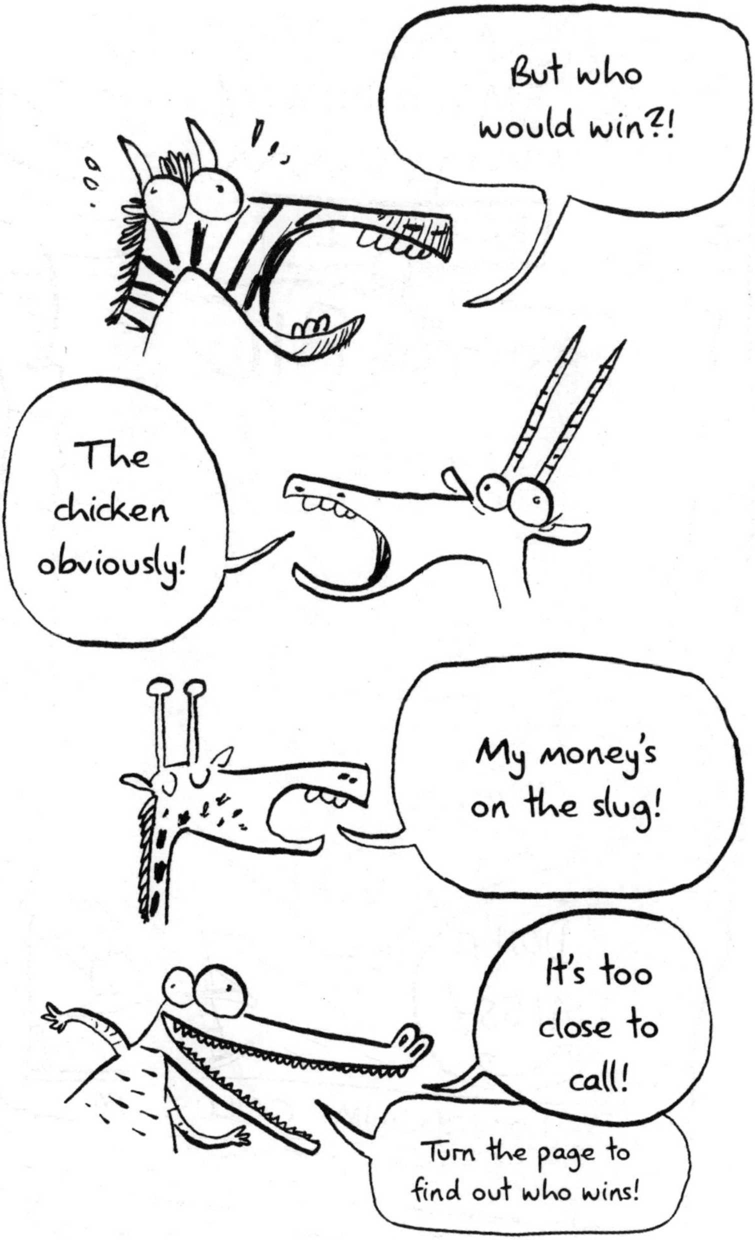
But who would win?!
The chicken obviously!
My money's on the slug!
It's too close to call!
Turn the page to find out who wins!

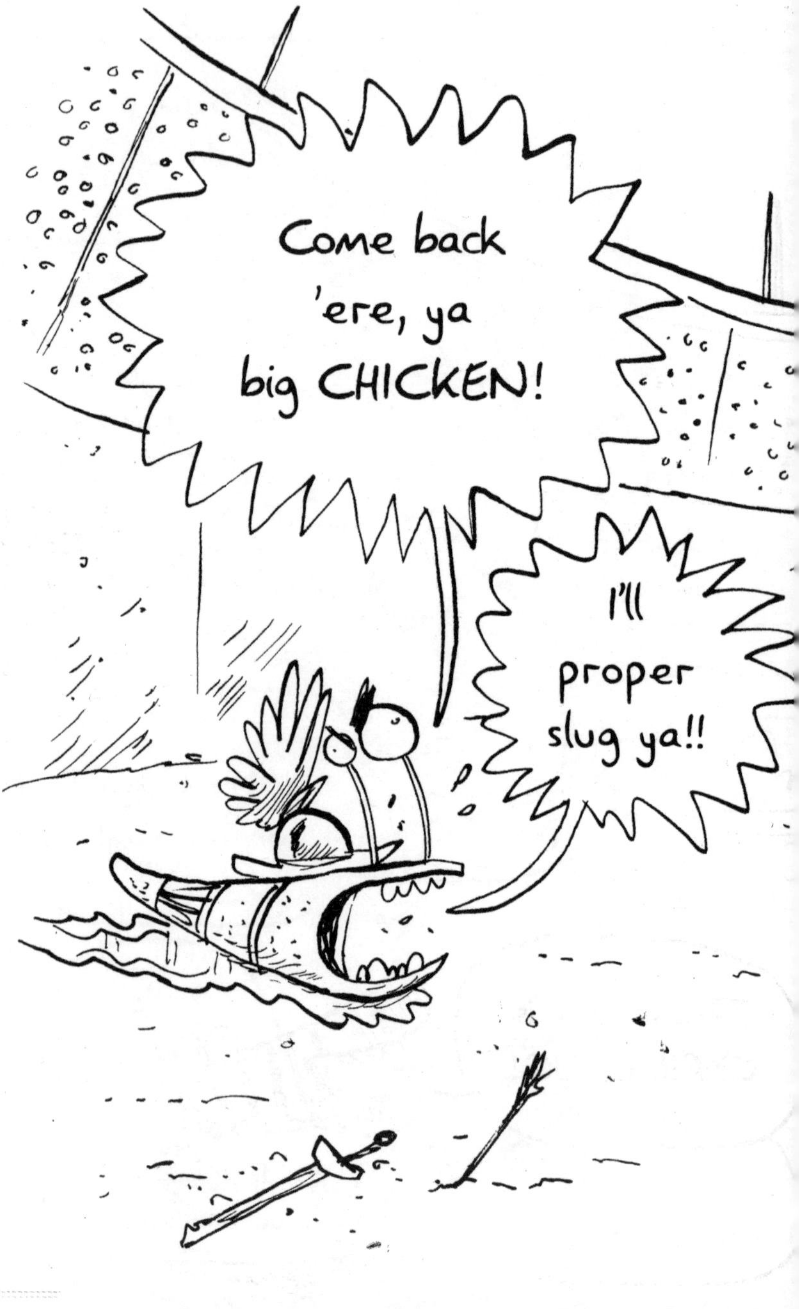
Come back 'ere, ya big CHICKEN!
I'll proper slug ya!!

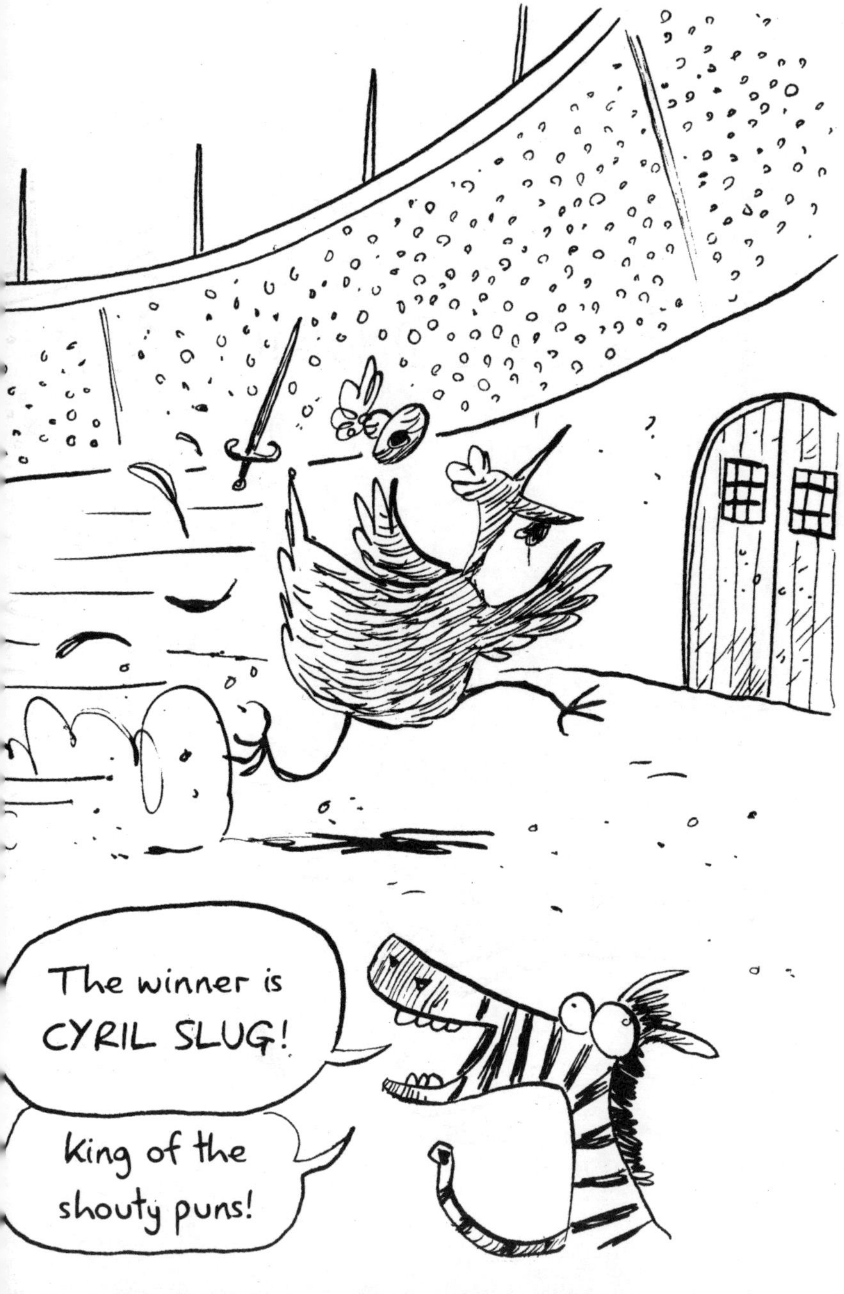
The winner is CYRIL SLUG!
King of the shouty puns!

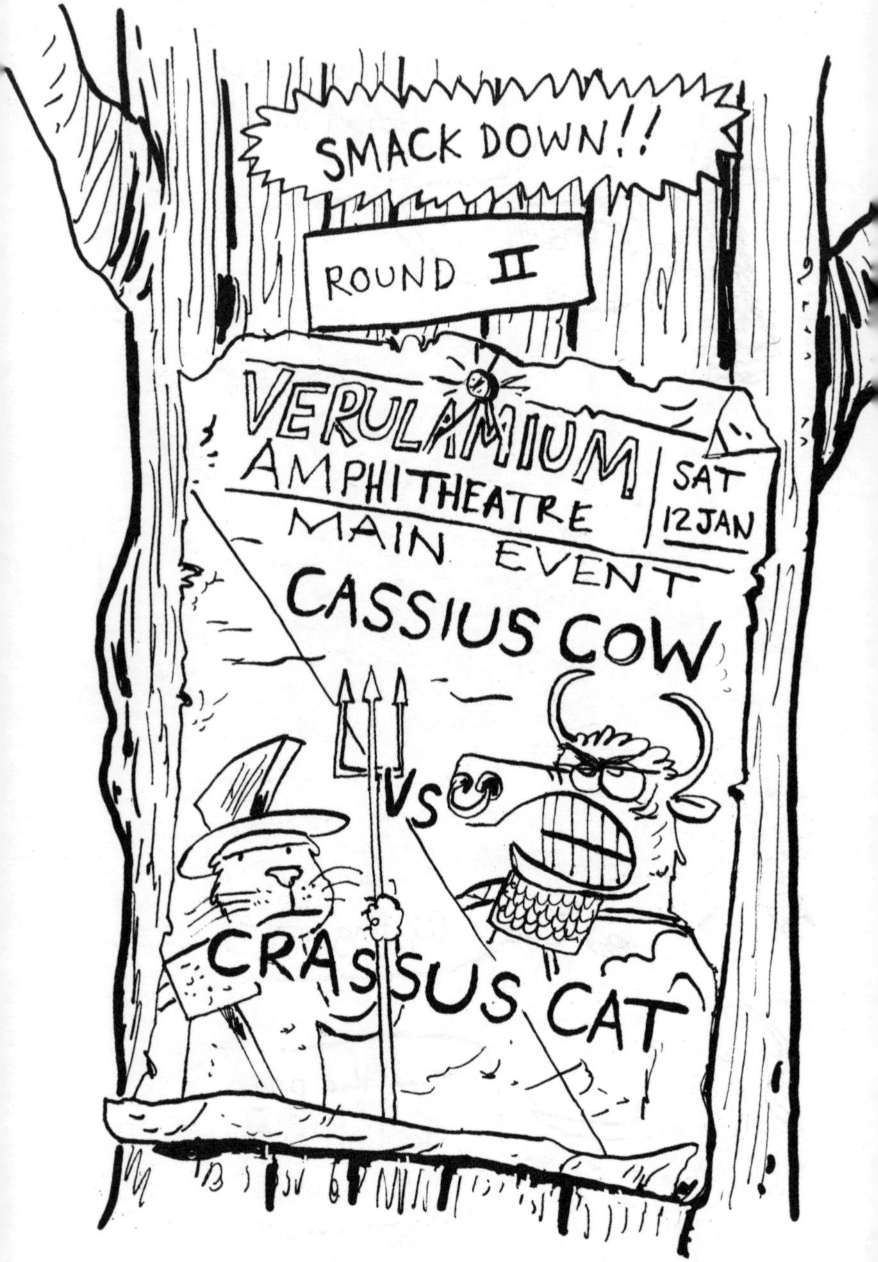
SMACK DOWN!!
ROUND II
VERULAMIUM
AMPHITHEATRE
SAT
12 JAN
MAIN EVENT
CASSIUS COW
VS
CRASSUS CAT

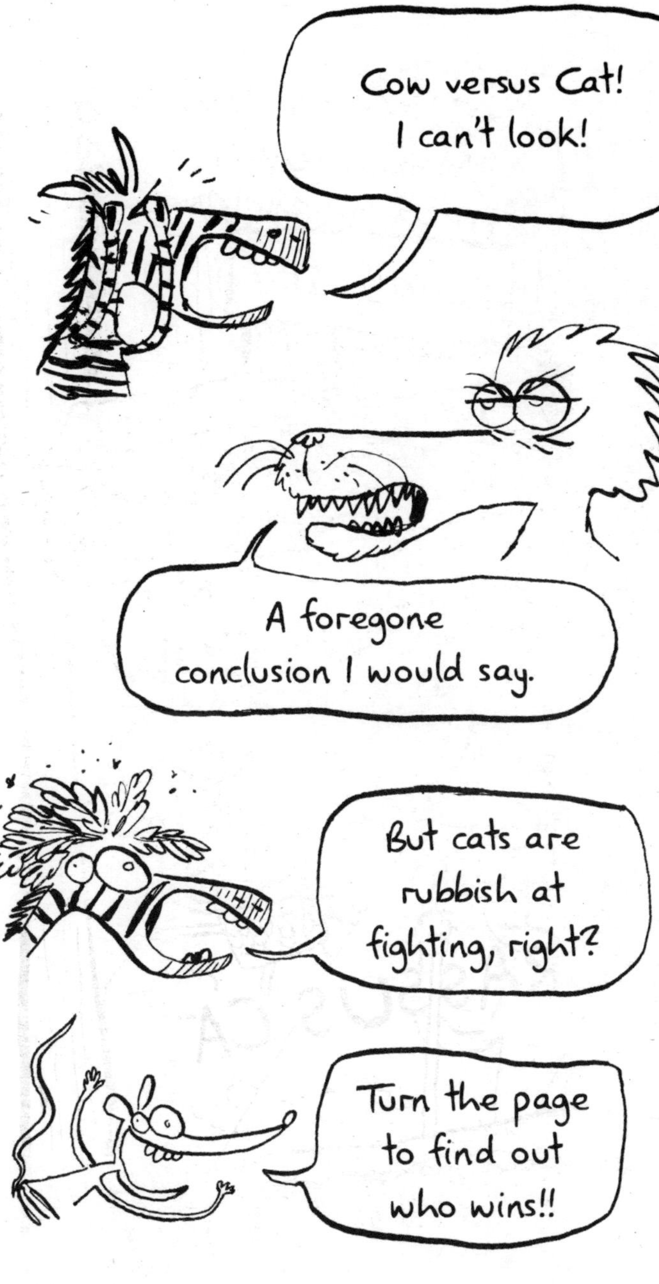
Cow versus Cat! I can't look!
A foregone conclusion I would say.
But cats are rubbish at fighting, right?
Turn the page to find out who wins!!

BRITONS' SMACKDOWN II

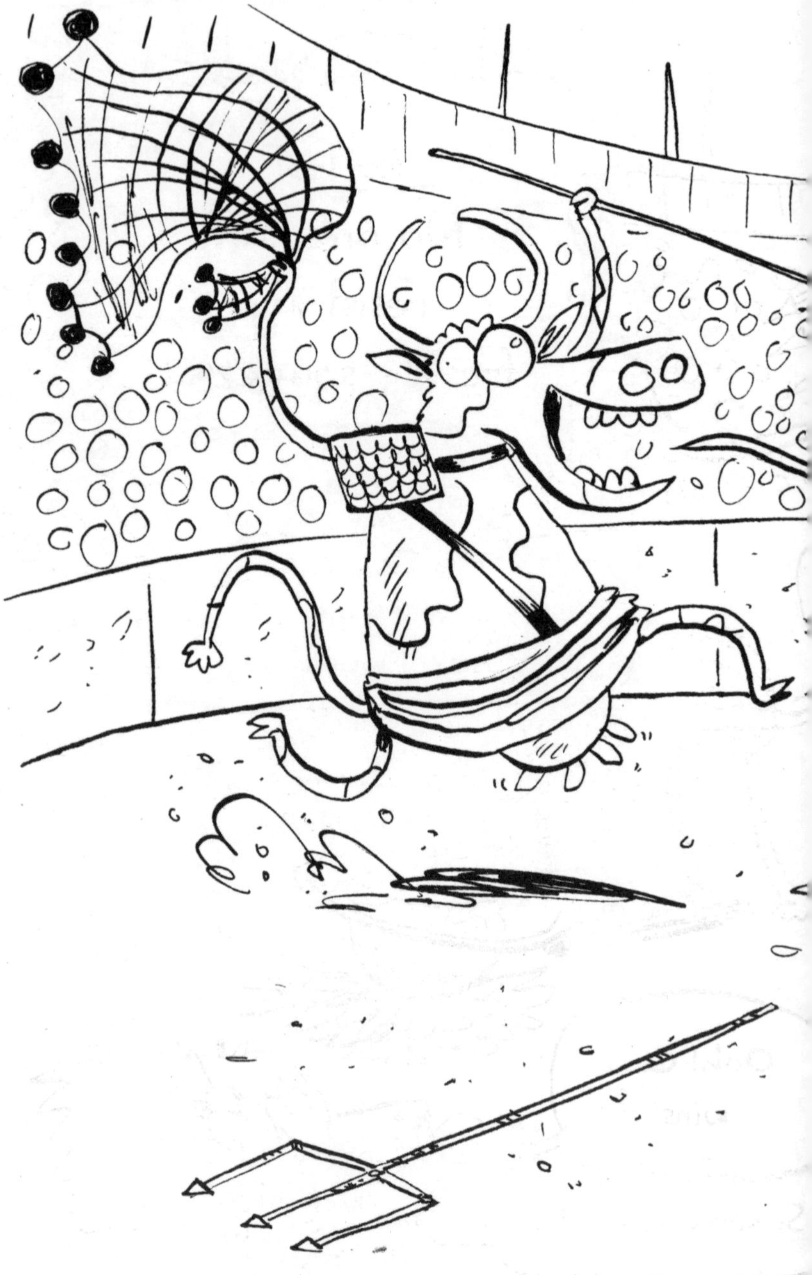

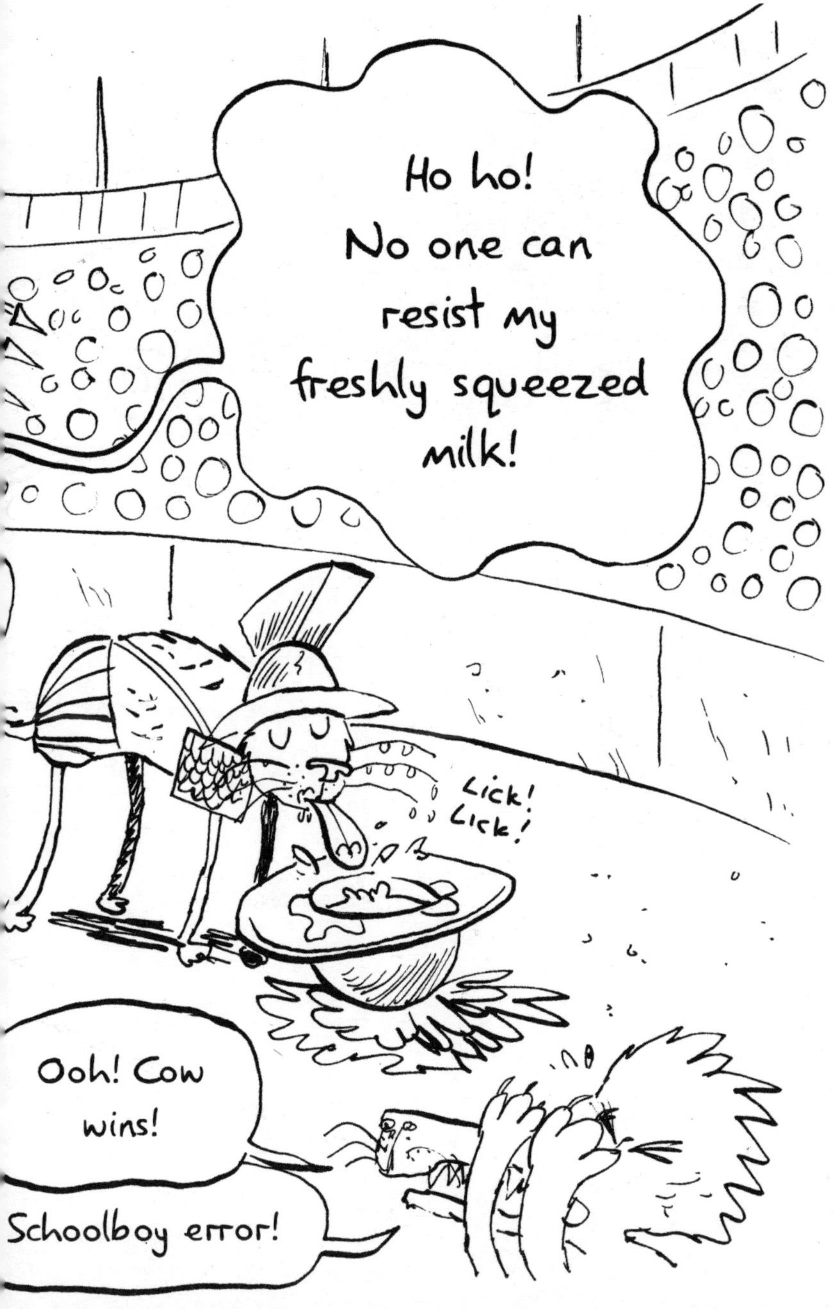
Ho ho! No one can resist my freshly squeezed milk!
Lick! Lick!
Ooh! Cow wins!
Schoolboy error!

CELTIC MOUSTACHE MANUAL

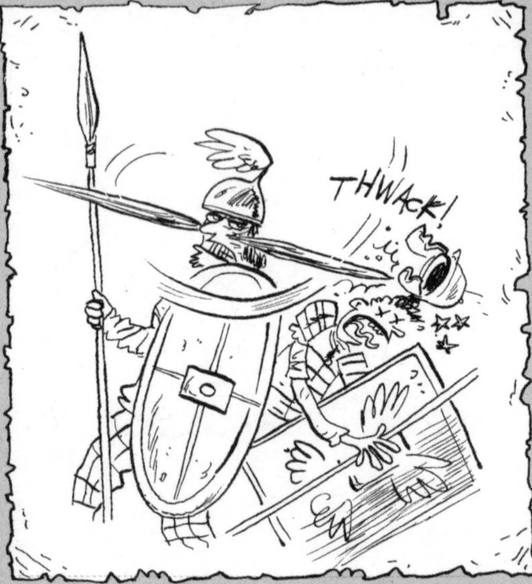
THWACK!

The double-edged sword

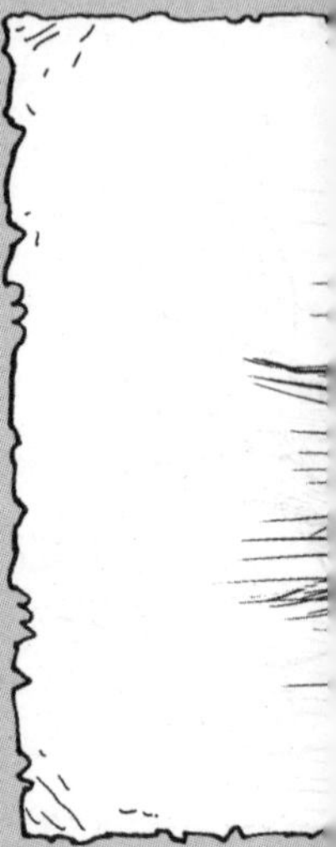

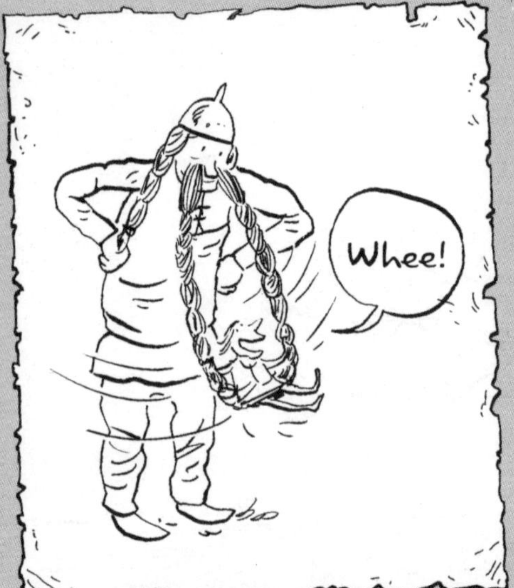
Whee!

The swing

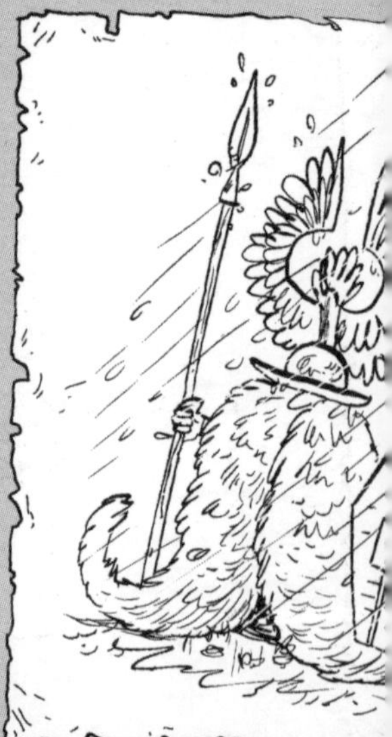

The rain coat

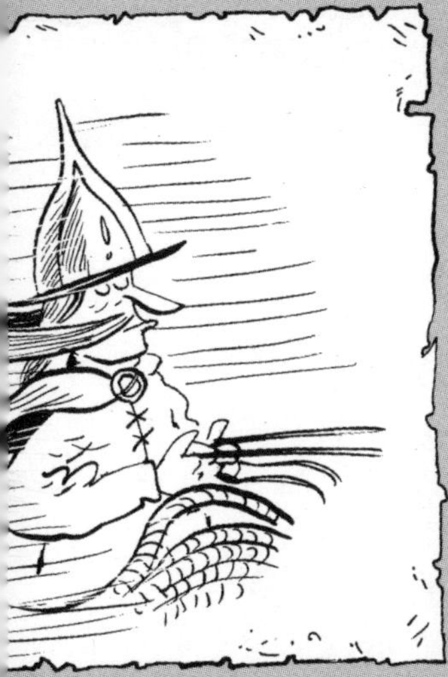

The Aerodynamic

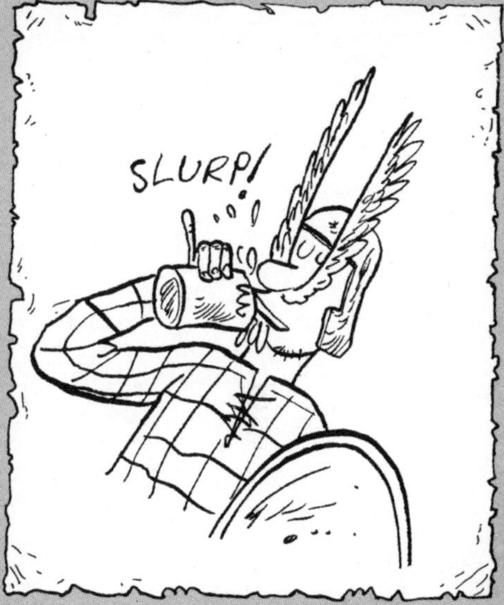
SLURP!

The Froth-Free

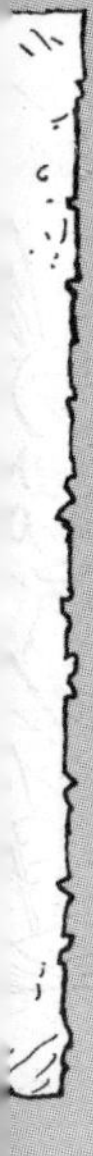

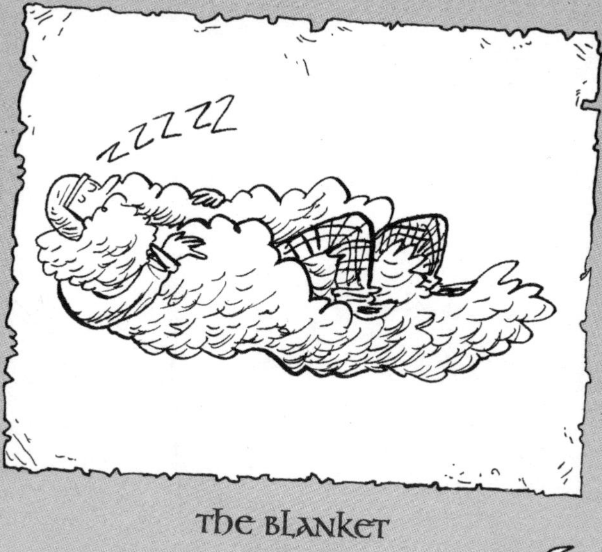
ZZZZZ

The Blanket

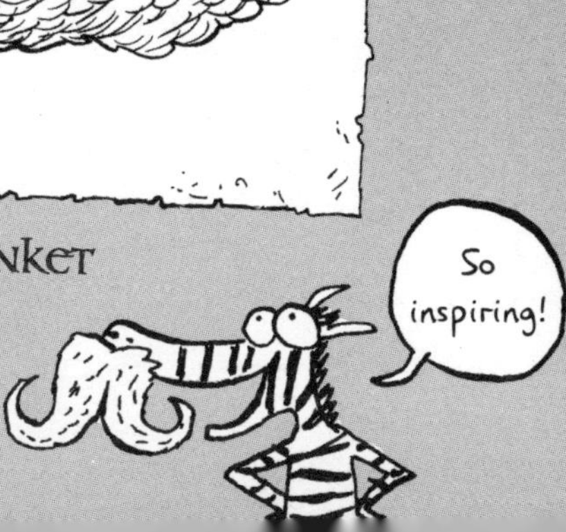
So inspiring!

SPACE INVADERS

THE ROMANS CAME, CONQUERED AND GAVE THE BRUTAL BRITS ALL OF THESE!

I. CATS

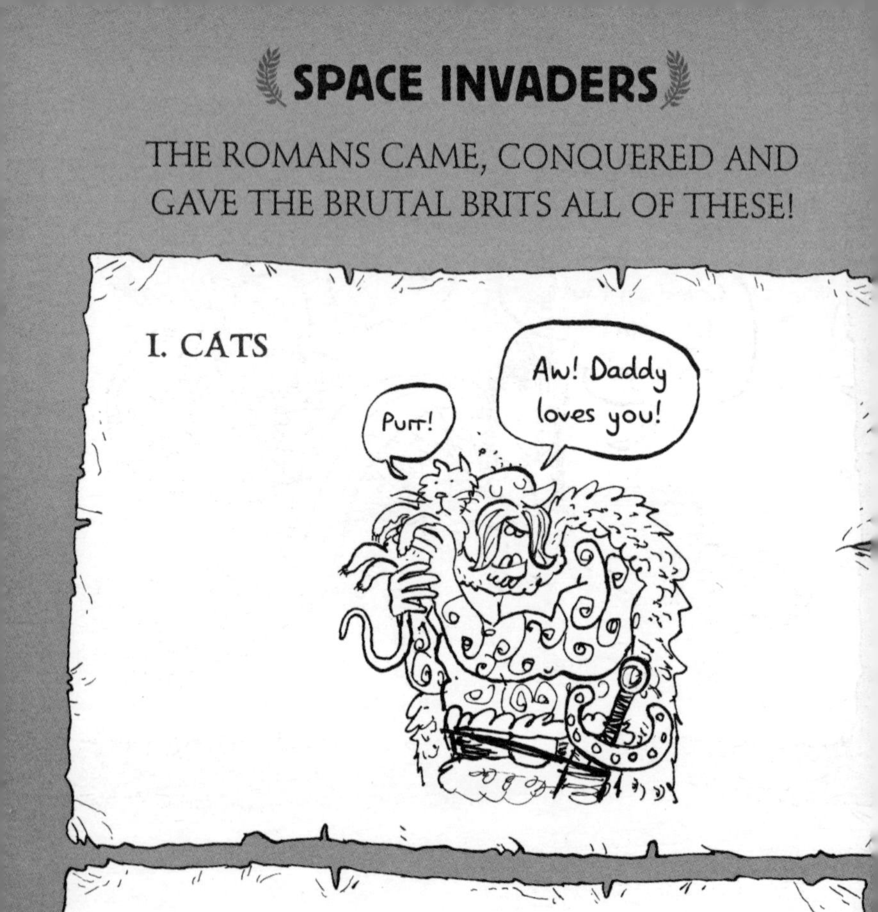
Purr!
Aw! Daddy loves you!

II. TURNIPS, CARROTS, CABBAGES AND PEAS

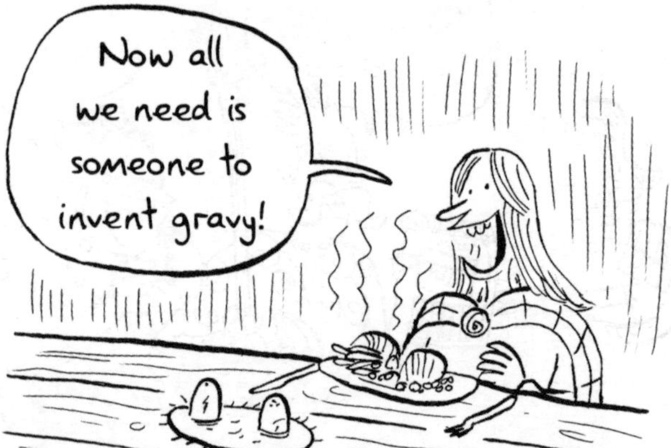
Now all we need is someone to invent gravy!

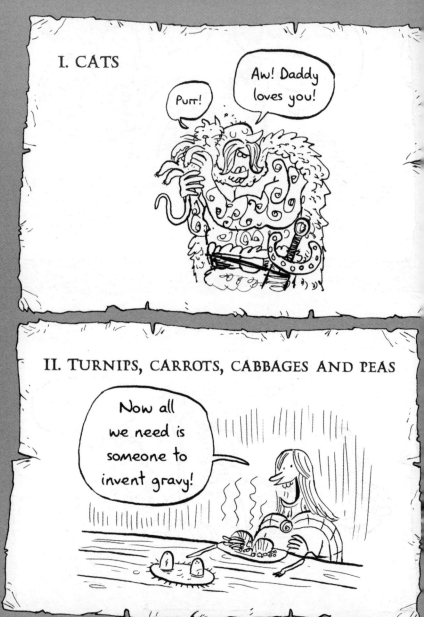

III. RABBITS

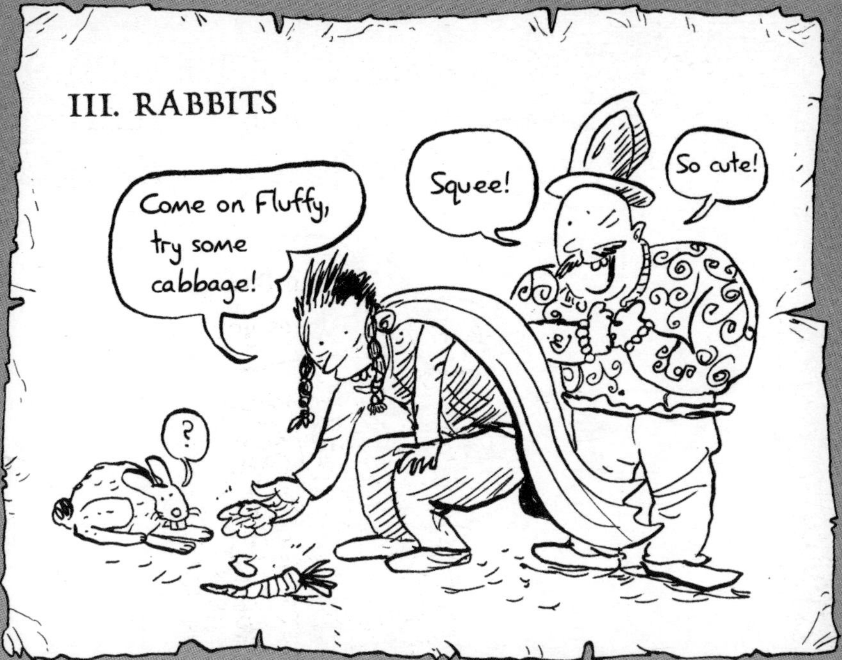

Come on Fluffy, try some cabbage!
?
Squee!
So cute!

IV. CALENDARS

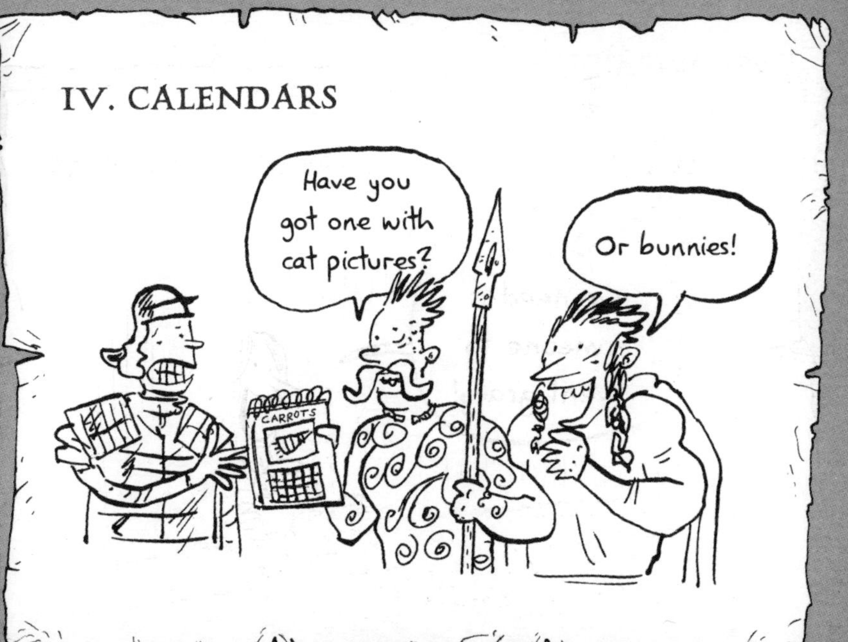

Have you got one with cat pictures?
Or bunnies!
CARROTS

V. BATHS

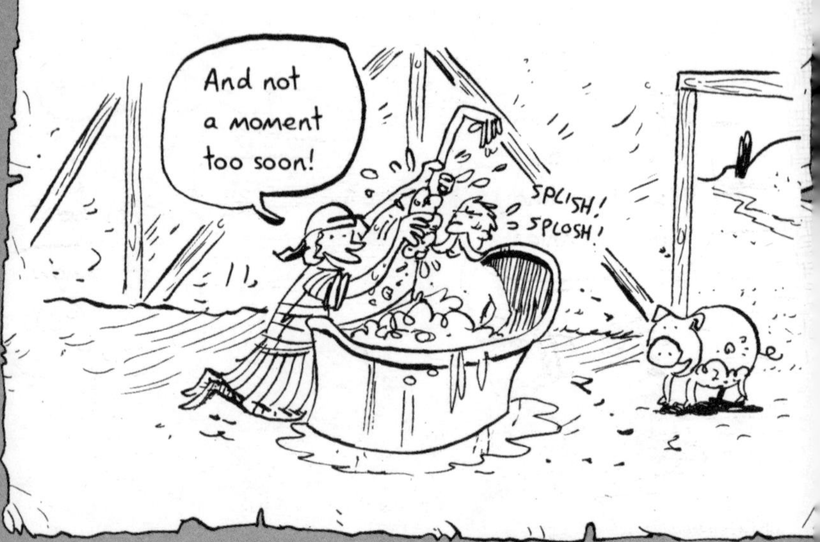
And not a moment too soon!
SPLISH!
SPLOSH!

VI. ROADS

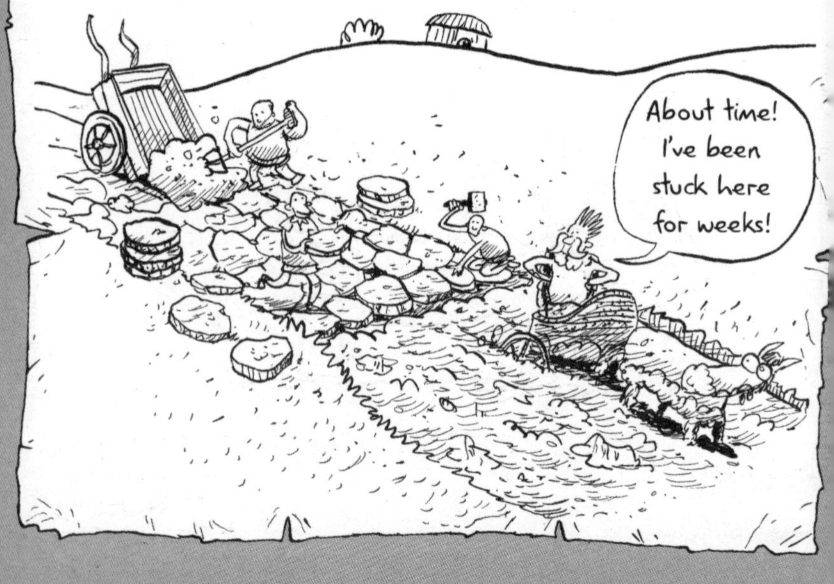
About time! I've been stuck here for weeks!

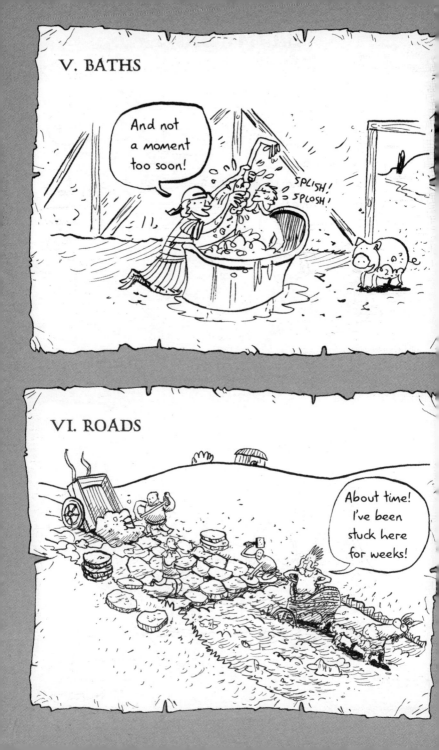

BARMY BRITS

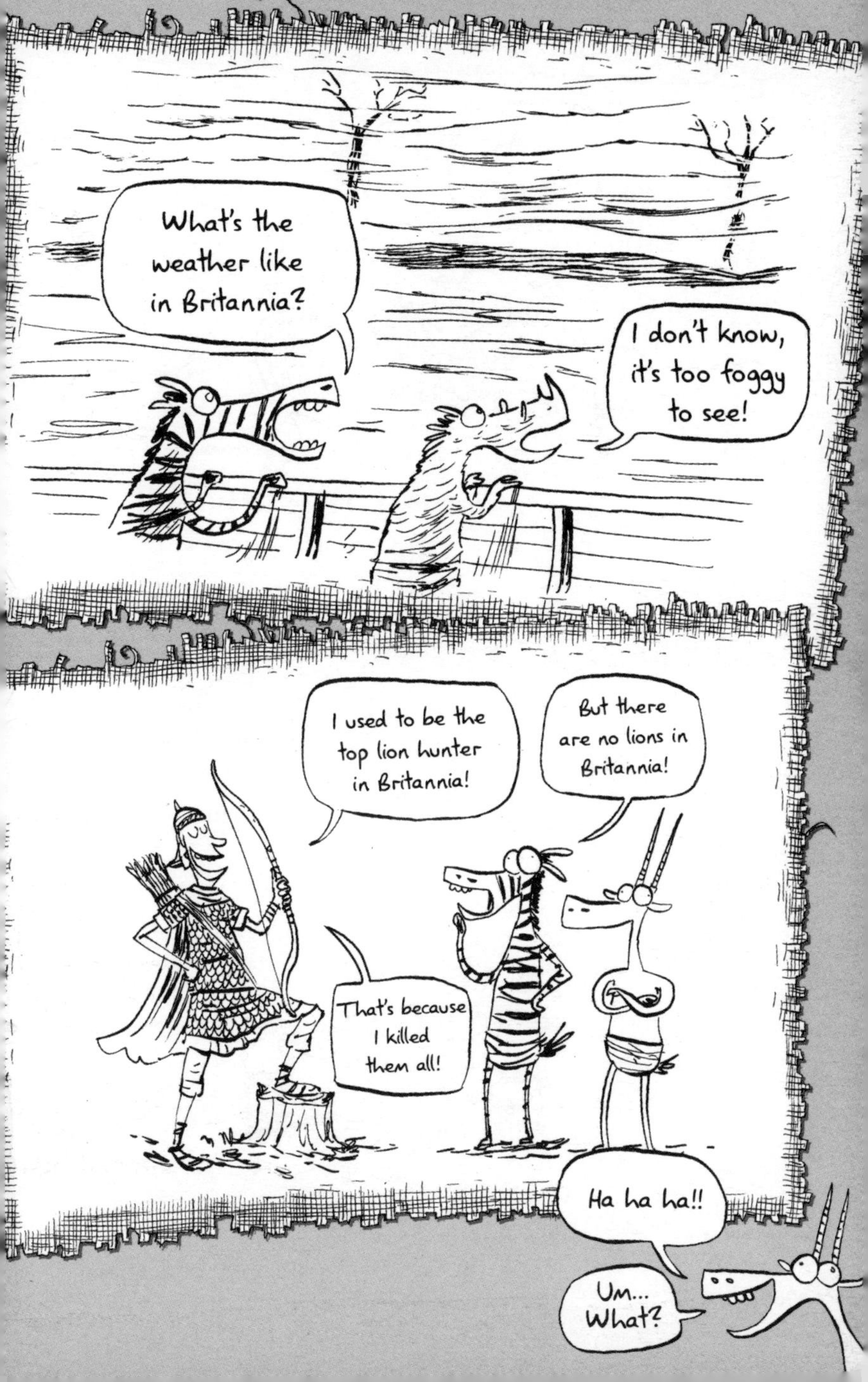
What's the weather like in Britannia?
I don't know, it's too foggy to see!
I used to be the top lion hunter in Britannia!
But there are no lions in Britannia!
That's because I killed them all!
Ha ha ha!!
Um... What?

MORE AMAZING JULIUS FACTS

BOUDICCA

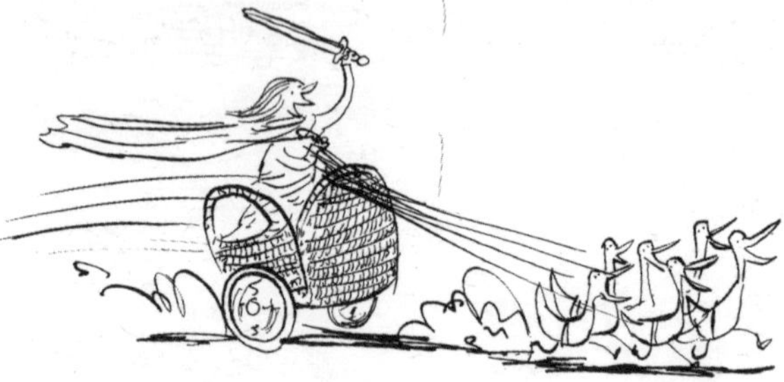

HER CHARIOT WAS PULLED BY A GAGGLE OF GEESE.

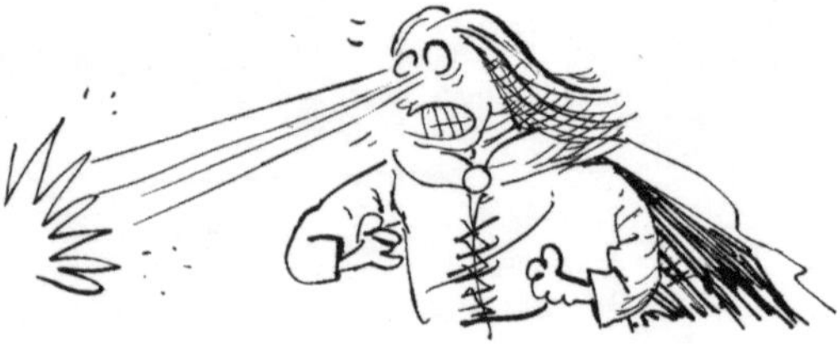

SHE SHOT BEAMS OF LIGHT FROM HER EYES.

BOUDICCA IS ACTUALLY SHORT FOR BOUDI-KAREN.

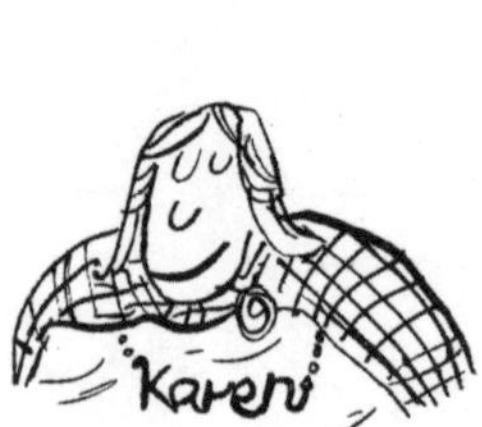
Karen

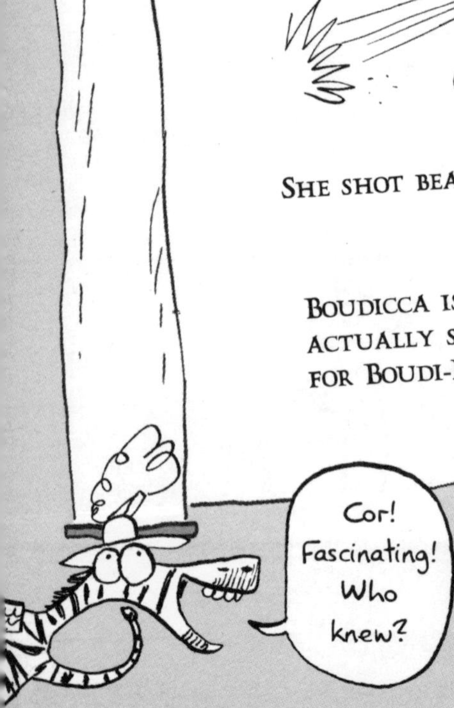
Cor! Fascinating! Who knew?

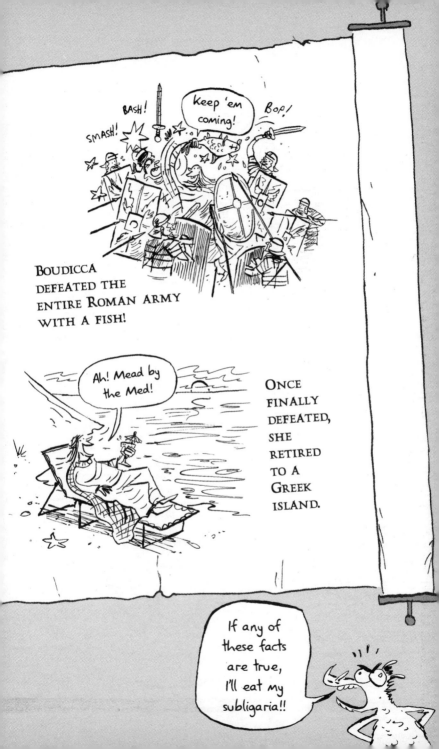

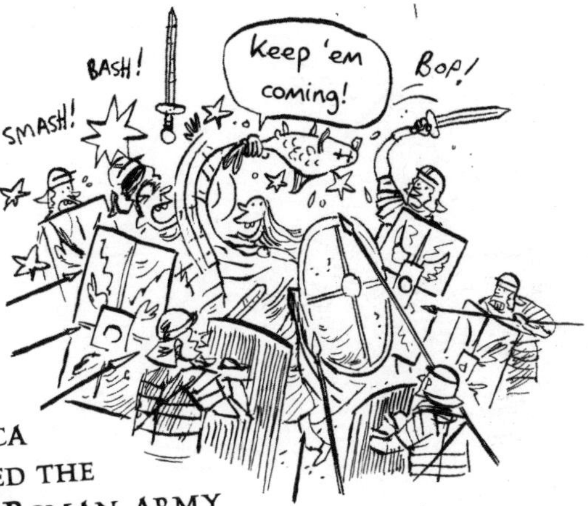
BASH!
Keep 'em coming!
Bop!
SMASH!

BOUDICCA DEFEATED THE ENTIRE ROMAN ARMY WITH A FISH!

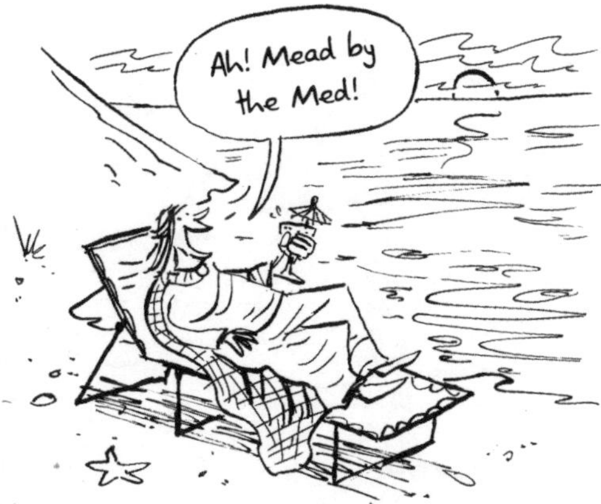
Ah! Mead by the Med!

ONCE FINALLY DEFEATED, SHE RETIRED TO A GREEK ISLAND.

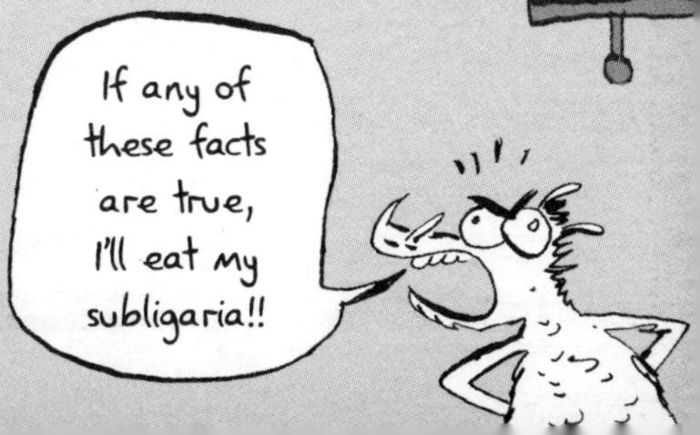
If any of these facts are true, I'll eat my subligaria!!

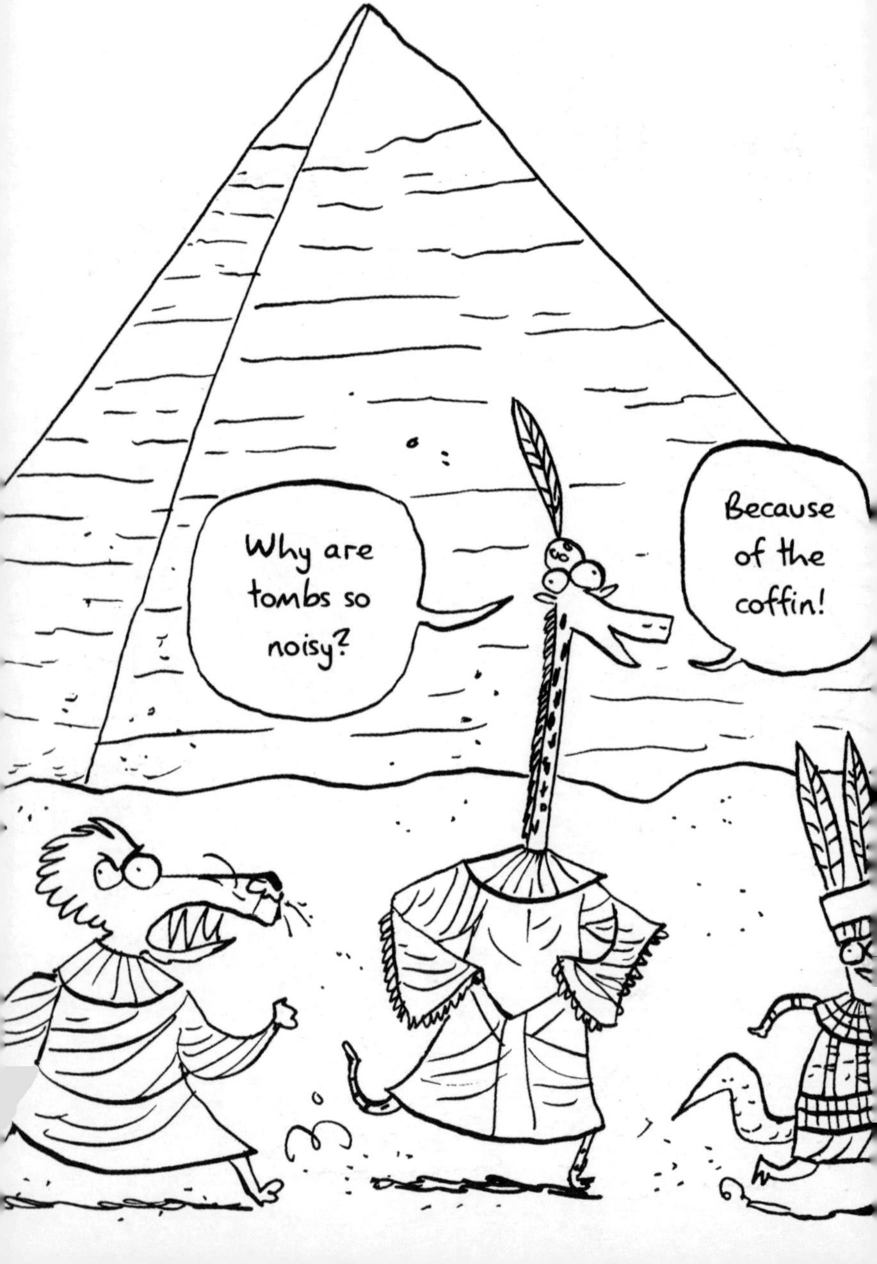
Why are tombs so noisy?
Because of the coffin!

PART III
ANCIENT EGYPTIANS

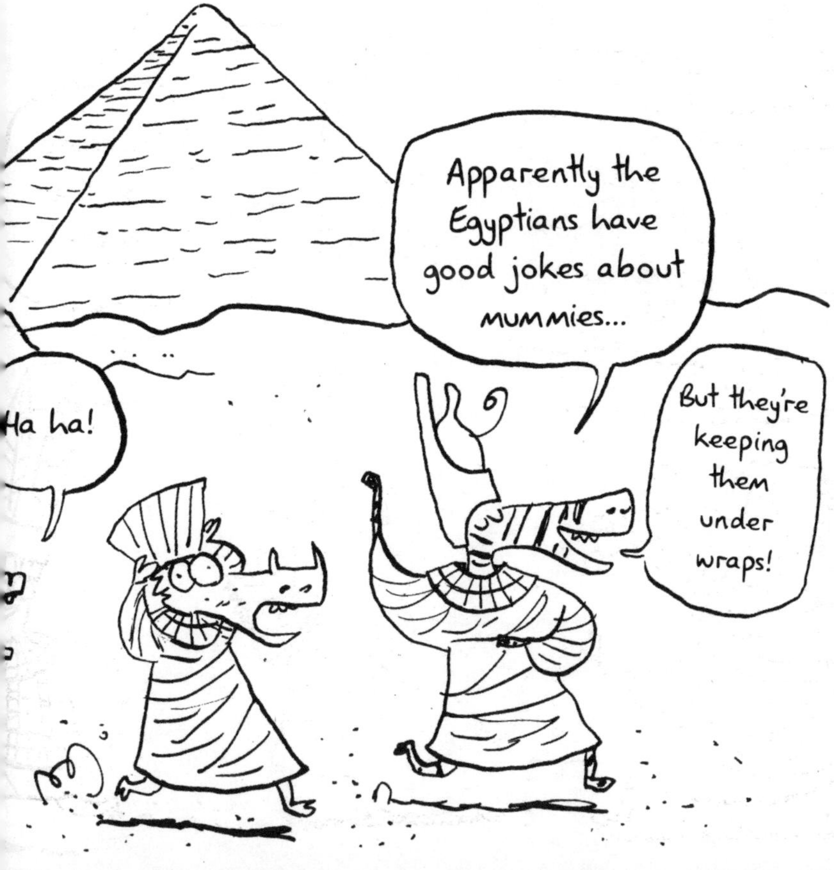
Apparently the Egyptians have good jokes about mummies...
Ha ha!
But they're keeping them under wraps!

MEET THE EGYPTIAN GODS

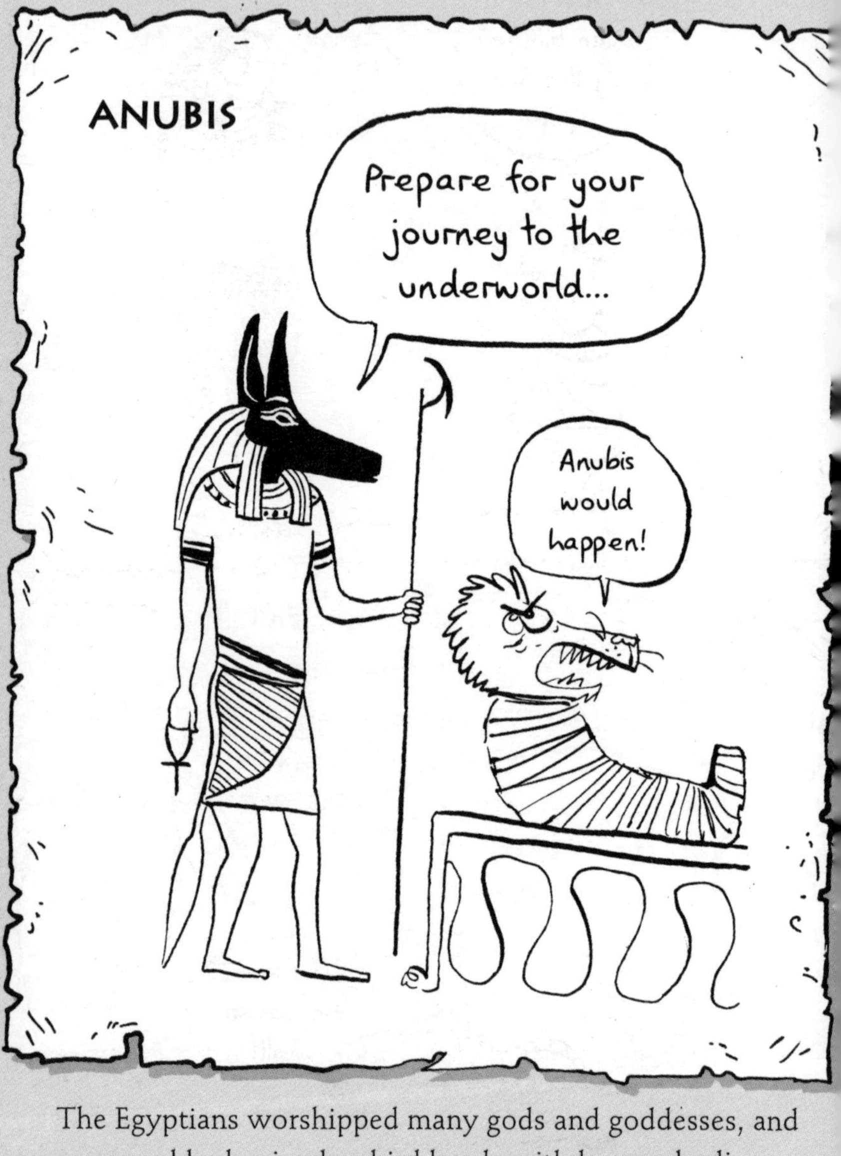
ANUBIS
Prepare for your journey to the underworld...
Anubis would happen!

The Egyptians worshipped many gods and goddesses, and several had animal or bird heads with human bodies.

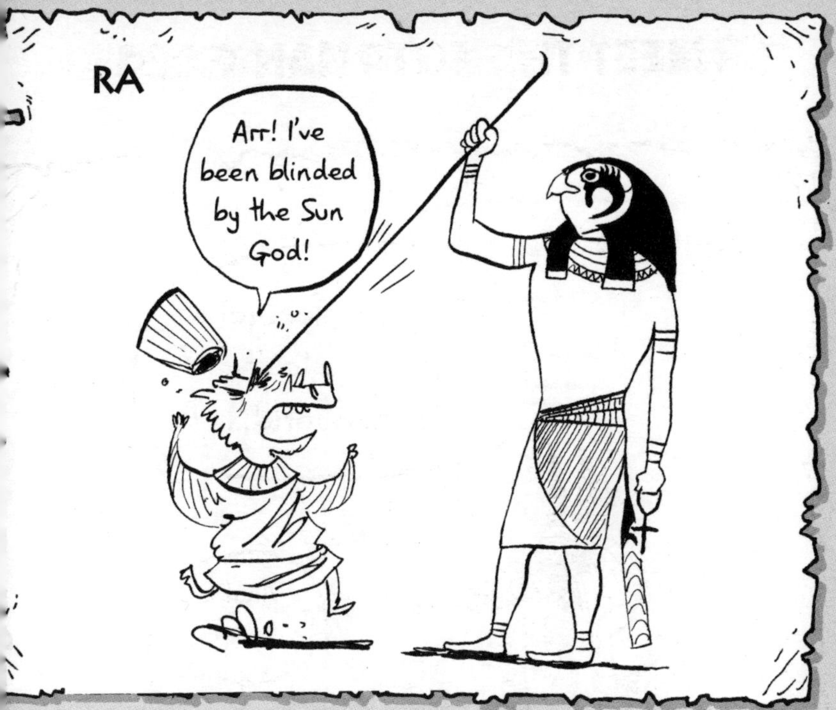
RA
Arr! I've been blinded by the Sun God!

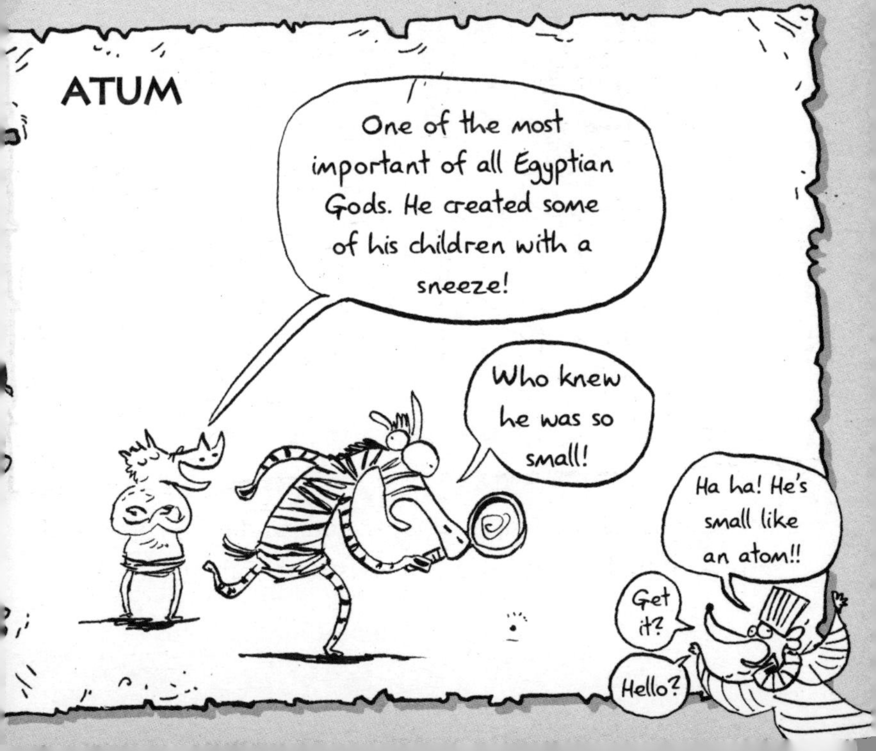
ATUM
One of the most important of all Egyptian Gods. He created some of his children with a sneeze!
Who knew he was so small!
Ha ha! He's small like an atom!!
Get it?
Hello?

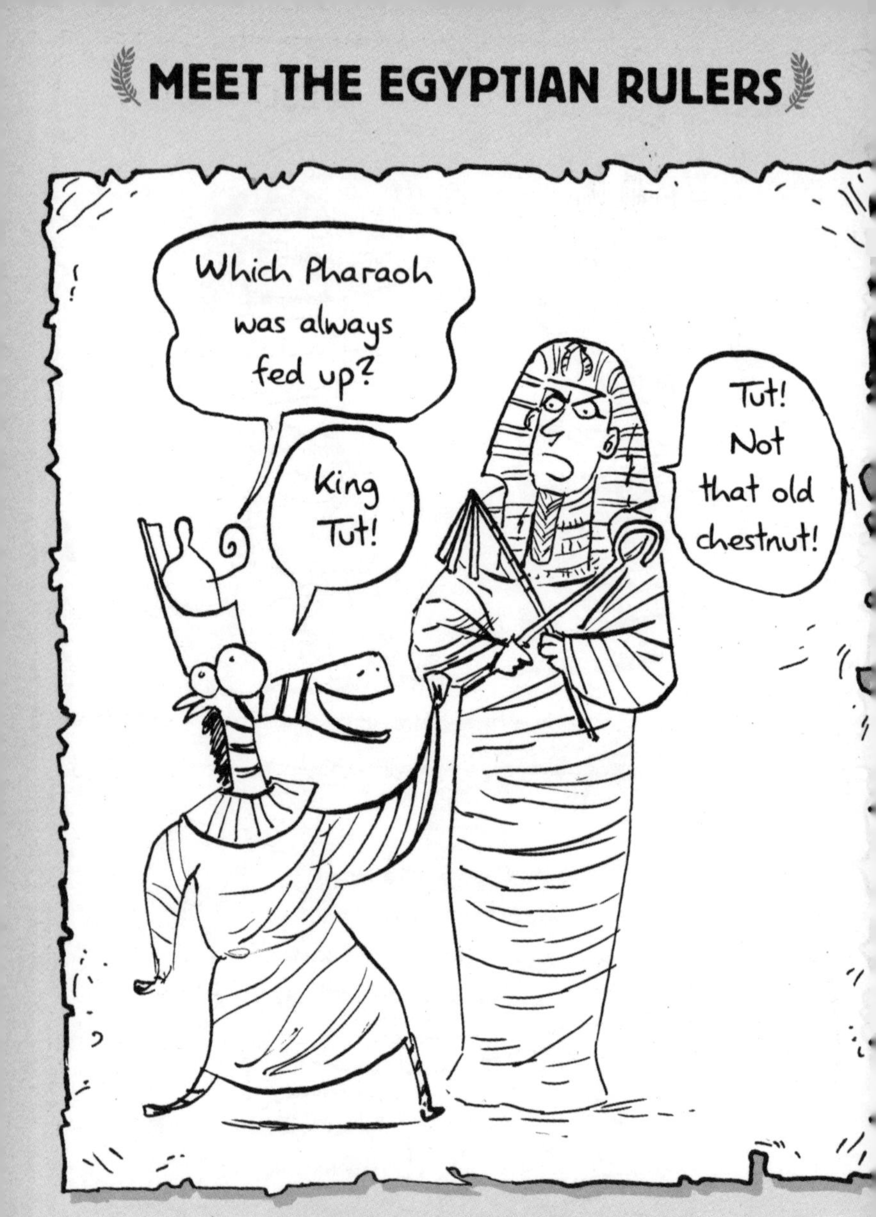
Which Pharaoh was always fed up?
King Tut!
Tut! Not that old chestnut!

TUTANHKAMUN

Tutankhamun was one of the youngest pharaohs (he died aged 18) and Cleopatra was the second female pharaoh. Pharaohs could talk to the gods.

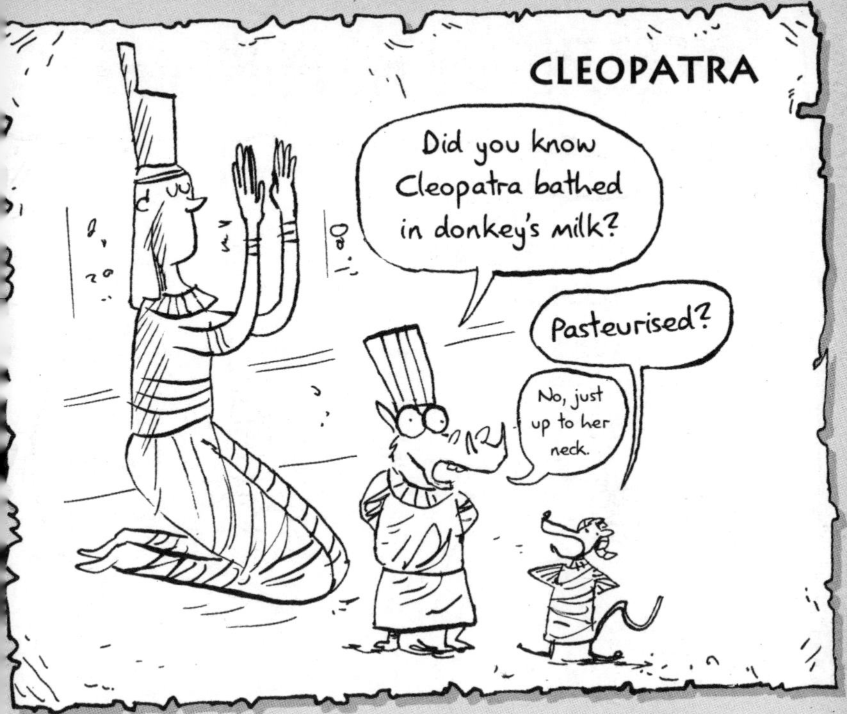
CLEOPATRA
Did you know Cleopatra bathed in donkey's milk?
Pasteurised?
No, just up to her neck.

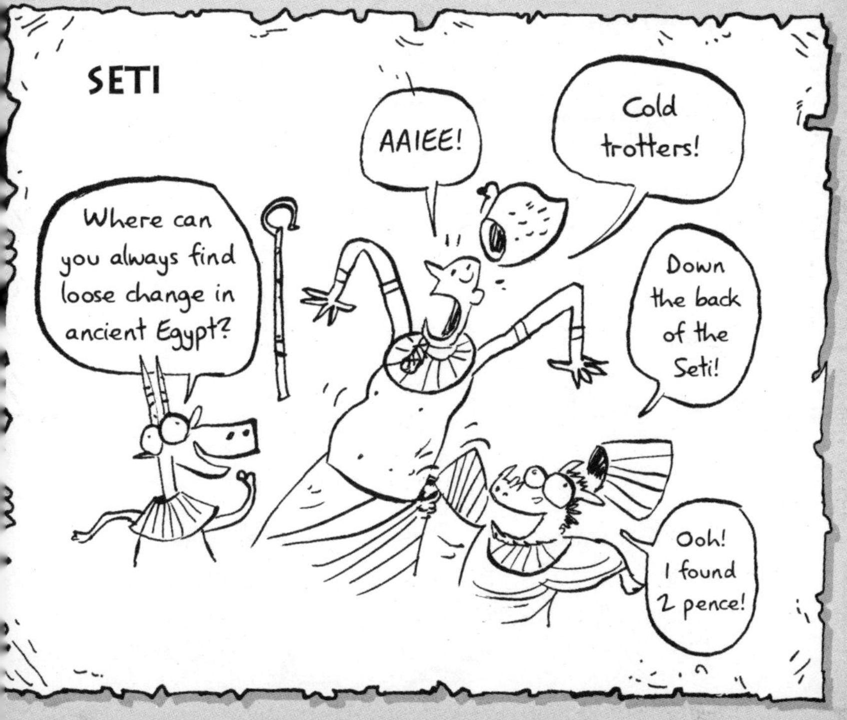
SETI
Where can you always find loose change in ancient Egypt?
AAIEE!
Cold trotters!
Down the back of the Seti!
Ooh! I found 2 pence!

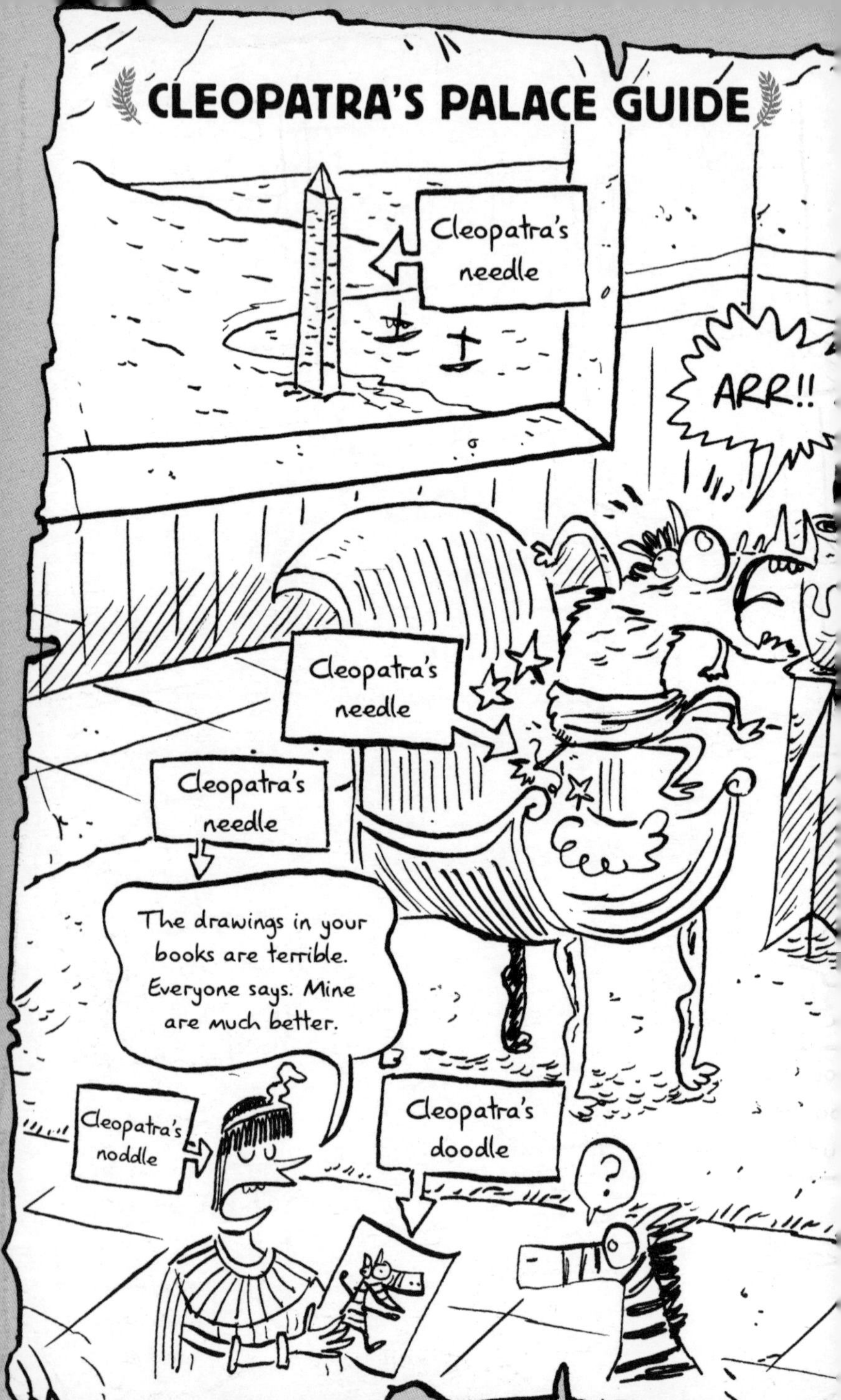
CLEOPATRA'S PALACE GUIDE
Cleopatra's needle
ARR!!
Cleopatra's needle
Cleopatra's needle
The drawings in your books are terrible. Everyone says. Mine are much better.
Cleopatra's noddle
Cleopatra's doodle
?

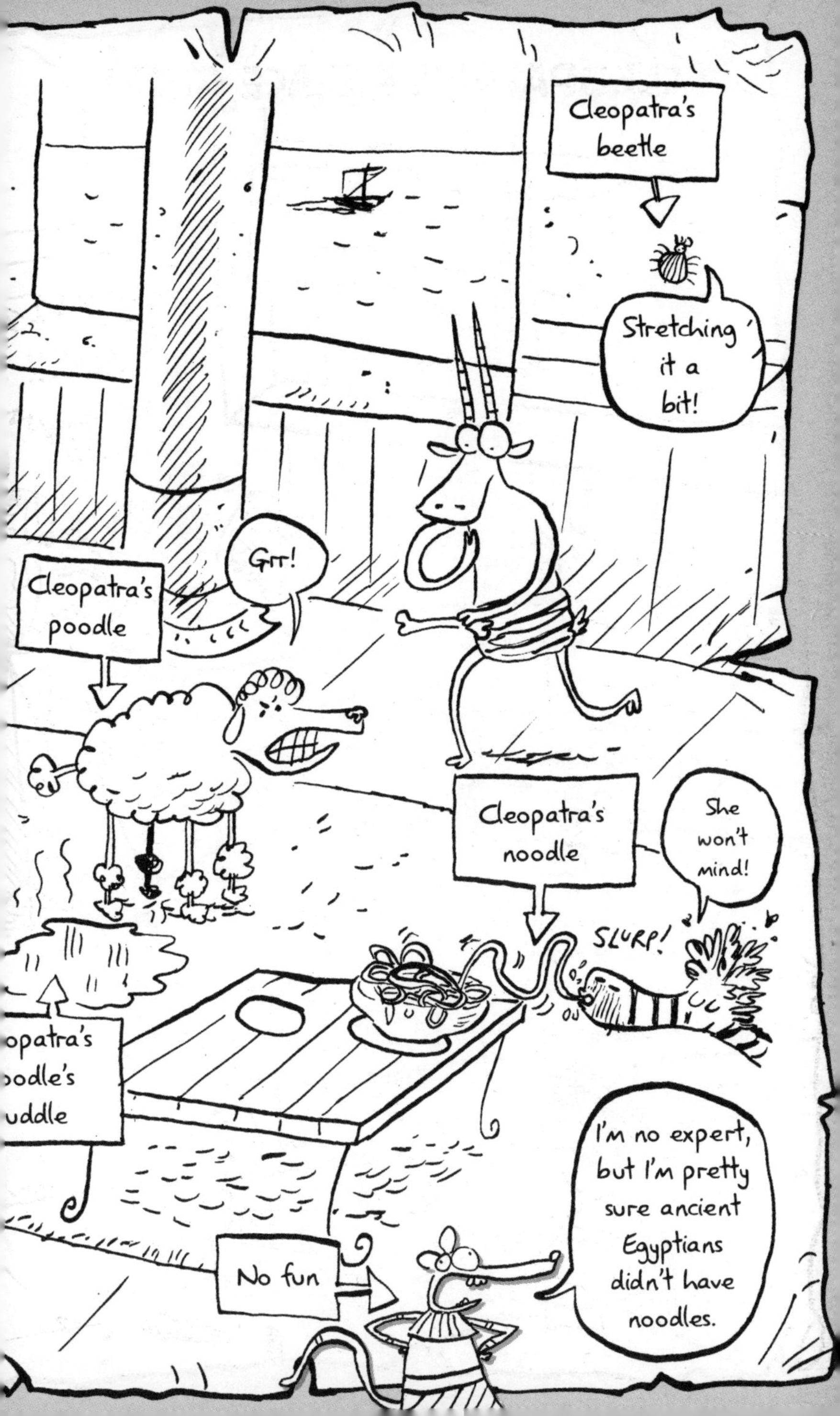

Cleopatra's beetle
Stretching it a bit!
Cleopatra's poodle
GIT!
Cleopatra's noodle
She won't mind!
SLURP!
opatra's
oodle's
uddle
No fun
I'm no expert, but I'm pretty sure ancient Egyptians didn't have noodles.

CHUCKLE WITH THE CROCS

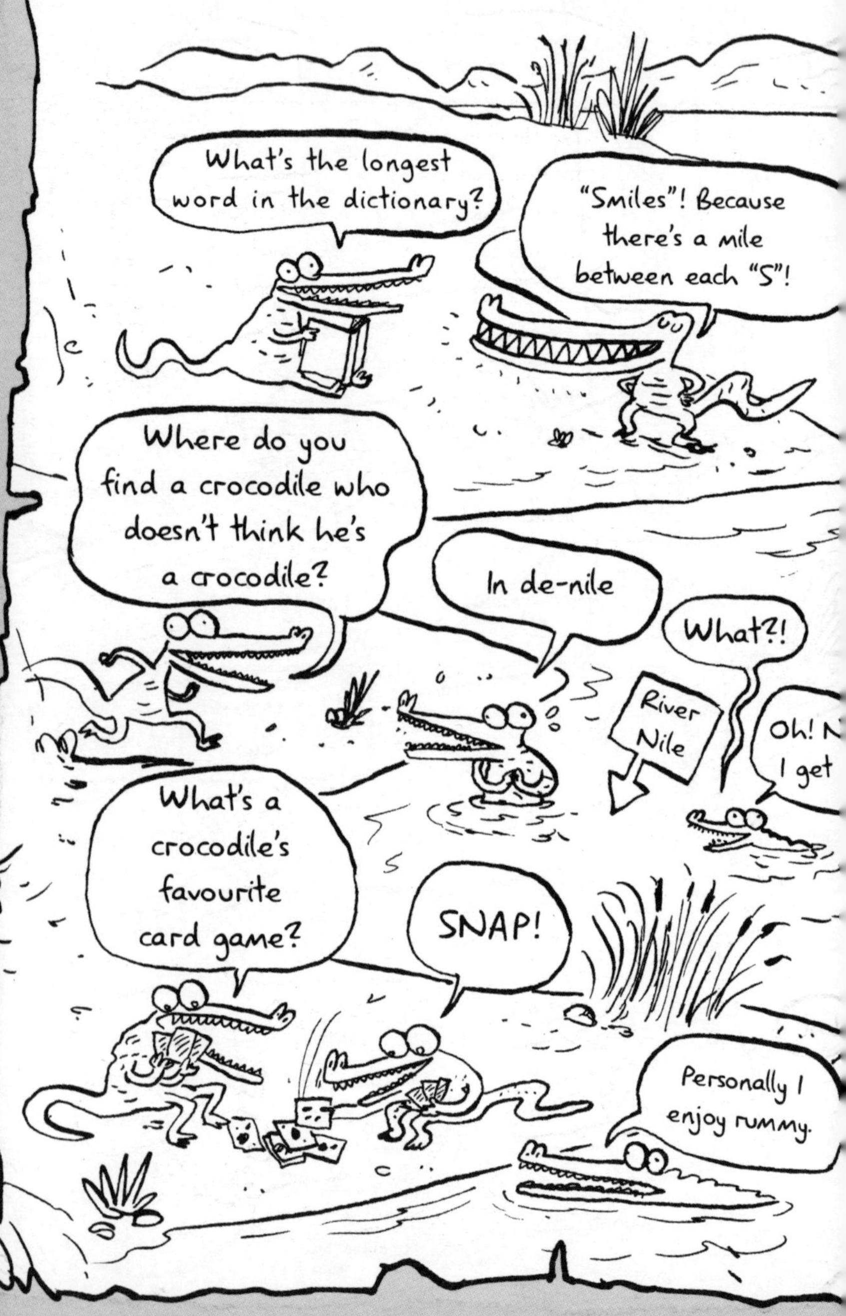

What's the longest word in the dictionary?
"Smiles"! Because there's a mile between each "S"!
Where do you find a crocodile who doesn't think he's a crocodile?
In de-nile
What?!
River Nile
Oh! N
I get
What's a crocodile's favourite card game?
SNAP!
Personally I enjoy rummy.

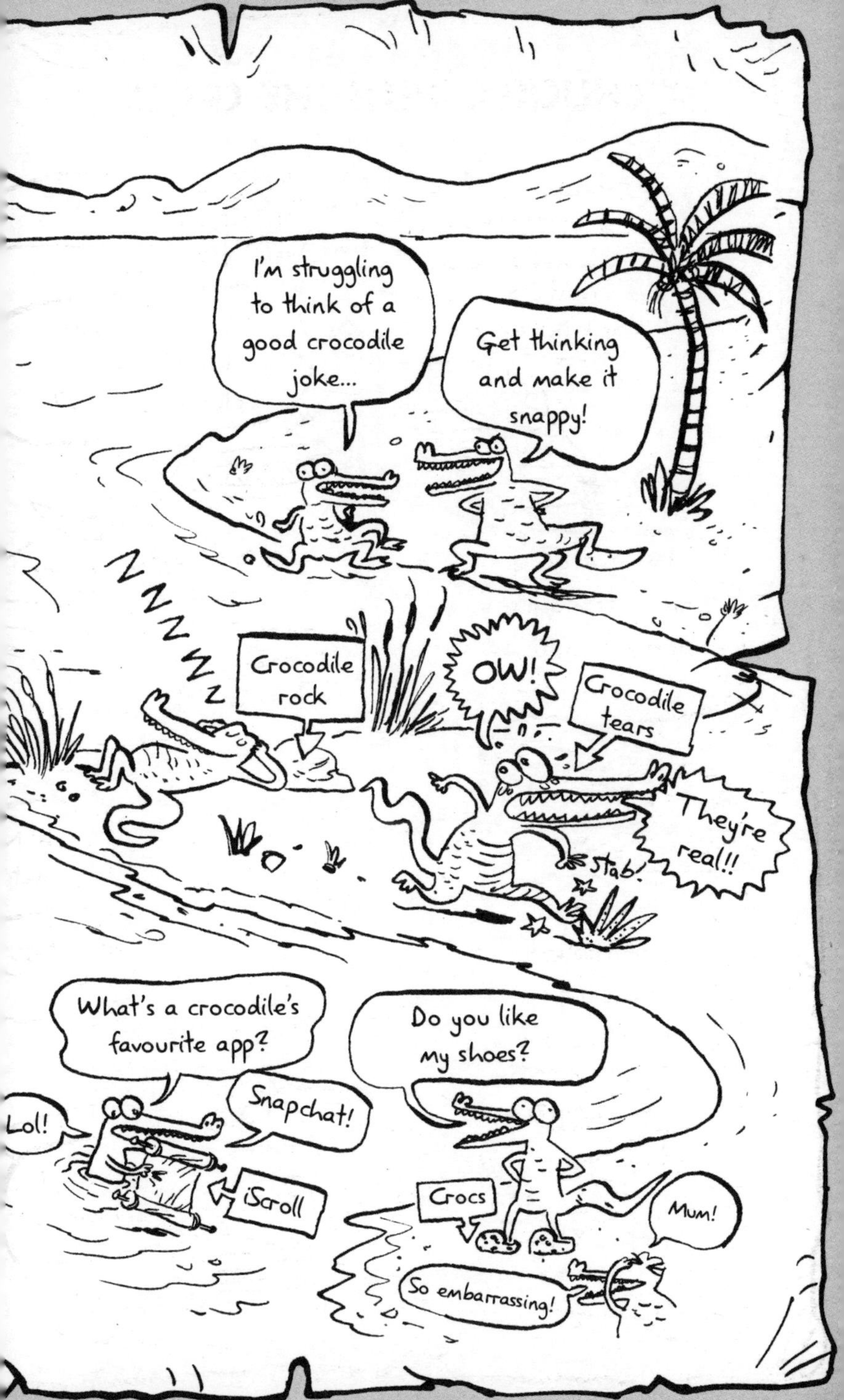
I'm struggling to think of a good crocodile joke...
Get thinking and make it snappy!
ZZZZZ
Crocodile rock
OW!
Crocodile tears
They're real!!
Stab!
What's a crocodile's favourite app?
Lol!
Snapchat!
iScroll
Do you like my shoes?
Crocs
Mum!
So embarrassing!

LIBRARY LAUGHS

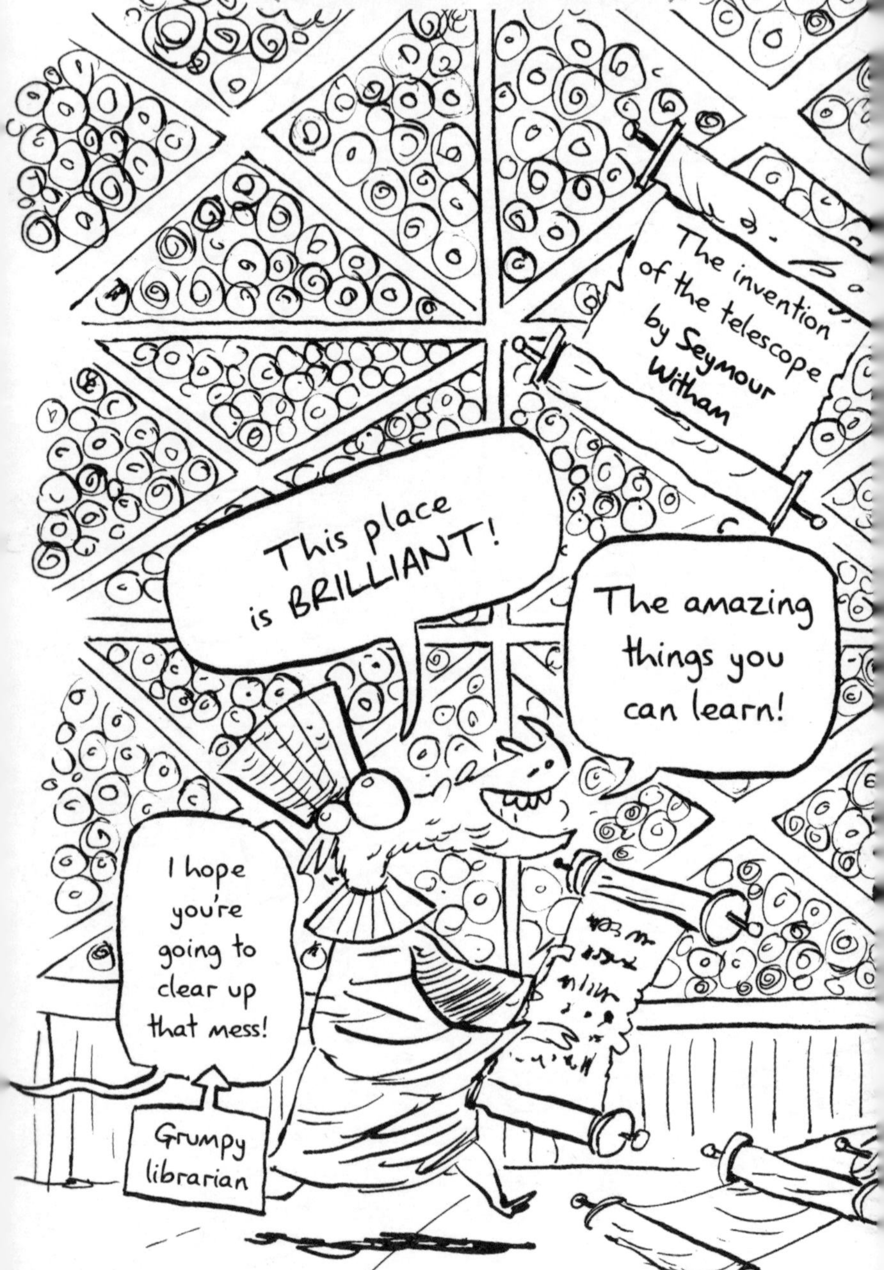
The invention of the telescope by Seymour Witham
This place is BRILLIANT!
The amazing things you can learn!
I hope you're going to clear up that mess!
Grumpy librarian

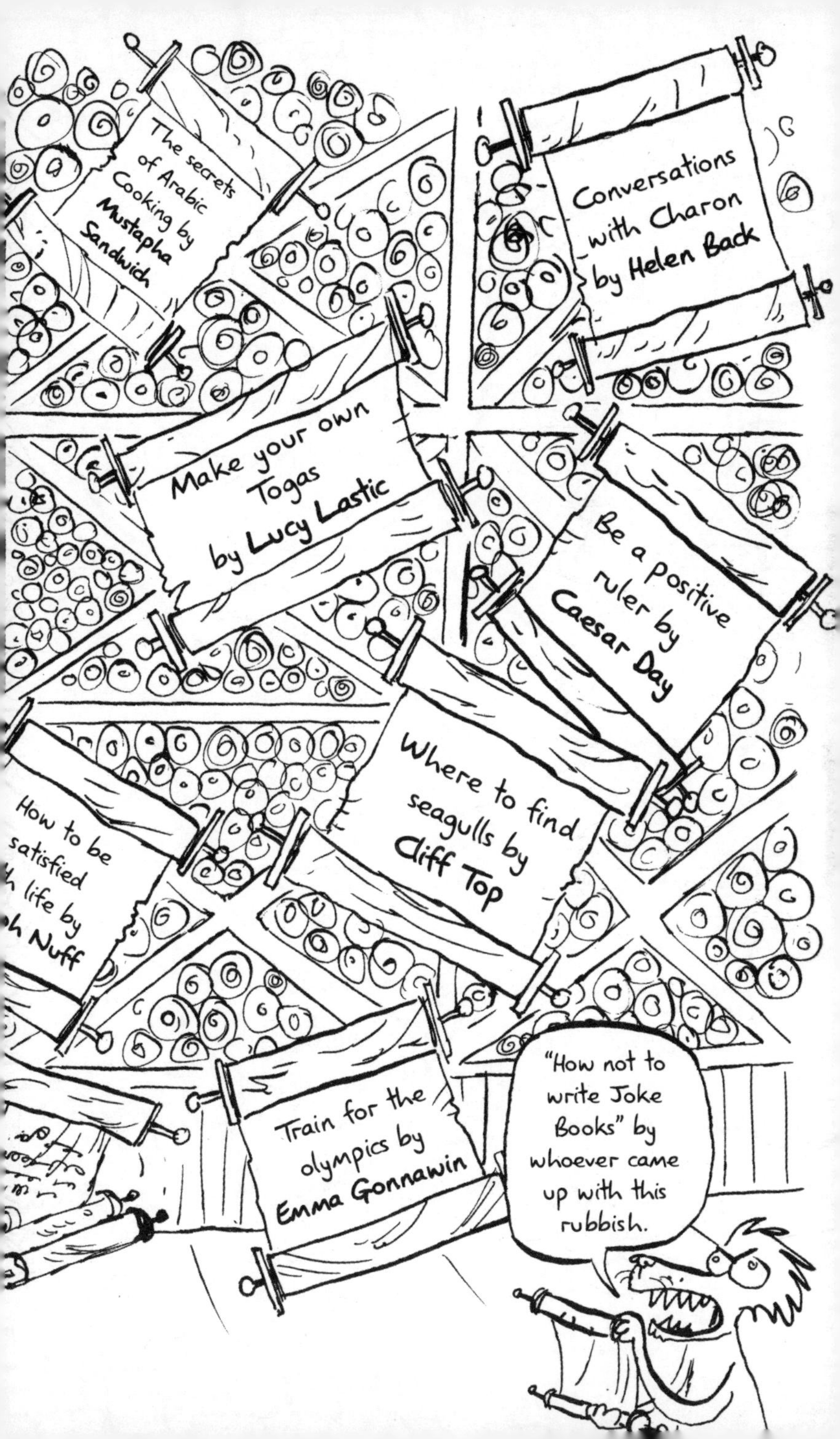
The secrets of Arabic Cooking by Mustapha Sandwich
Conversations with Charon by Helen Back
Make your own Togas by Lucy Lastic
Be a positive ruler by Caesar Day
Where to find seagulls by Cliff Top
How to be satisfied ...h life by ...h Nuff
Train for the olympics by Emma Gonnawin
"How not to write Joke Books" by whoever came up with this rubbish.

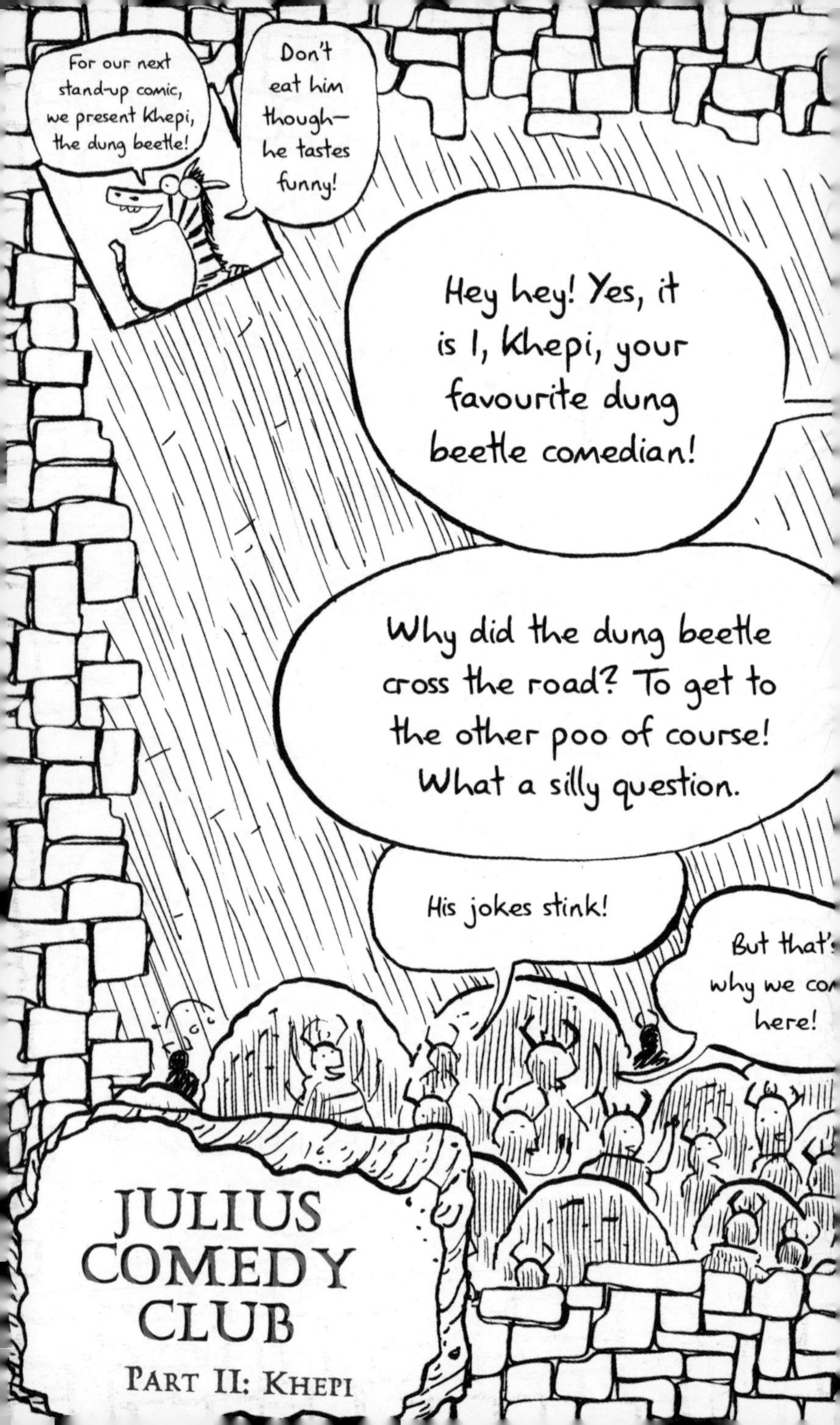
For our next stand-up comic, we present Khepi, the dung beetle!
Don't eat him though— he tastes funny!
Hey hey! Yes, it is I, Khepi, your favourite dung beetle comedian!
Why did the dung beetle cross the road? To get to the other poo of course! What a silly question.
His jokes stink!
But that' why we co here!
JULIUS COMEDY CLUB
PART II: KHEPI

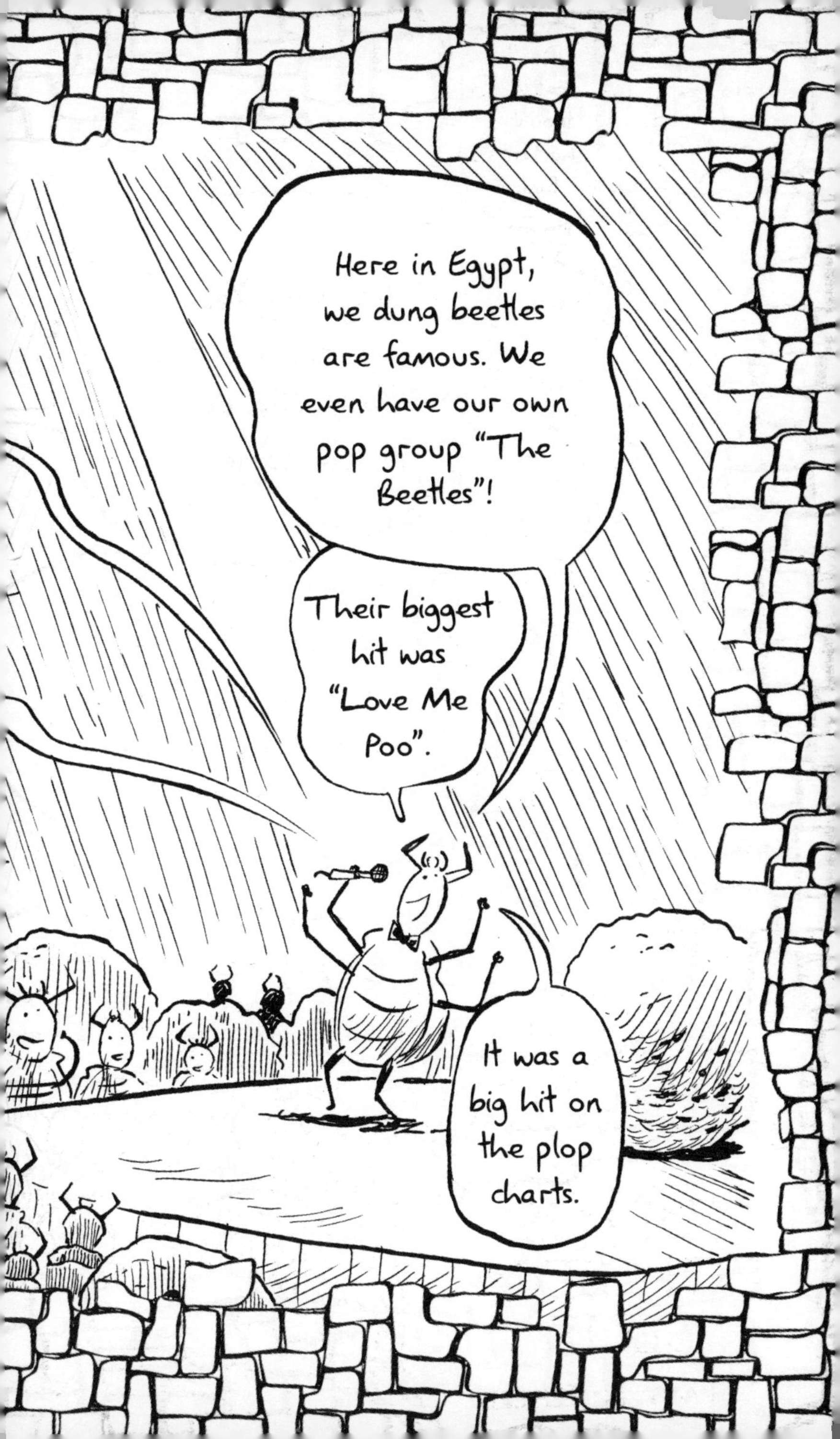
Here in Egypt, we dung beetles are famous. We even have our own pop group "The Beetles"!
Their biggest hit was "Love Me Poo".
It was a big hit on the plop charts.

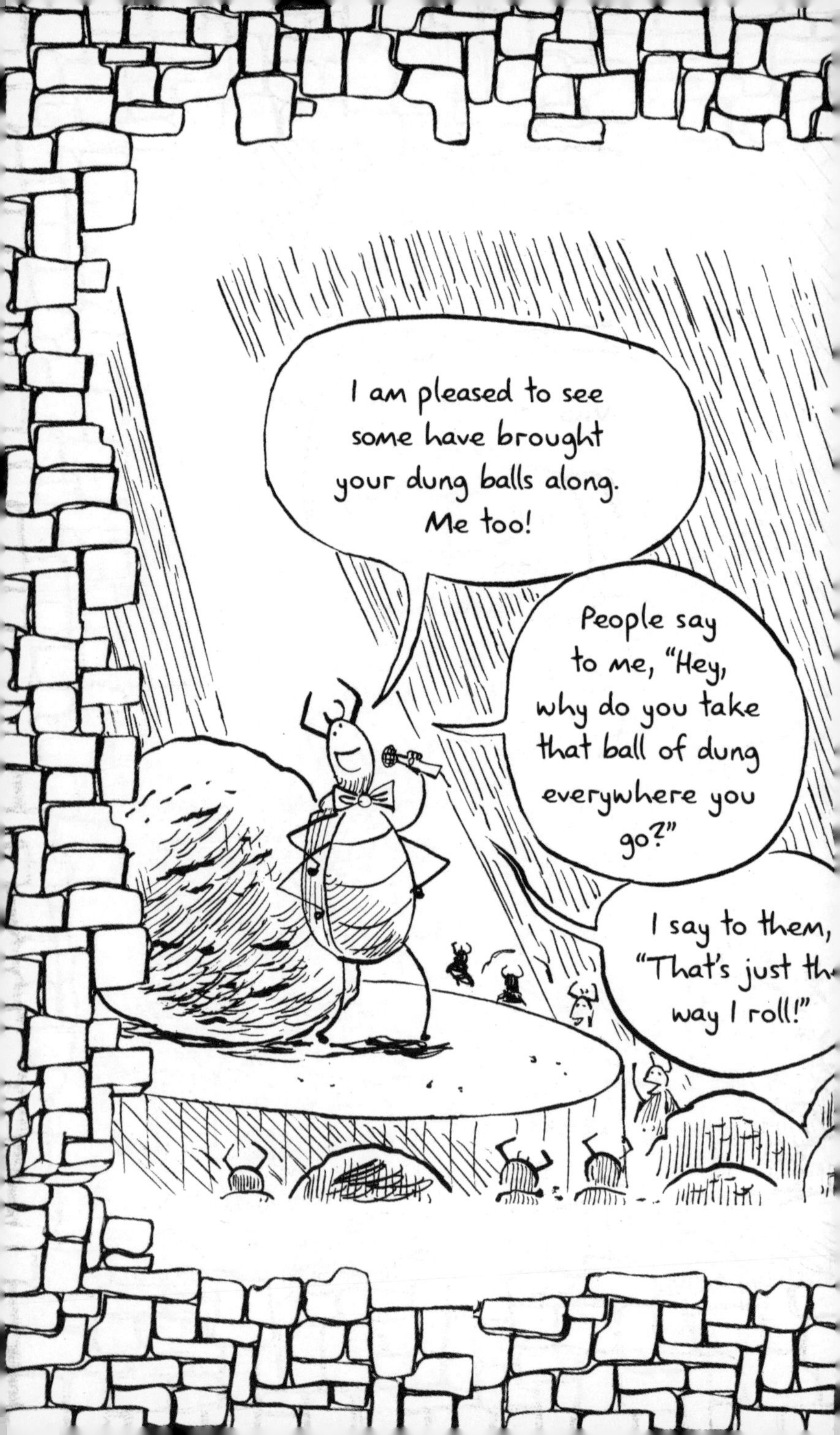
I am pleased to see some have brought your dung balls along. Me too!
People say to me, "Hey, why do you take that ball of dung everywhere you go?"
I say to them, "That's just th way I roll!"

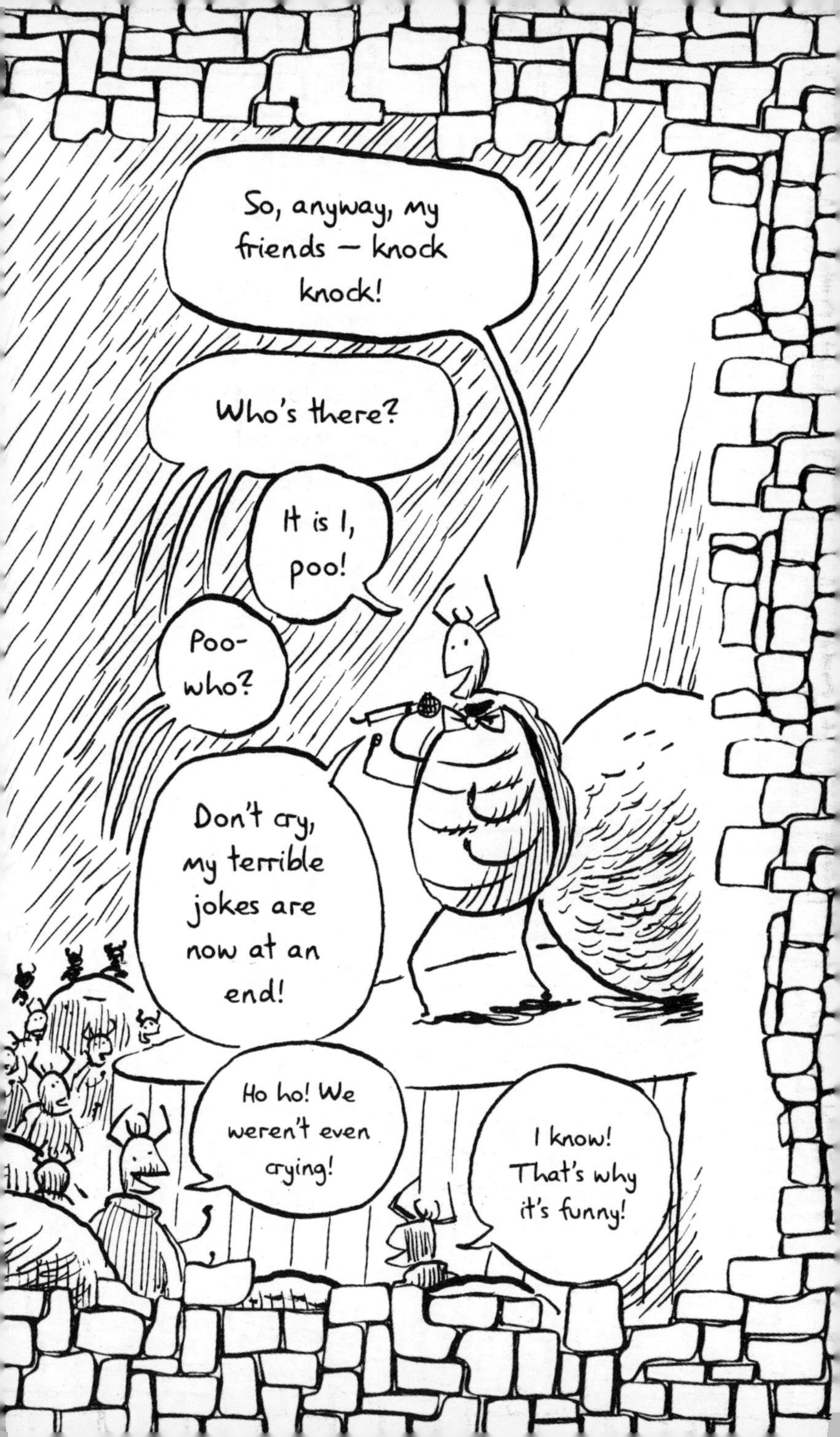
So, anyway, my friends – knock knock!
Who's there?
It is I, poo!
Poo-who?
Don't cry, my terrible jokes are now at an end!
Ho ho! We weren't even crying!
I know! That's why it's funny!

THE RIDDLE OF THE SPHINX

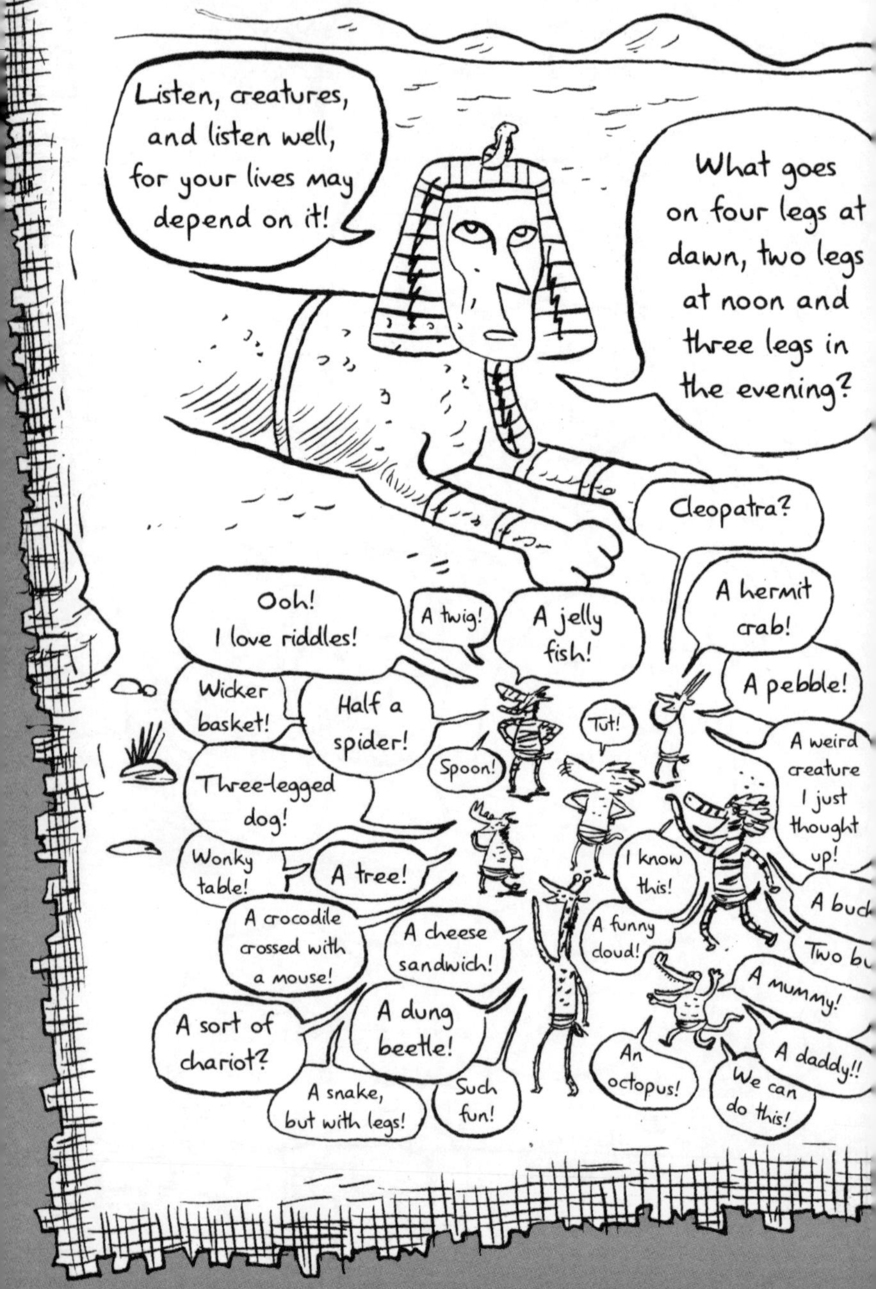

Listen, creatures, and listen well, for your lives may depend on it!
What goes on four legs at dawn, two legs at noon and three legs in the evening?
Cleopatra?
Ooh! I love riddles!
A twig!
A jelly fish!
A hermit crab!
A pebble!
Wicker basket!
Half a spider!
Tut!
Spoon!
Three-legged dog!
A weird creature I just thought up!
Wonky table!
A tree!
I know this!
A crocodile crossed with a mouse!
A cheese sandwich!
A funny cloud!
A mummy!
A sort of chariot?
A dung beetle!
An octopus!
A daddy!!
A snake, but with legs!
Such fun!
We can do this!

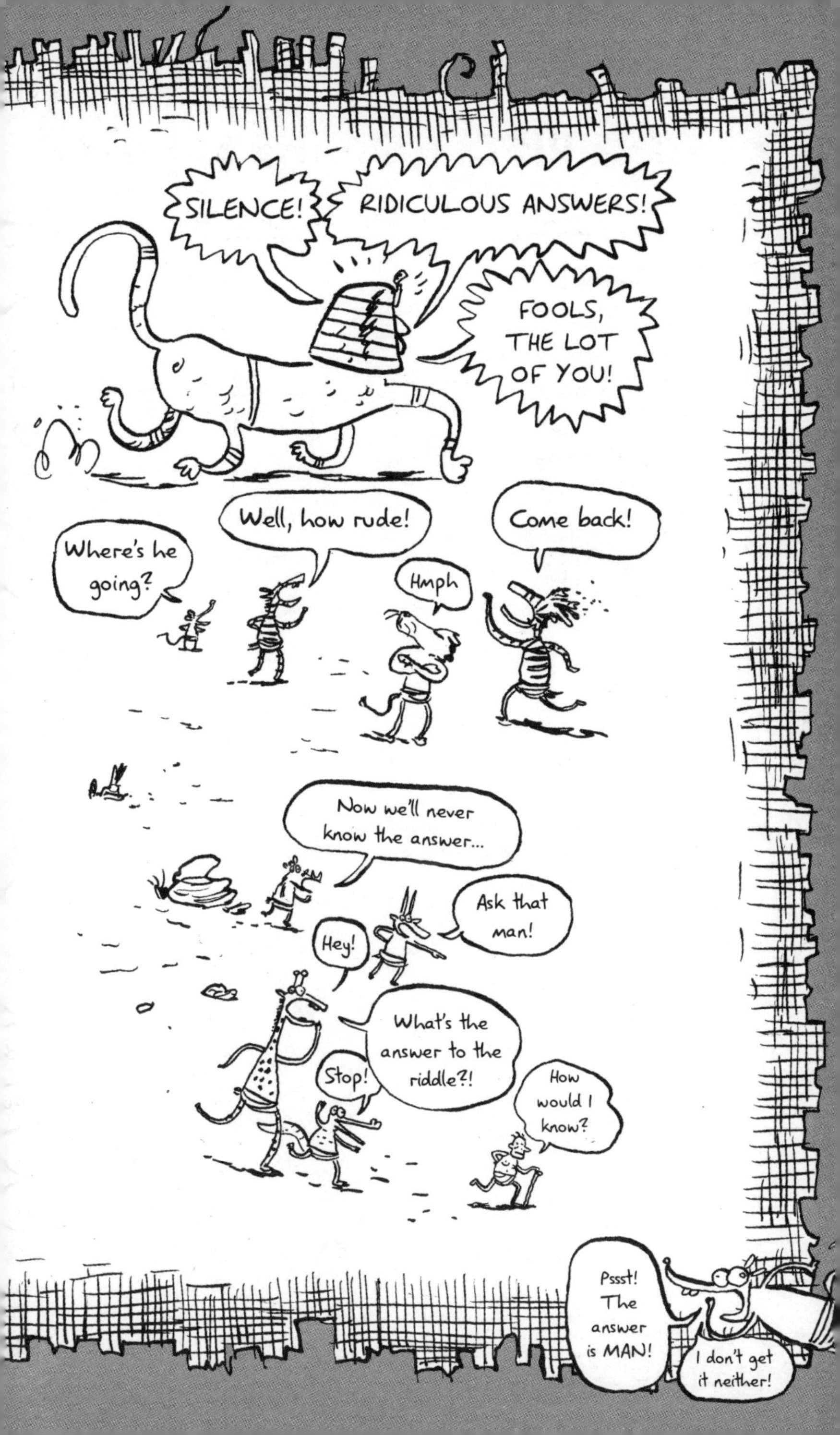
SILENCE!
RIDICULOUS ANSWERS!
FOOLS, THE LOT OF YOU!
Where's he going?
Well, how rude!
Hmph
Come back!
Now we'll never know the answer...
Ask that man!
Hey!
What's the answer to the riddle?!
Stop!
How would I know?
Pssst! The answer is MAN!
I don't get it neither!

FELIX'S ROCK COLLECTION

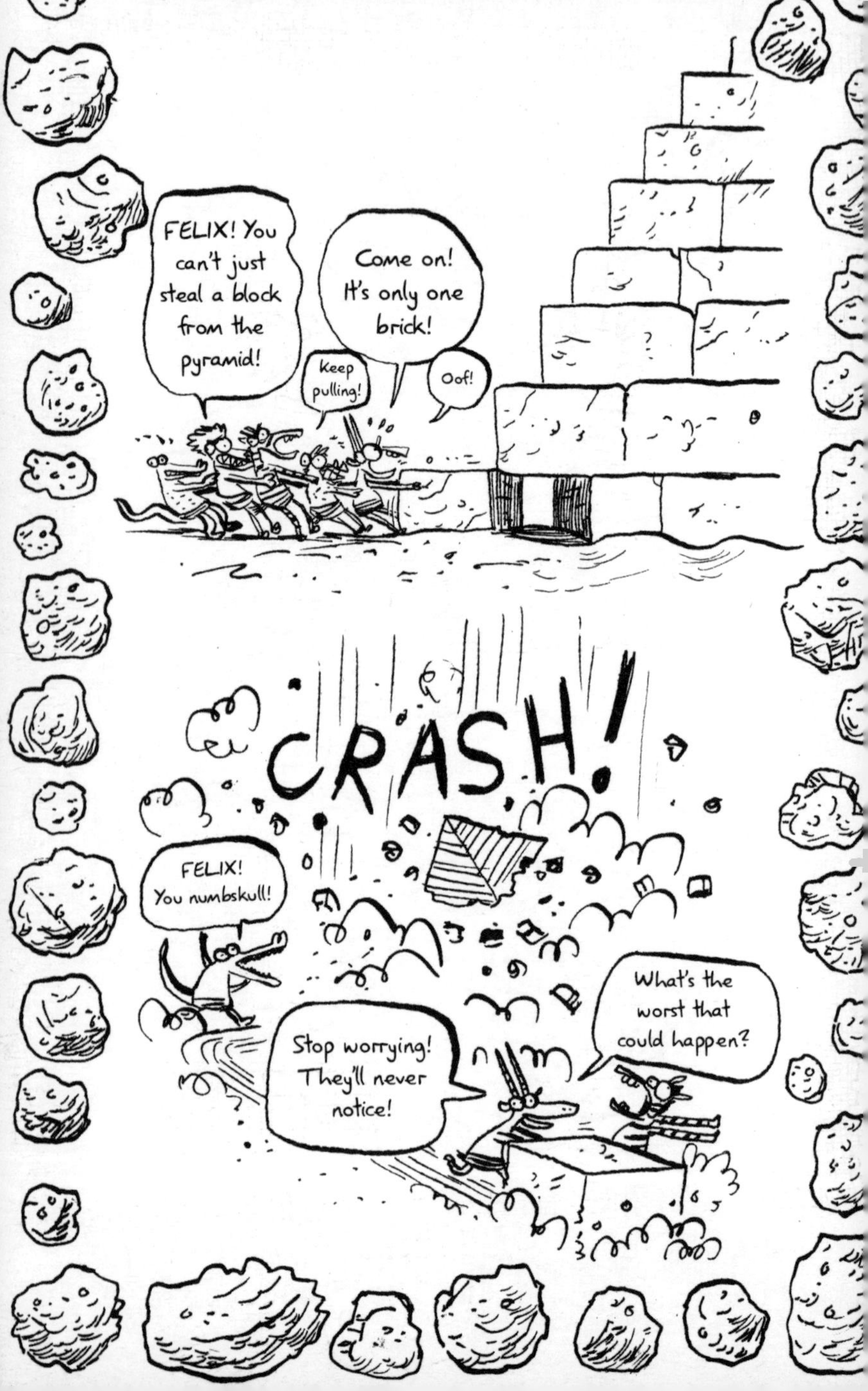
FELIX! You can't just steal a block from the pyramid!
Come on! It's only one brick!
Keep pulling!
Oof!
CRASH!
FELIX! You numbskull!
Stop worrying! They'll never notice!
What's the worst that could happen?

PHARAOH FUNNIES

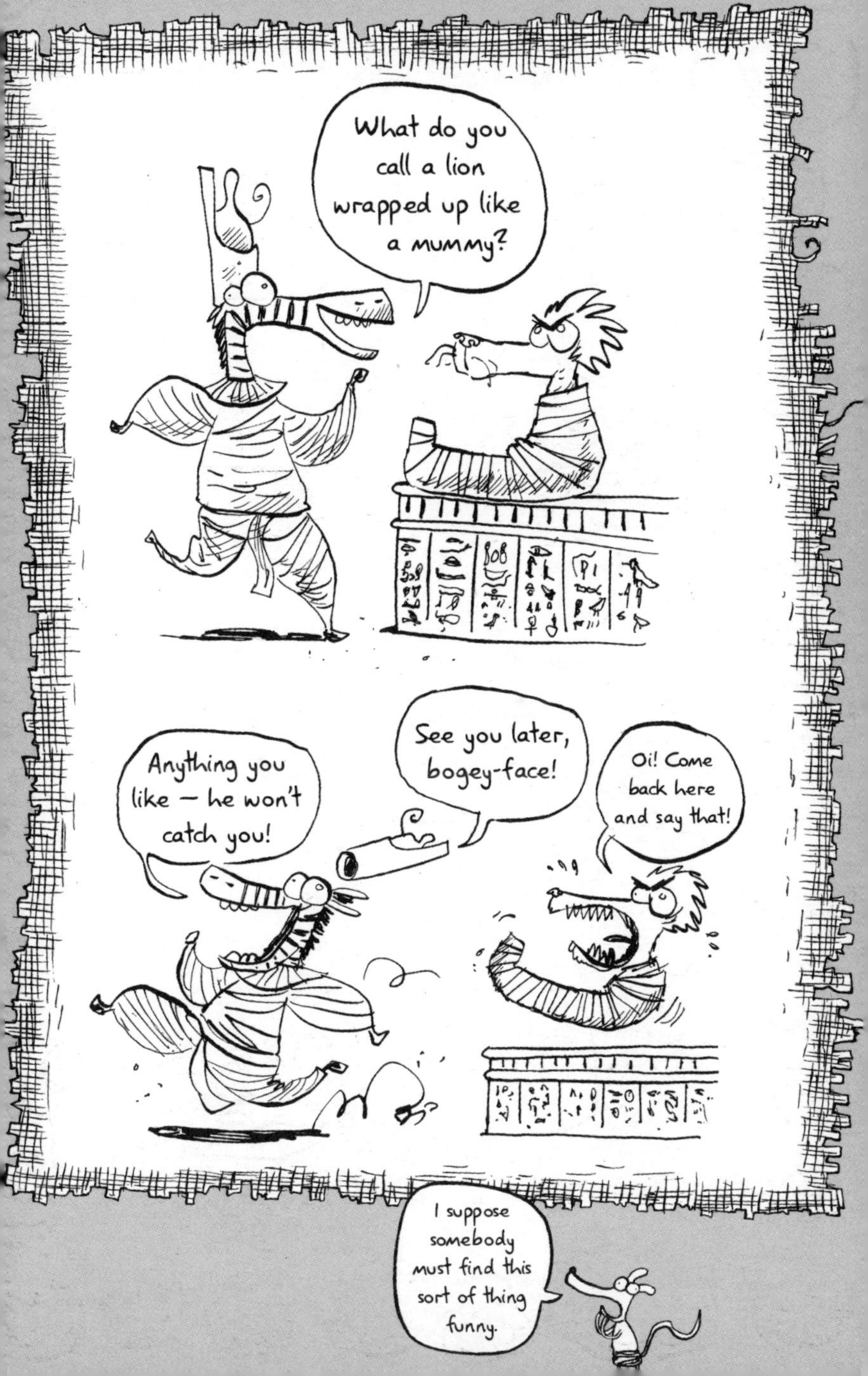
What do you call a lion wrapped up like a mummy?
Anything you like – he won't catch you!
See you later, bogey-face!
Oi! Come back here and say that!
I suppose somebody must find this sort of thing funny.

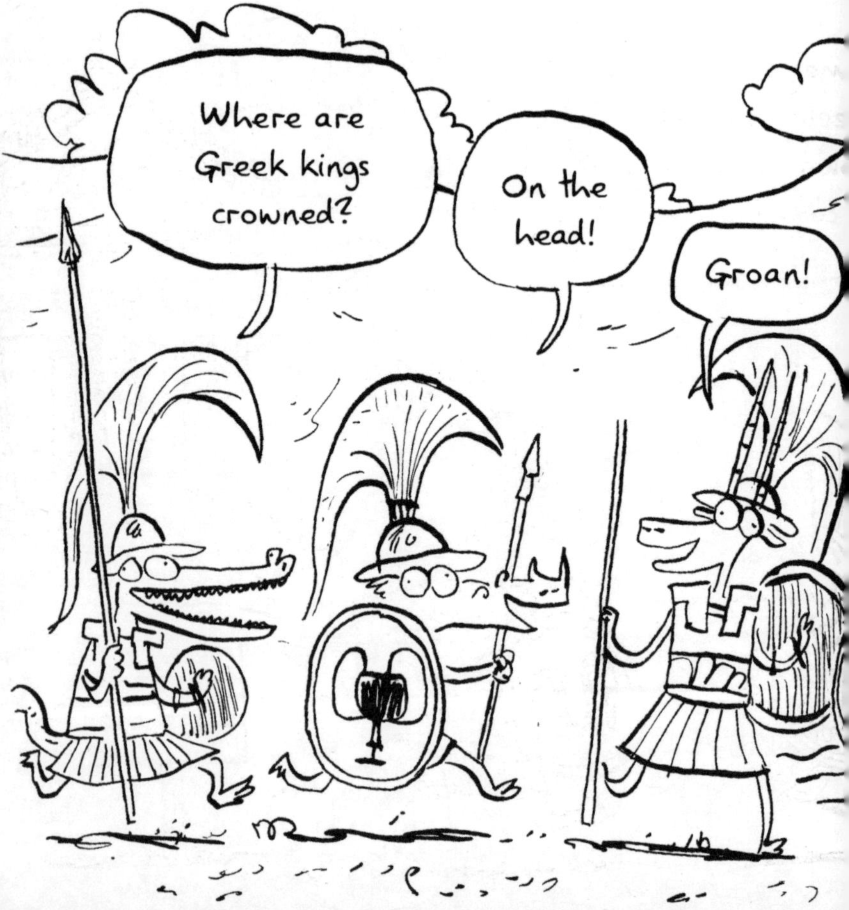
Where are Greek kings crowned?
On the head!
Groan!

PART IV
ANCIENT GREEKS

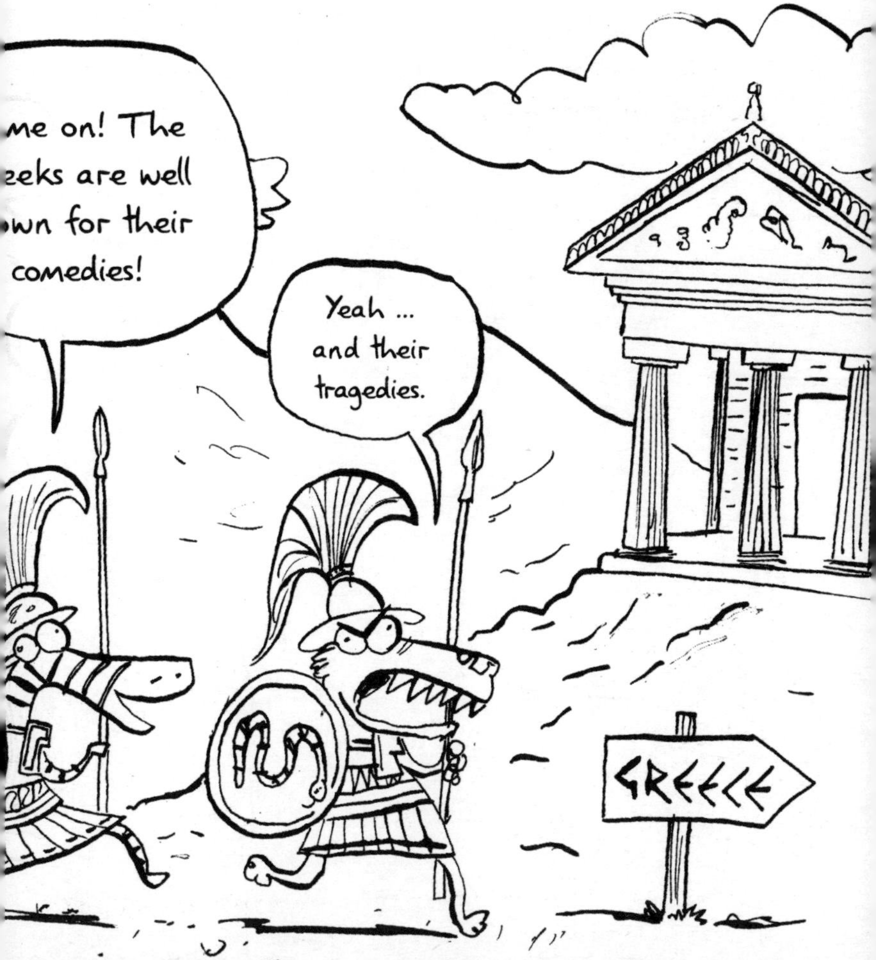
me on! The eeks are well wn for their comedies!
Yeah ... and their tragedies.
GREECE

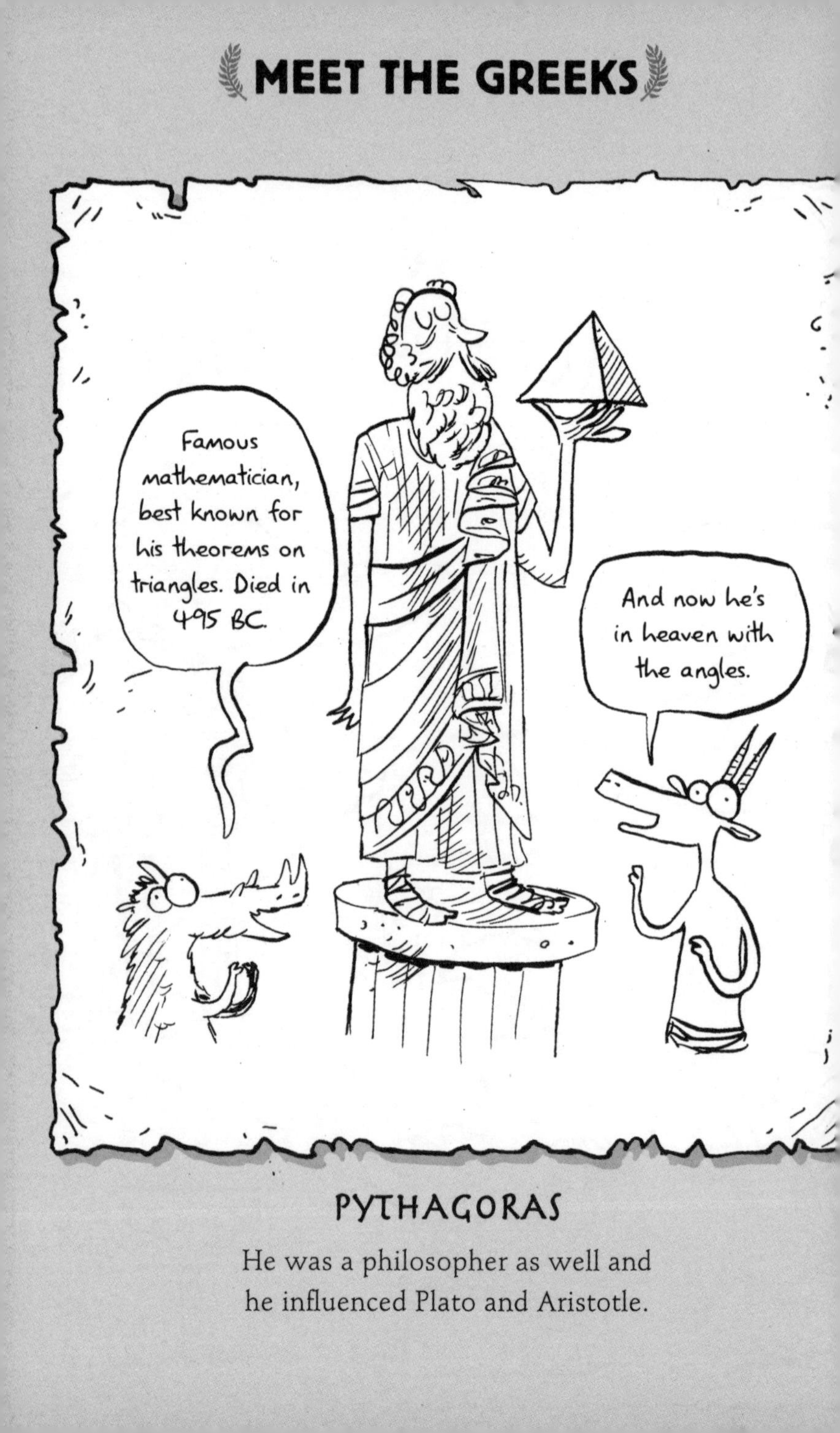
Famous mathematician, best known for his theorems on triangles. Died in 495 BC.
And now he's in heaven with the angles.

PYTHAGORAS

He was a philosopher as well and he influenced Plato and Aristotle.

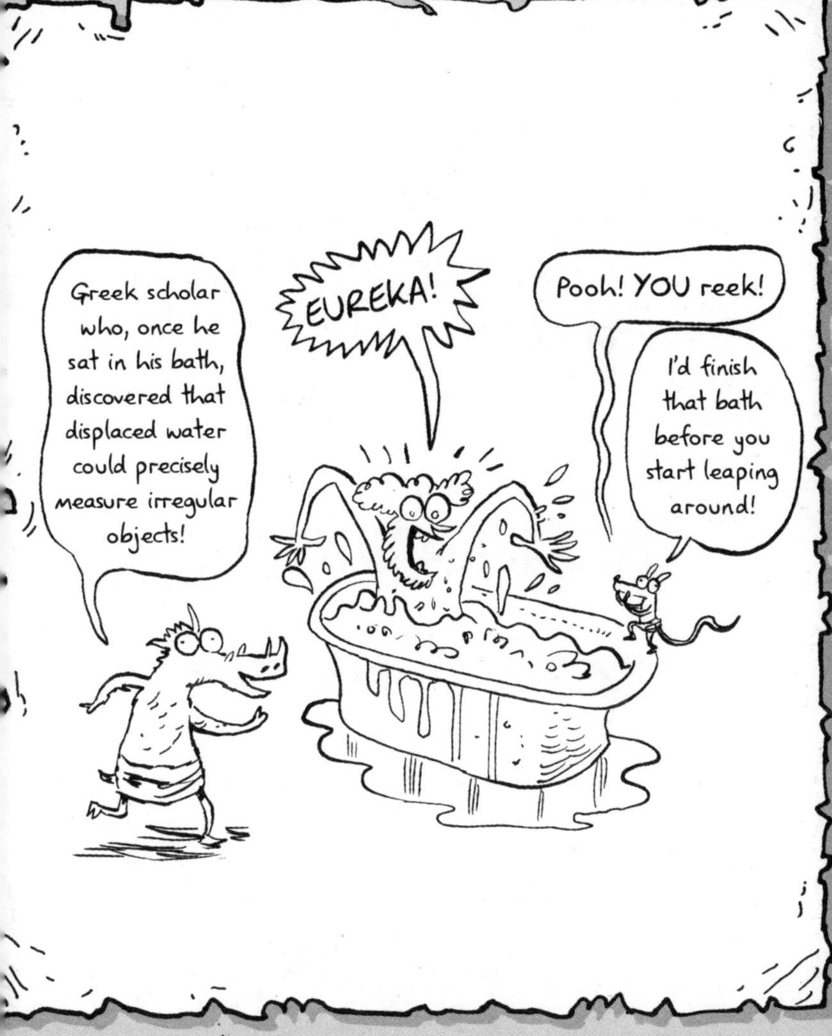
Greek scholar who, once he sat in his bath, discovered that displaced water could precisely measure irregular objects!
EUREKA!
Pooh! YOU reek!
I'd finish that bath before you start leaping around!

ARCHIMEDES

He also calculated the value of pi, which is the circumference of a circle.

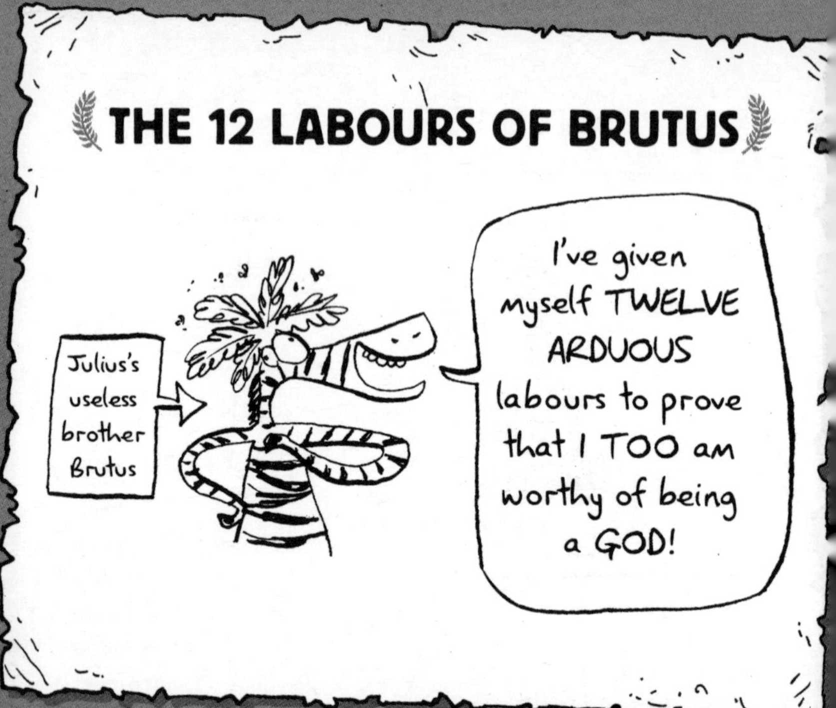
THE 12 LABOURS OF BRUTUS
Julius's useless brother Brutus
I've given myself TWELVE ARDUOUS labours to prove that I TOO am worthy of being a GOD!

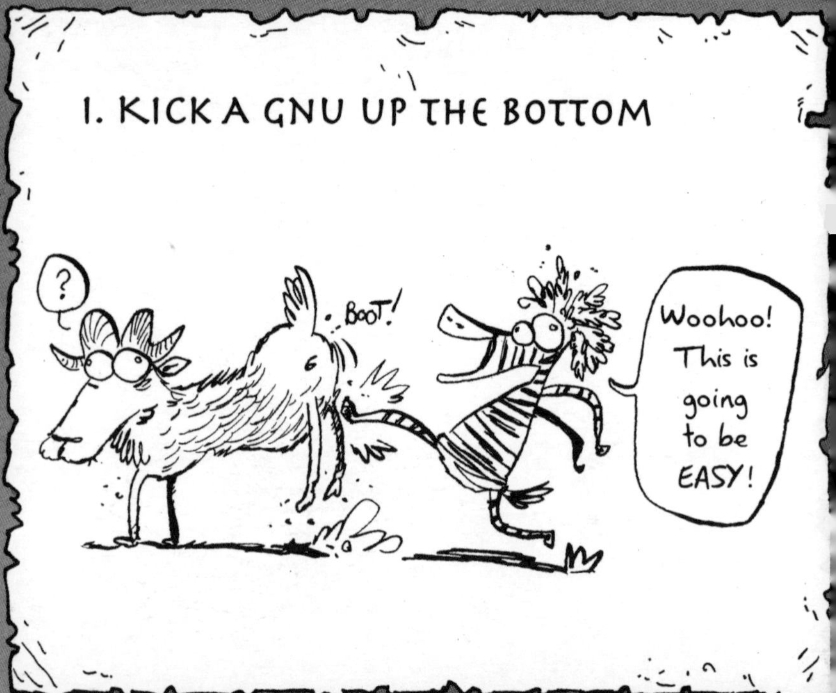
1. KICK A GNU UP THE BOTTOM
?
BOOT!
Woohoo! This is going to be EASY!

II. GO SHOPPING

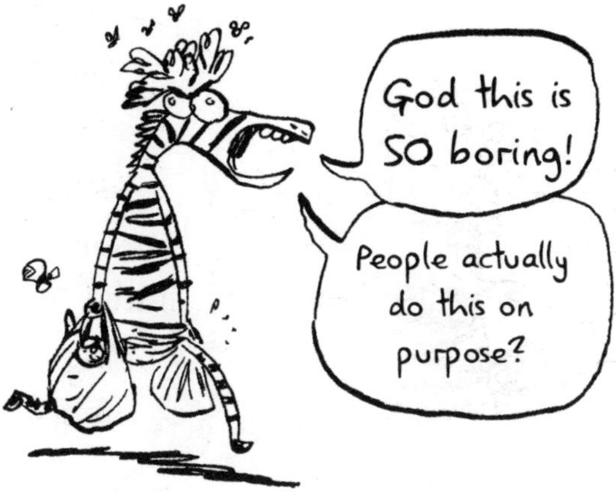
God this is SO boring!
People actually do this on purpose?

III. READ A SCROLL

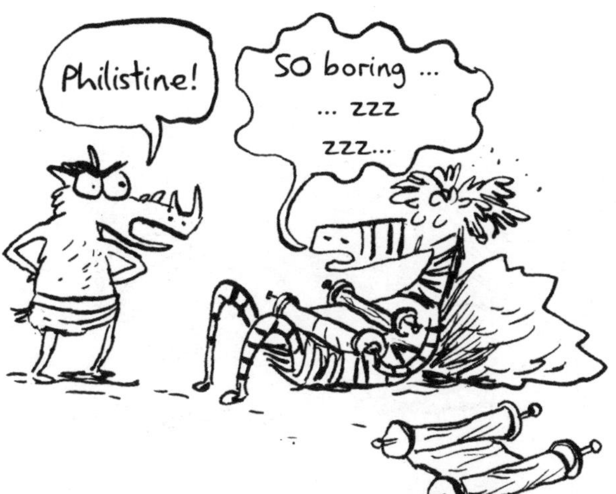
Philistine!
SO boring ... ... zzz zzz...

IV. WRESTLE A CAT

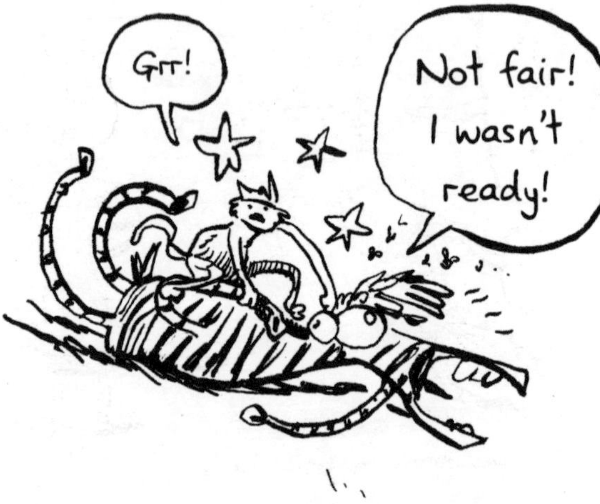
Grr!
Not fair! I wasn't ready!

V. DO THE WASHING UP

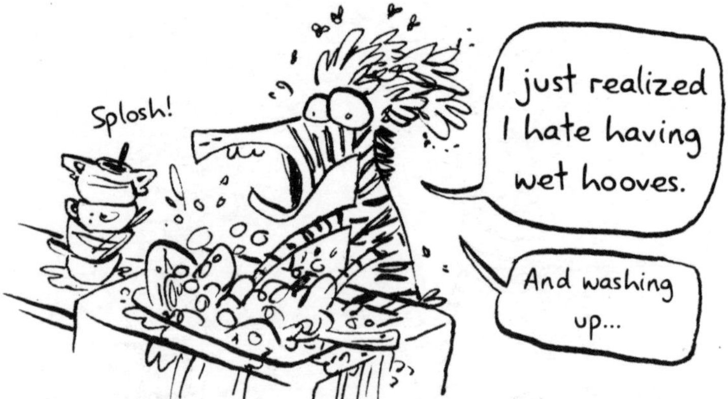
Splosh!
I just realized I hate having wet hooves.
And washing up...

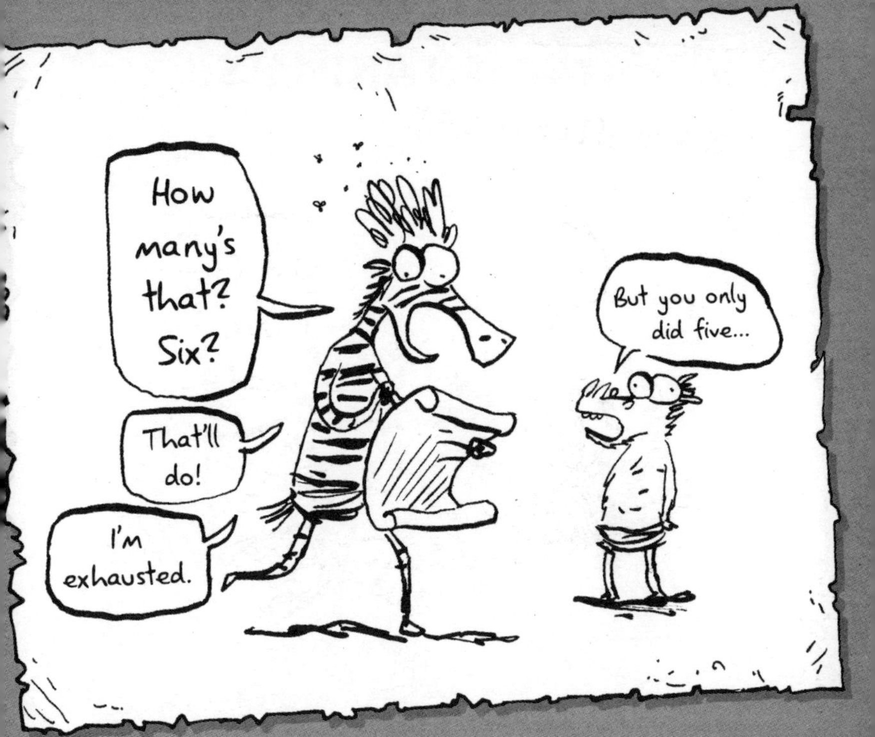
How many's that? Six?
That'll do!
I'm exhausted.
But you only did five...

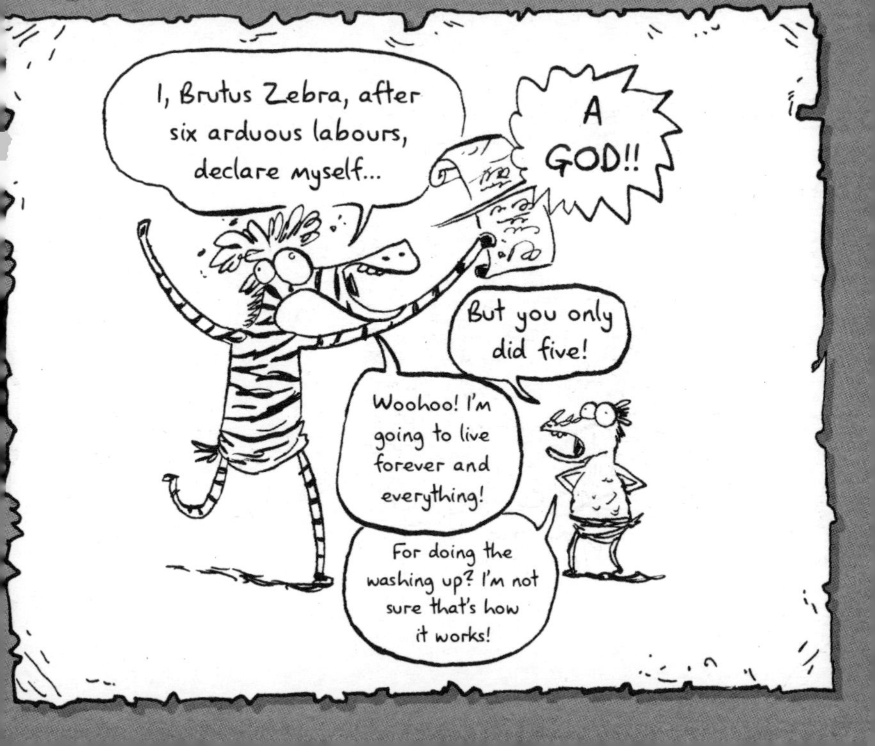
I, Brutus Zebra, after six arduous labours, declare myself...
A GOD!!
But you only did five!
Woohoo! I'm going to live forever and everything!
For doing the washing up? I'm not sure that's how it works!

TROJAN ANIMALS

REJECTED WOODEN ANIMALS
BUILT TO SNEAK INTO TROY!

I. HEDGEHOG

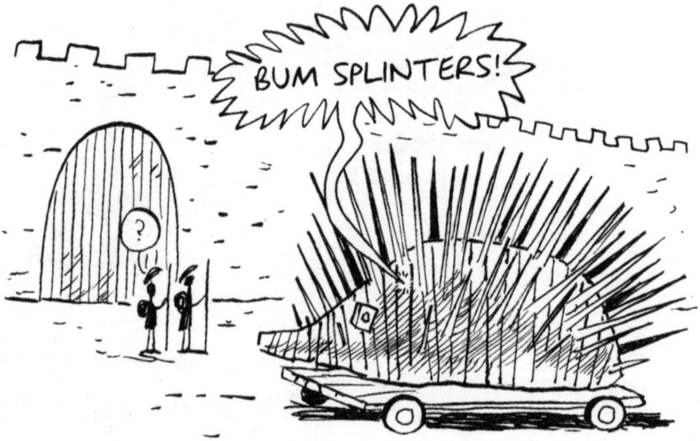
BUM SPLINTERS!
?

II. FROG

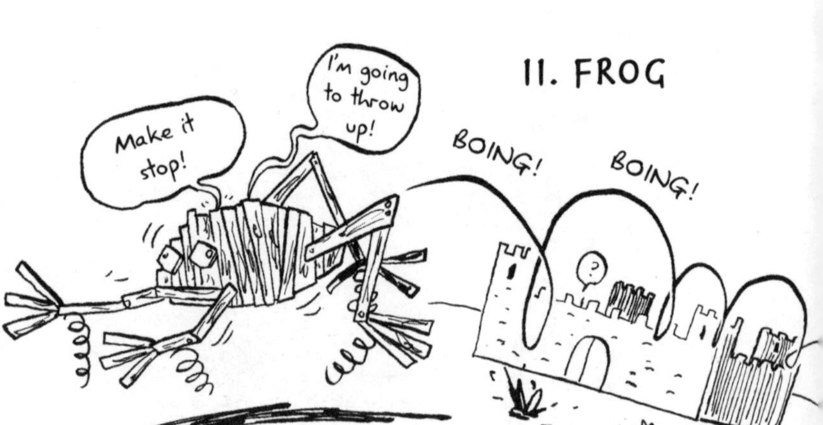
Make it stop!
I'm going to throw up!
BOING!
BOING!
?

III. SPIDER

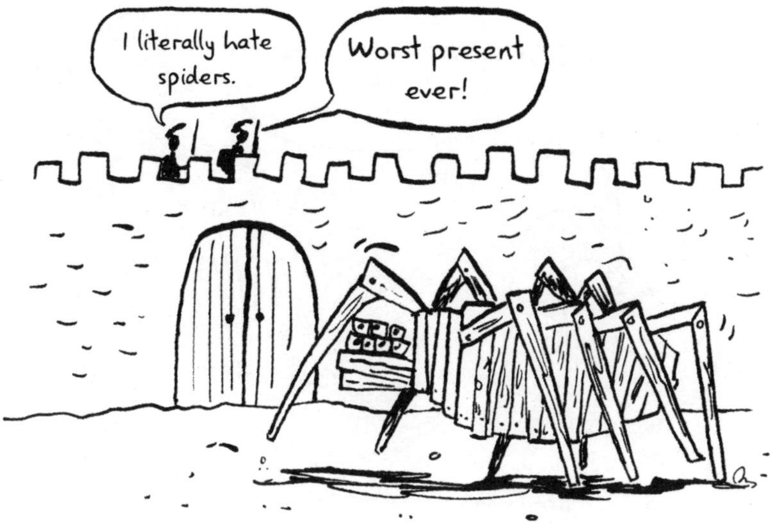
I literally hate spiders.
Worst present ever!

IV. FISH

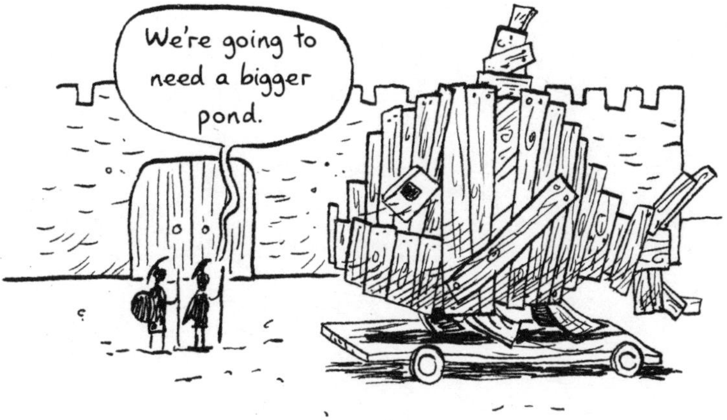
We're going to need a bigger pond.

GREEK GAGS

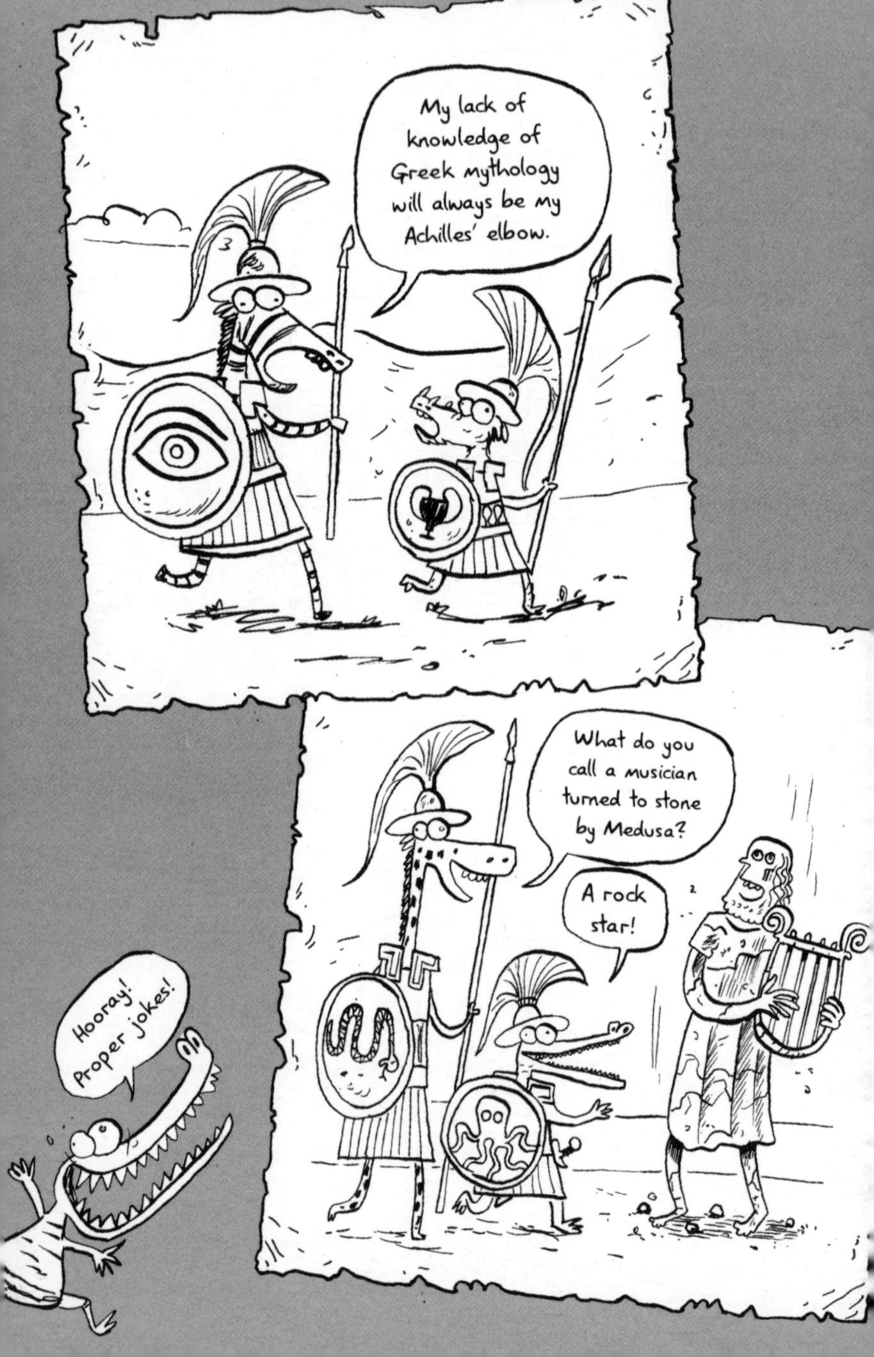
My lack of knowledge of Greek mythology will always be my Achilles' elbow.
What do you call a musician turned to stone by Medusa?
A rock star!
Hooray! Proper jokes!

FELIX'S ROCK COLLECTION

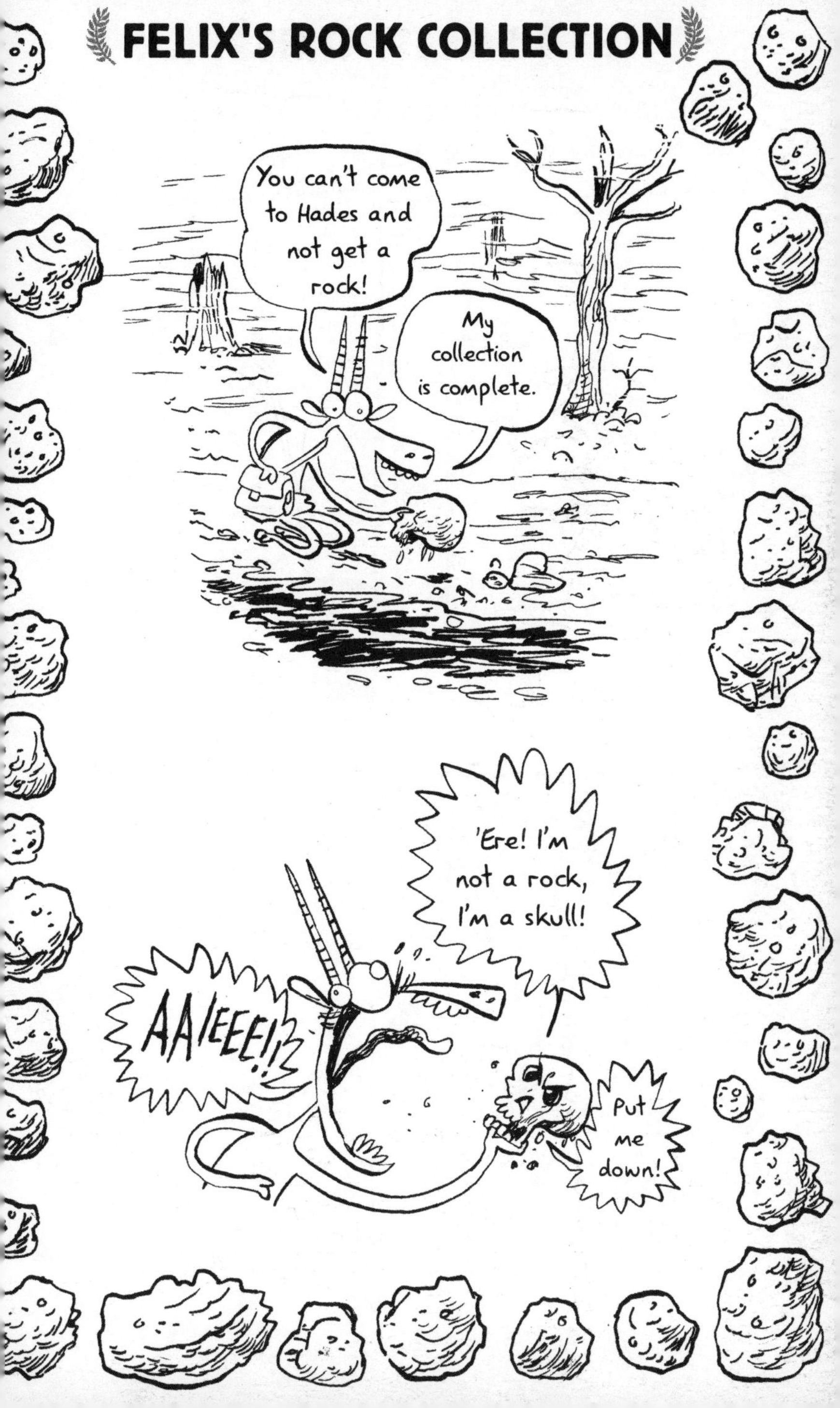
You can't come to Hades and not get a rock!
My collection is complete.
'Ere! I'm not a rock, I'm a skull!
AAIEEEE!!
Put me down!

HEAD-DRESS TO IMPRESS

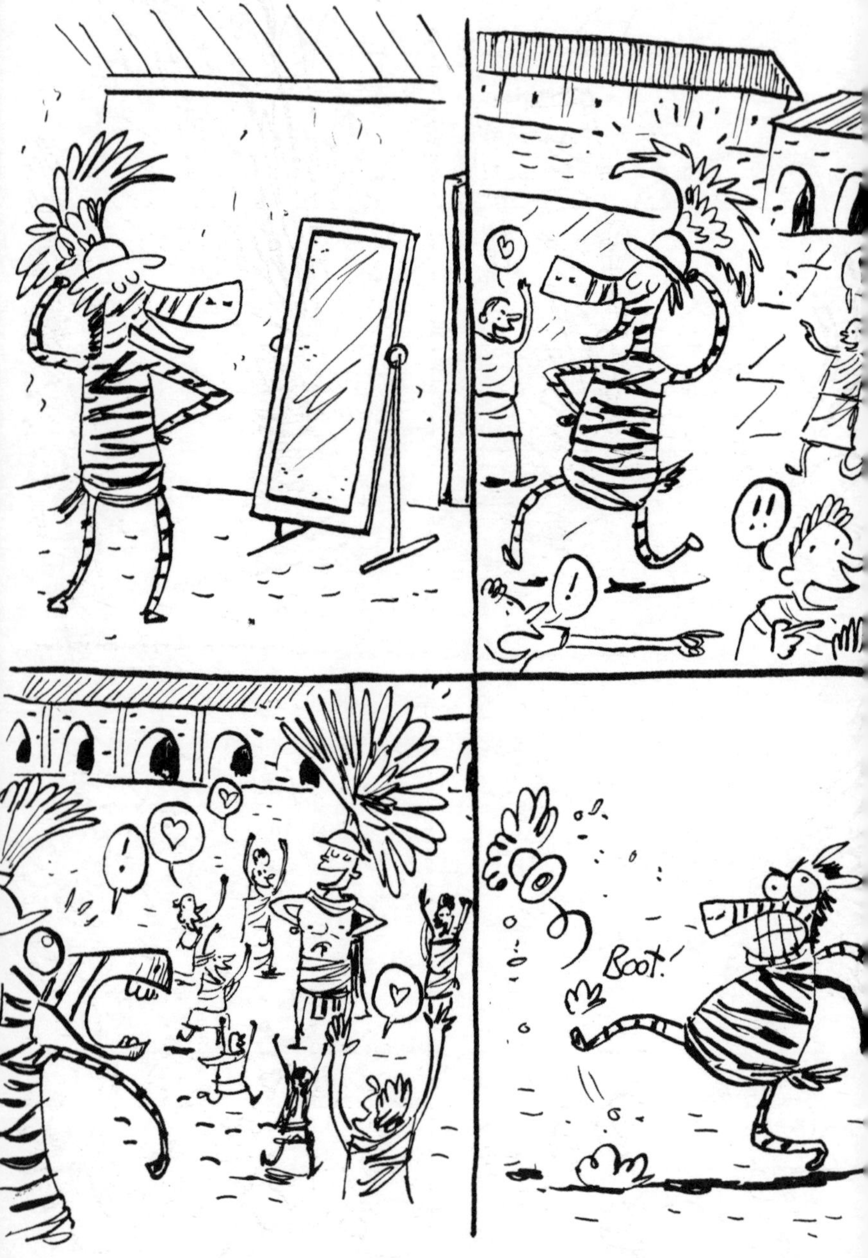

B
!!
!
!
Boot!

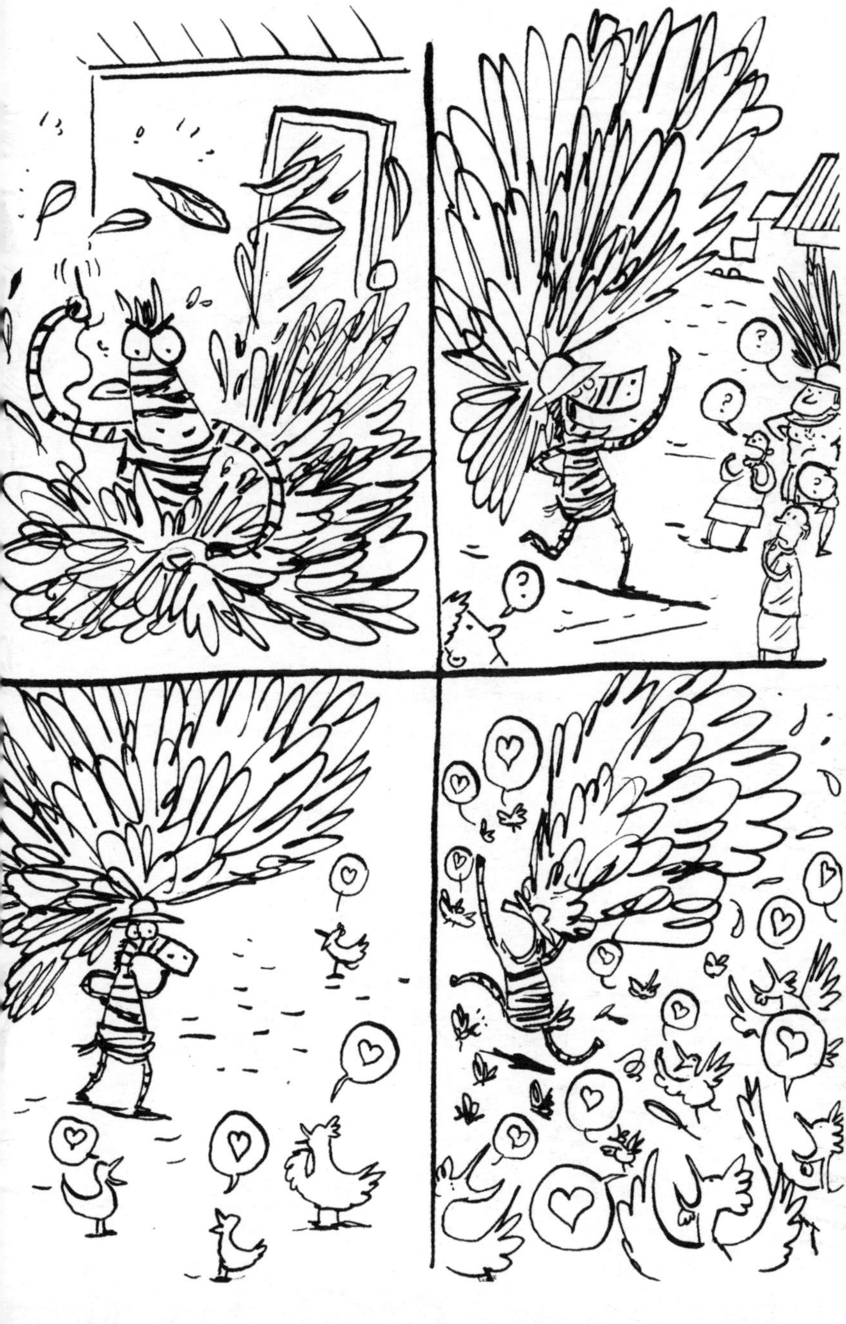

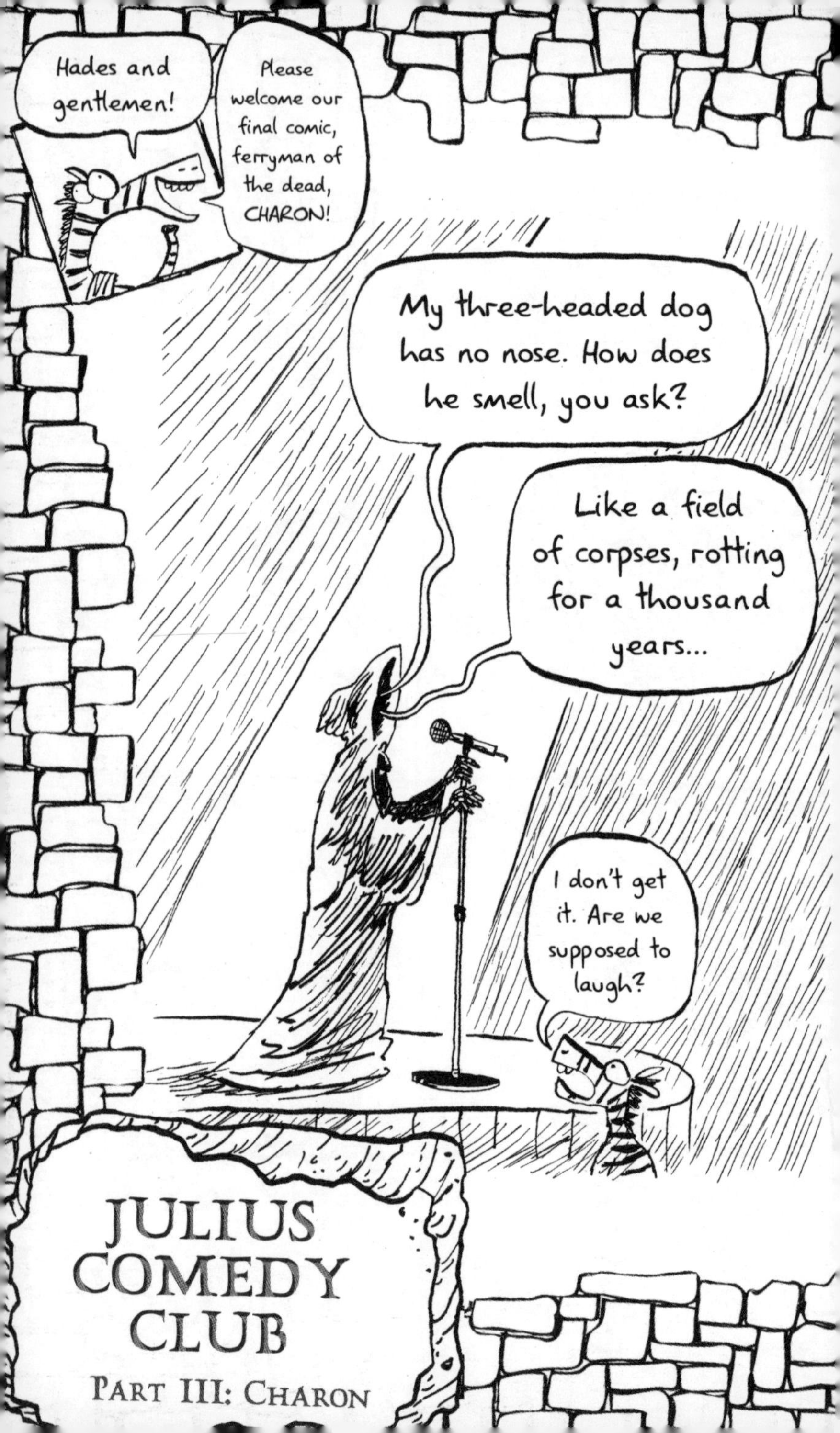
Hades and gentlemen!
Please welcome our final comic, ferryman of the dead, CHARON!
My three-headed dog has no nose. How does he smell, you ask?
Like a field of corpses, rotting for a thousand years...
I don't get it. Are we supposed to laugh?
JULIUS COMEDY CLUB
PART III: CHARON

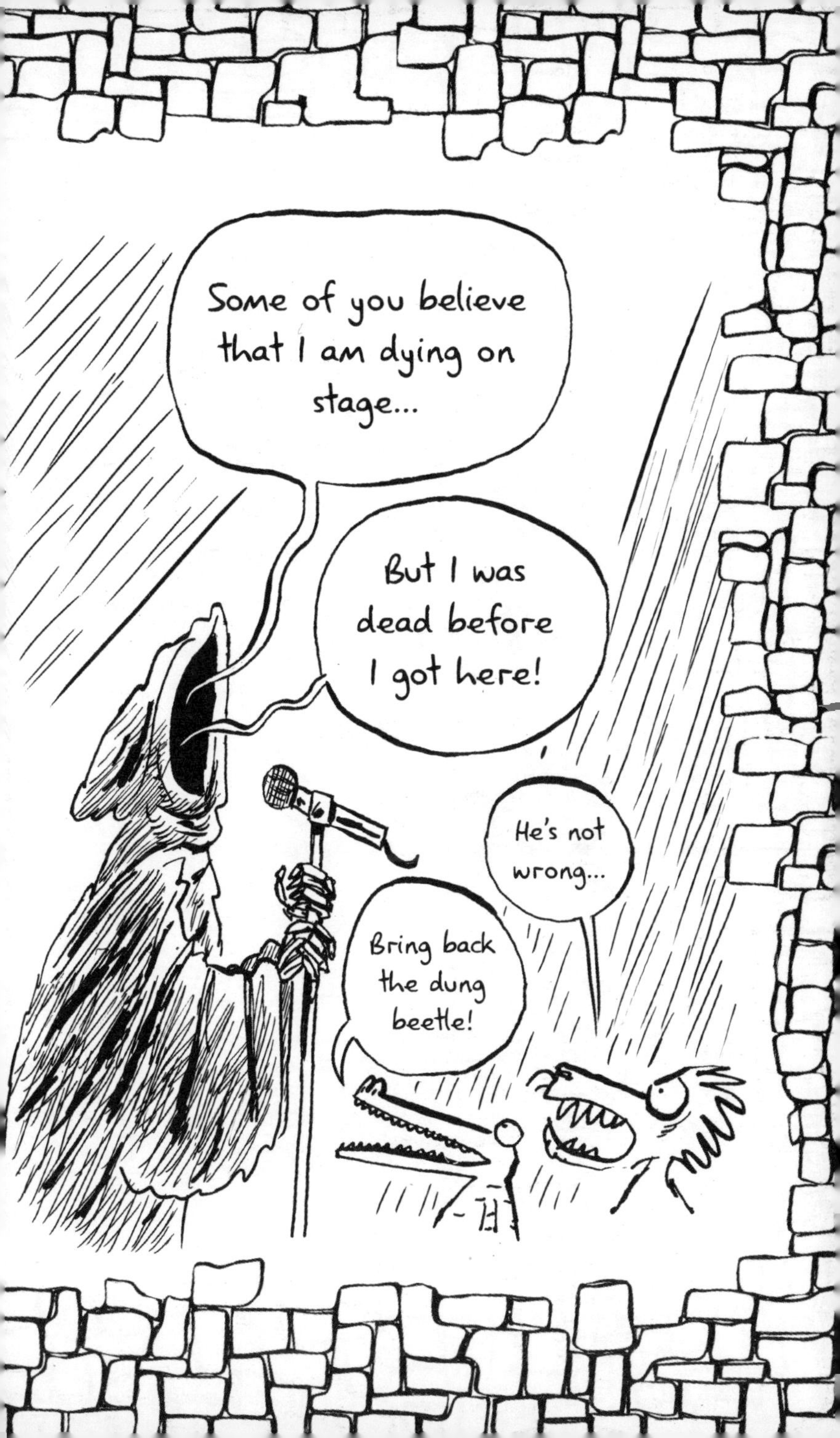
Some of you believe that I am dying on stage...
But I was dead before I got here!
He's not wrong...
Bring back the dung beetle!

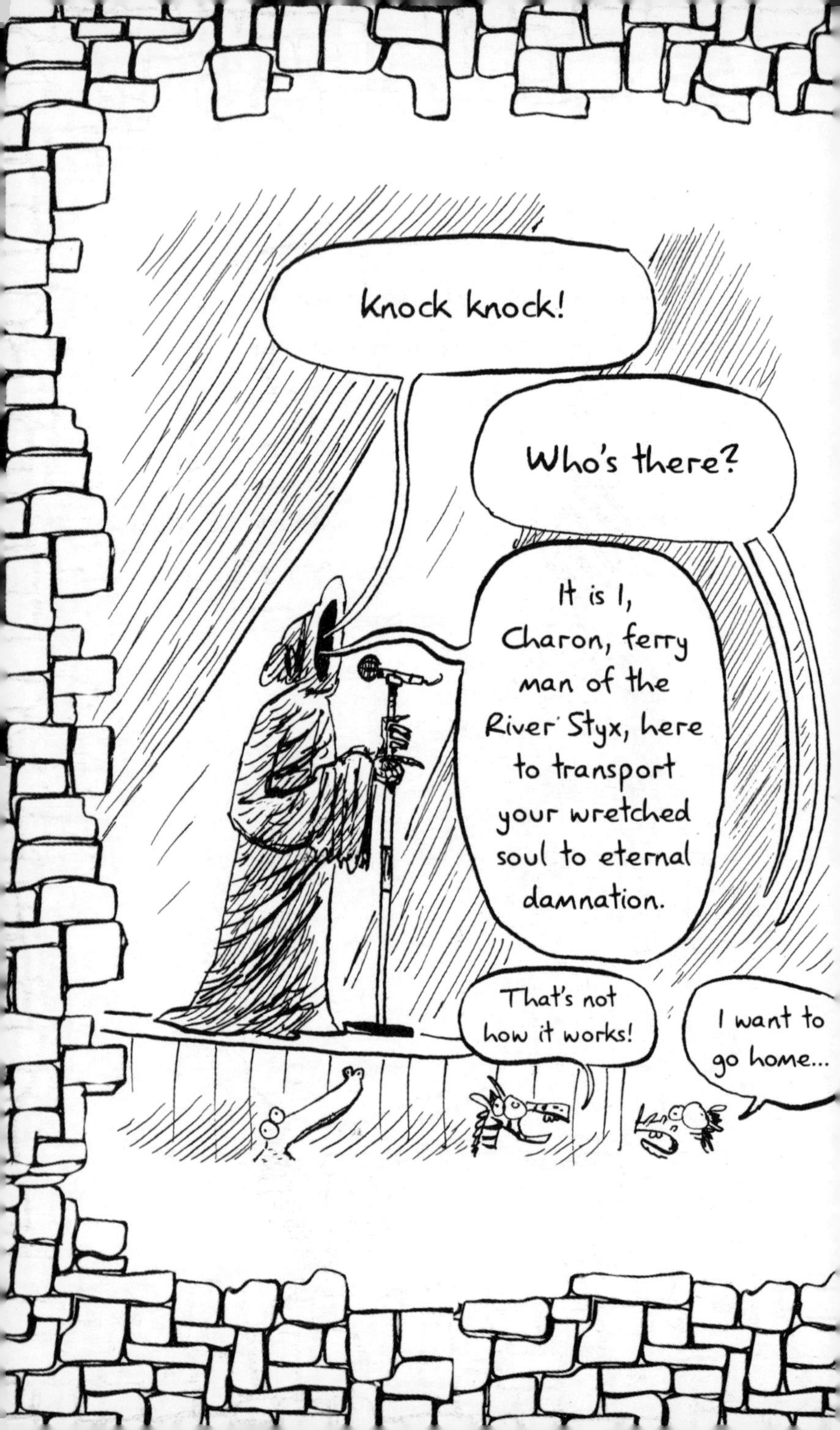
Knock knock!
Who's there?
It is I, Charon, ferry man of the River Styx, here to transport your wretched soul to eternal damnation.
That's not how it works!
I want to go home...

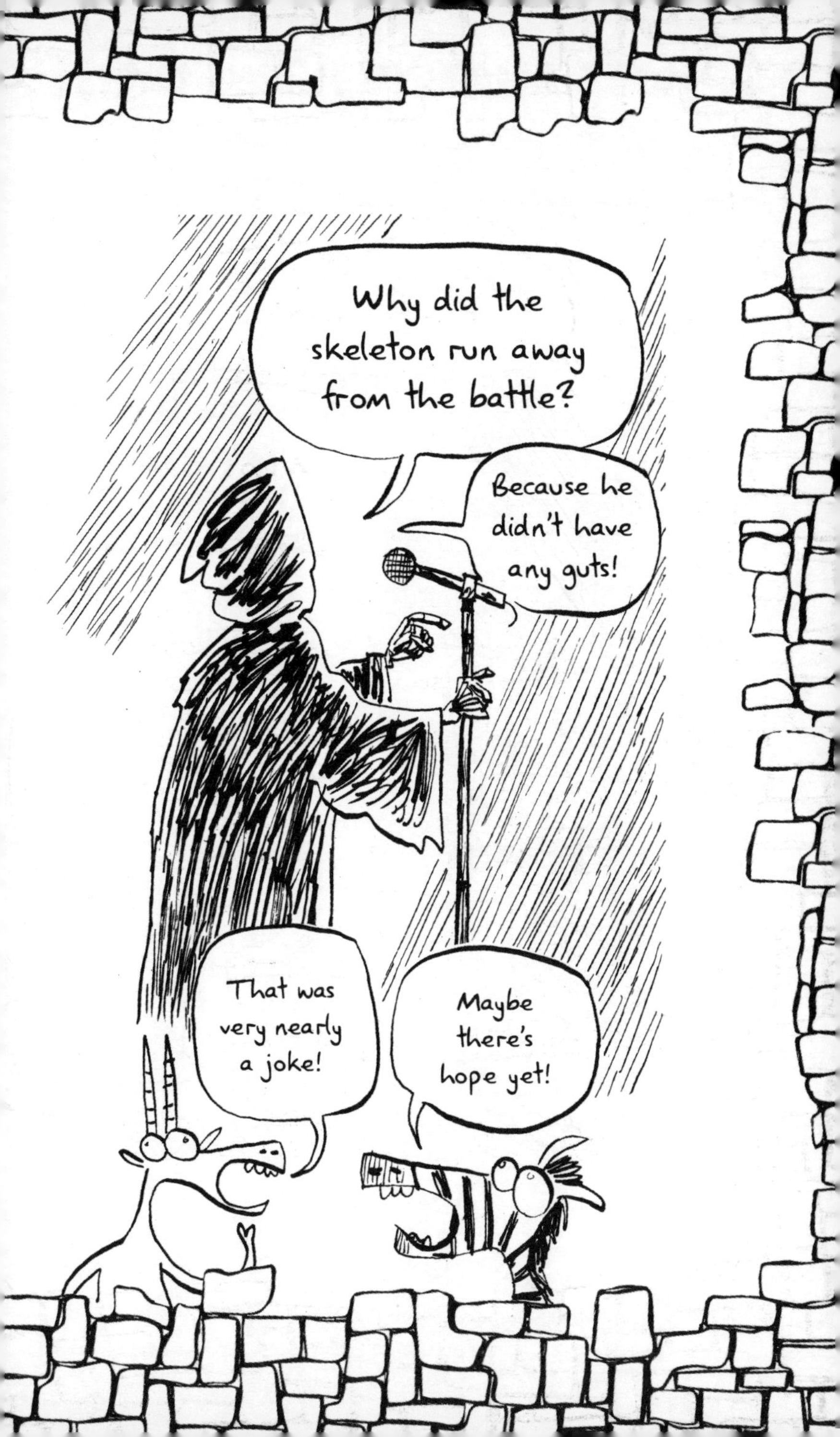
Why did the skeleton run away from the battle?
Because he didn't have any guts!
That was very nearly a joke!
Maybe there's hope yet!

EVEN MORE AMAZING JULIUS FACTS

LESSER GODS

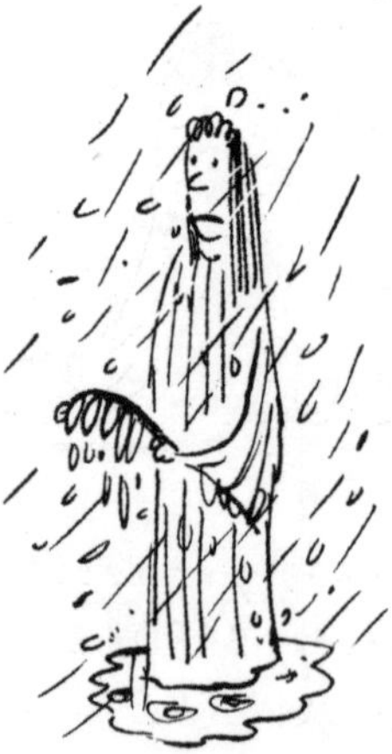

God of drizzly rain
– AESOPPY

God of tightly fitted clothes
– EURIPIDES TROUSERS

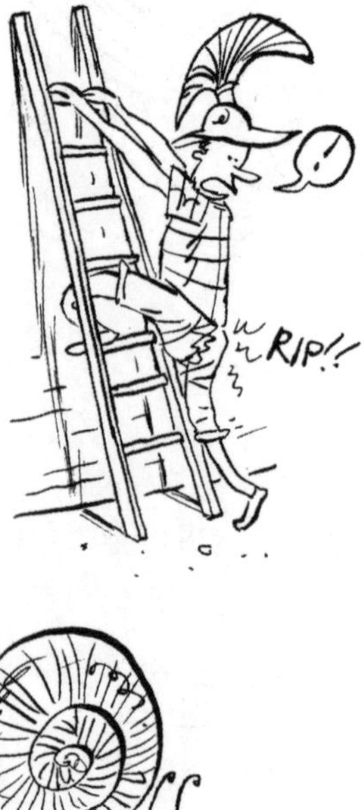
RIP!!

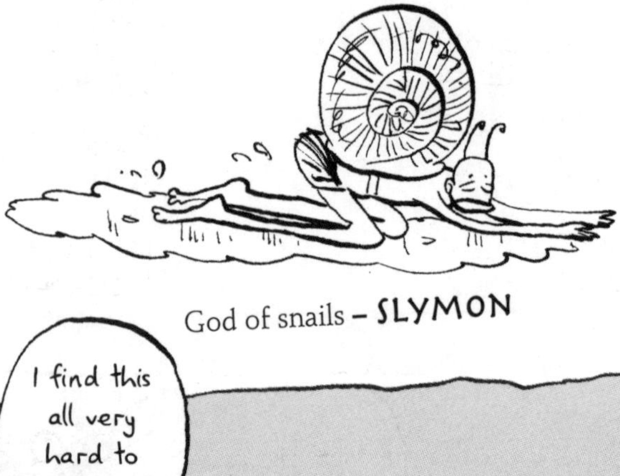

God of snails – SLYMON

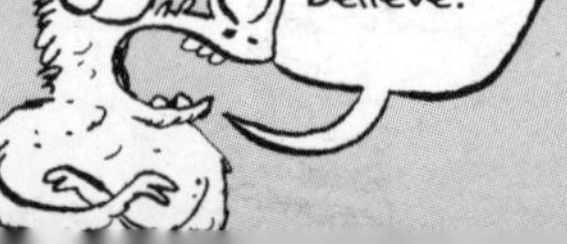
I find this all very hard to believe!

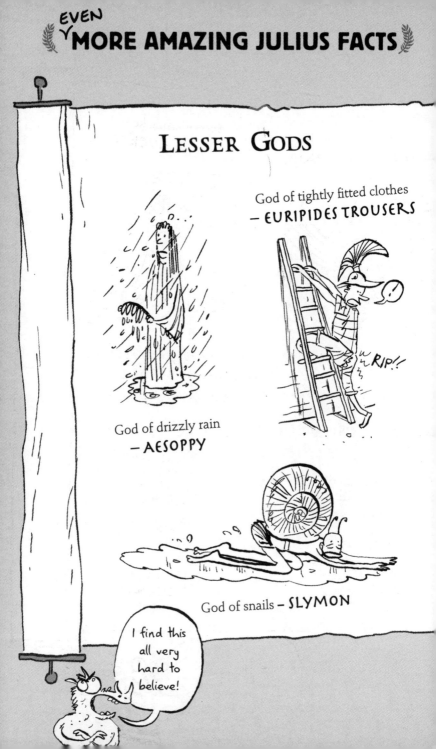

God of nice sandals
– **IONNA NICEPAIR**

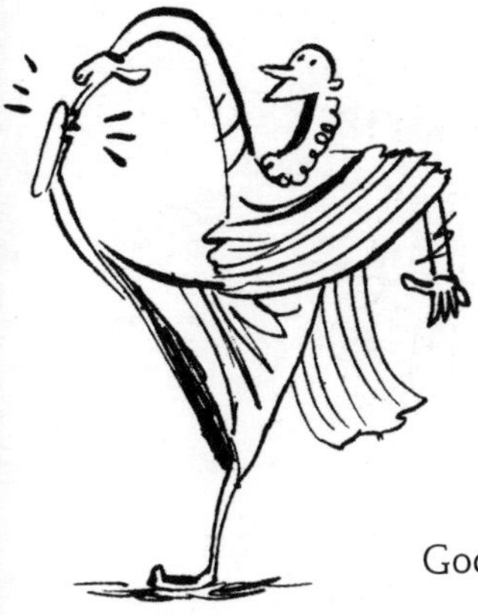

Goddess of losing keys
– **ISADORA LOCKED**

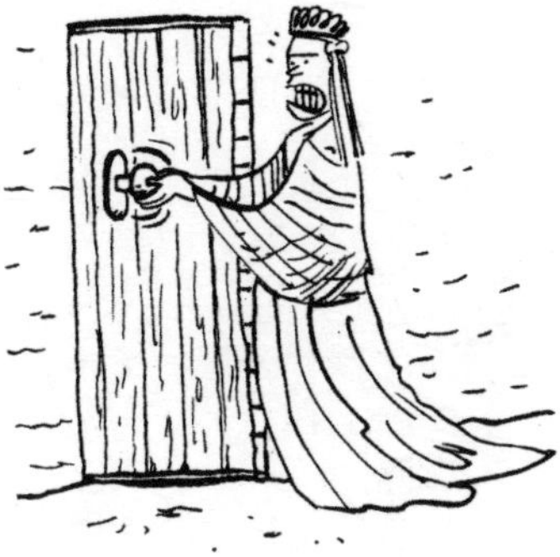

Goddess of forgetting people's names
– **ATHENA BEFORE SOMEWHERE**

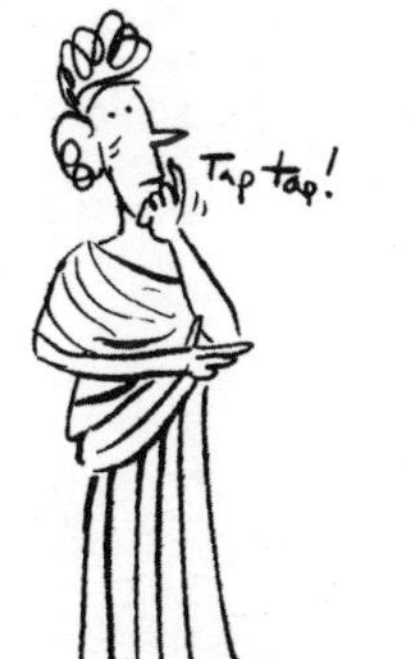
Tap tap!

Goddess of weeding
– **BACCHUS BREACHUS**

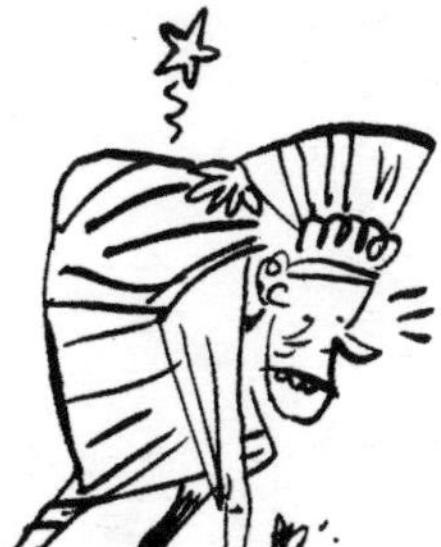

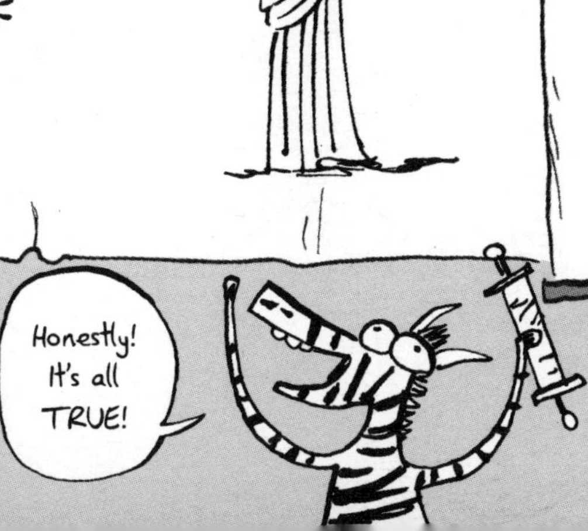
Honestly! It's all TRUE!

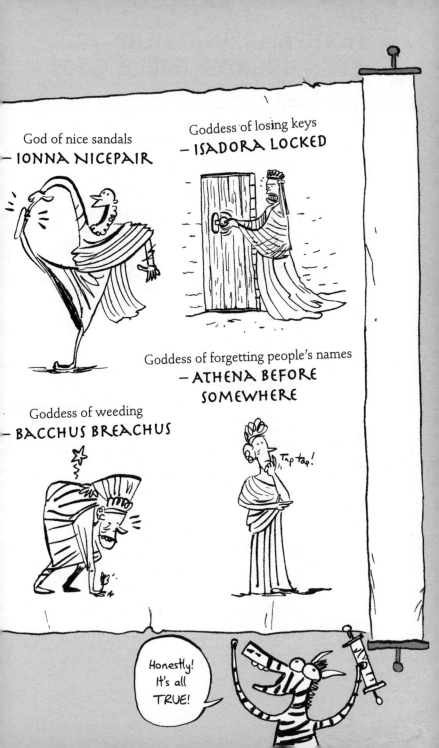

EVEN GREATER GREEK GAGS

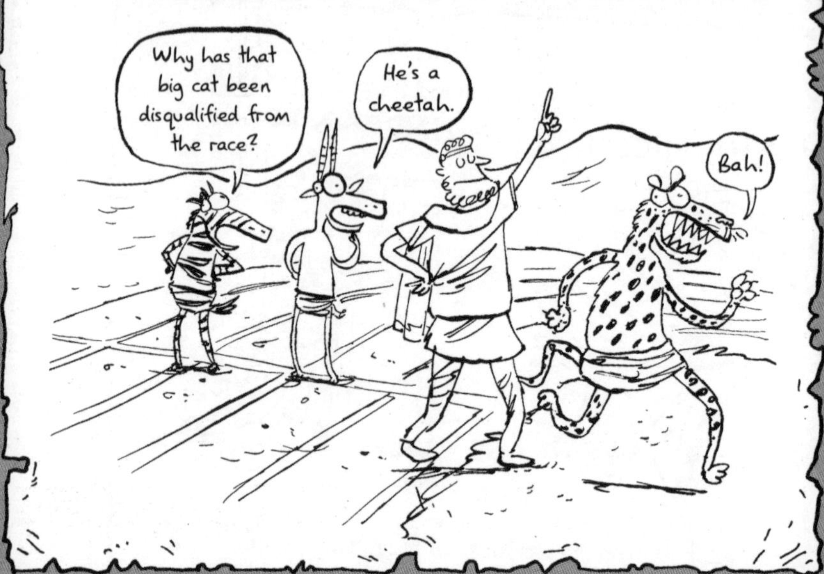
Why has that big cat been disqualified from the race?
He's a cheetah.
Bah!

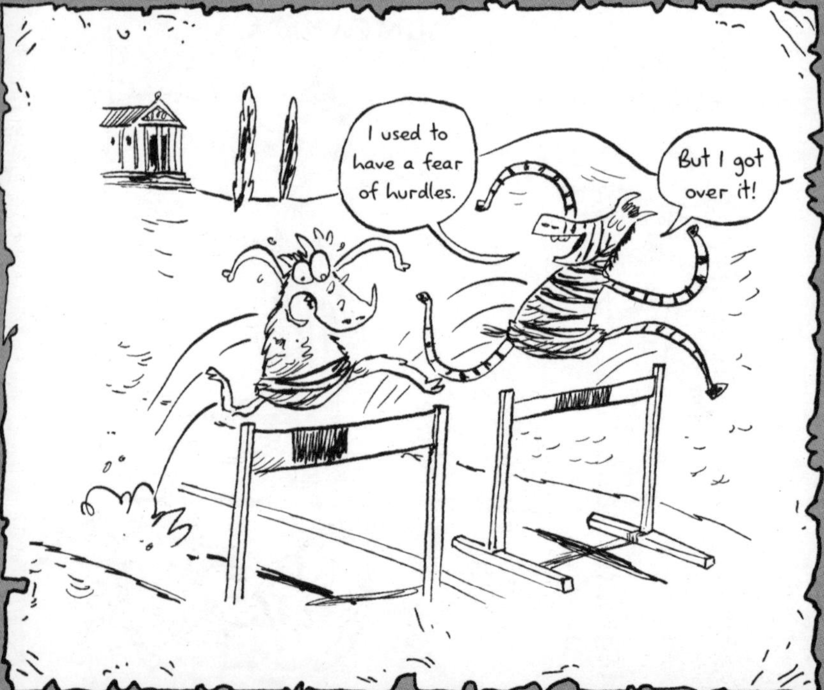
I used to have a fear of hurdles.
But I got over it!

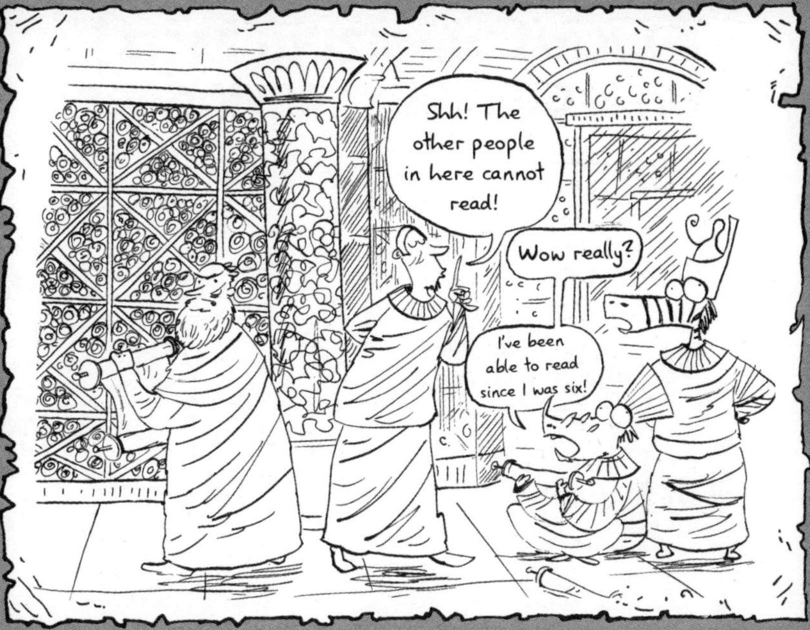
Shh! The other people in here cannot read!
Wow really?
I've been able to read since I was six!

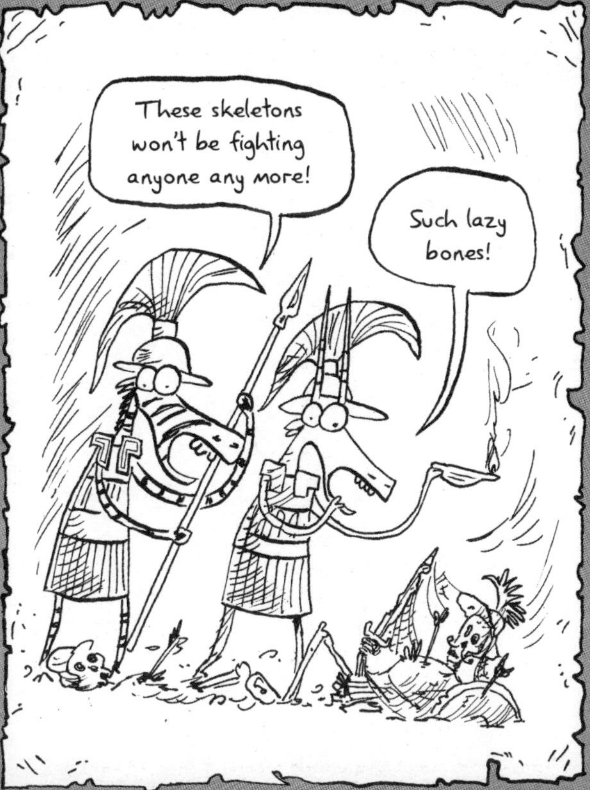
These skeletons won't be fighting anyone any more!
Such lazy bones!

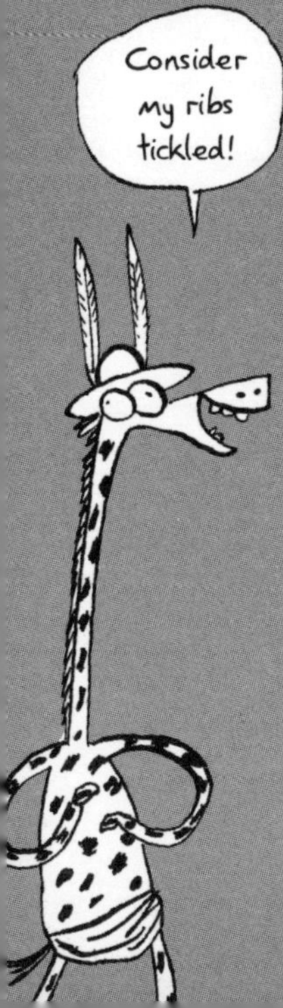
Consider my ribs tickled!

JULIUS'S AMAZING FACTS

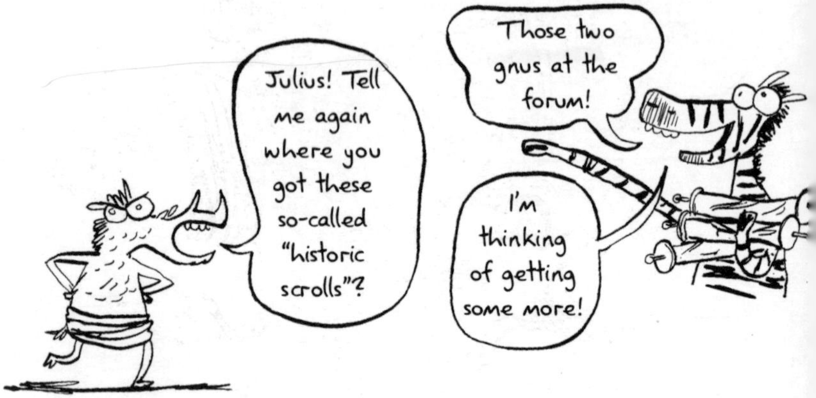
Julius! Tell me again where you got these so-called "historic scrolls"?
Those two gnus at the forum!
I'm thinking of getting some more!

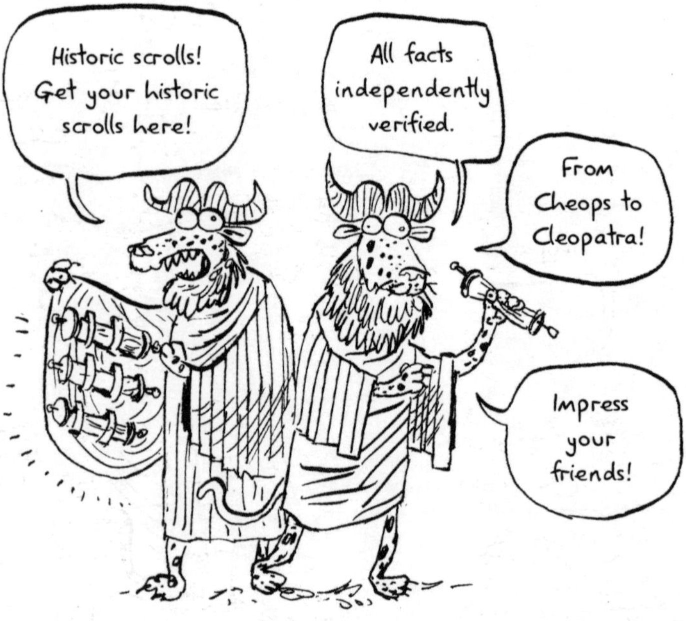
Historic scrolls! Get your historic scrolls here!
All facts independently verified.
From Cheops to Cleopatra!
Impress your friends!

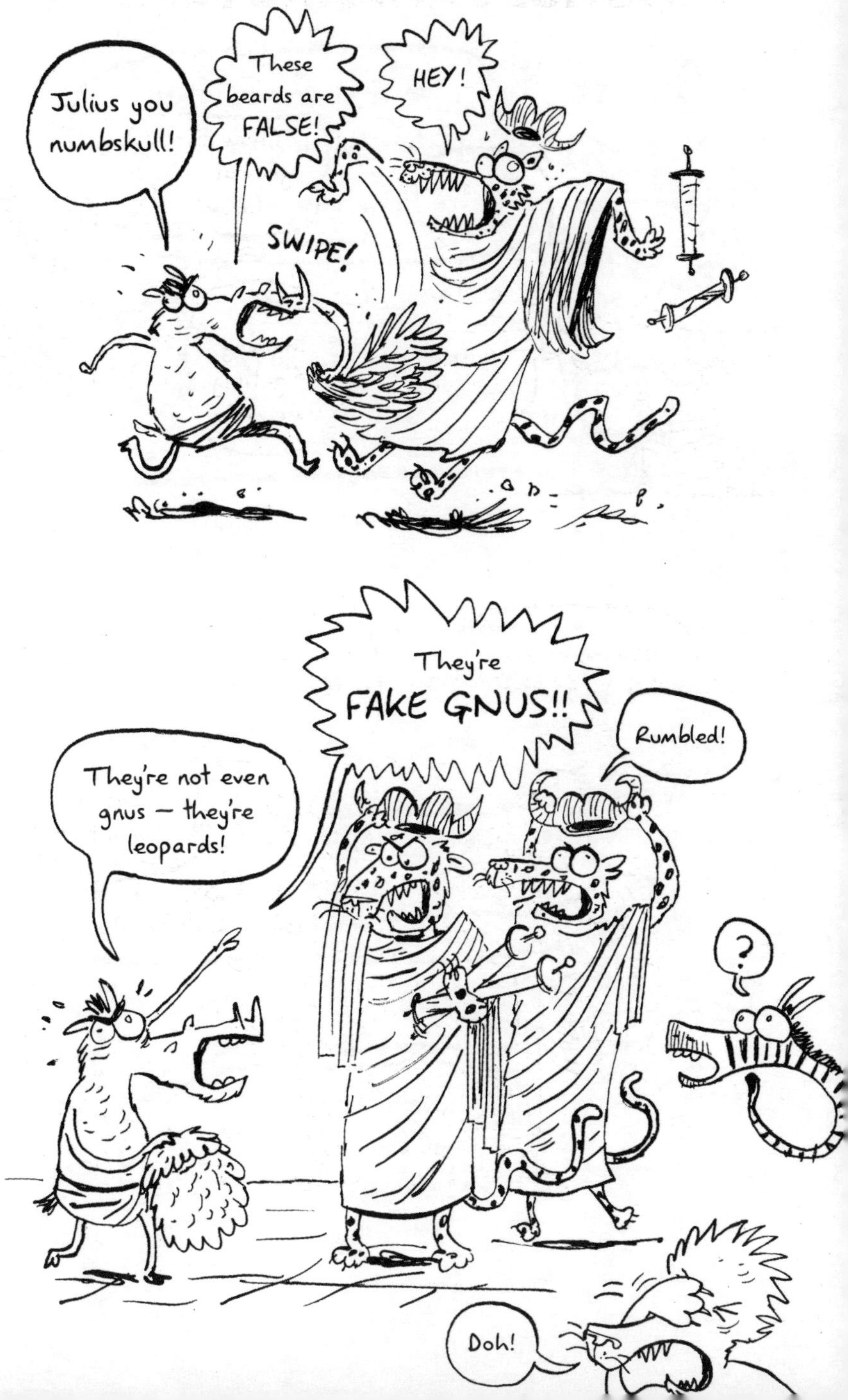
Julius you numbskull!
These beards are FALSE!
HEY!
SWIPE!
They're FAKE GNUS!!
Rumbled!
They're not even gnus – they're leopards!
?
Doh!

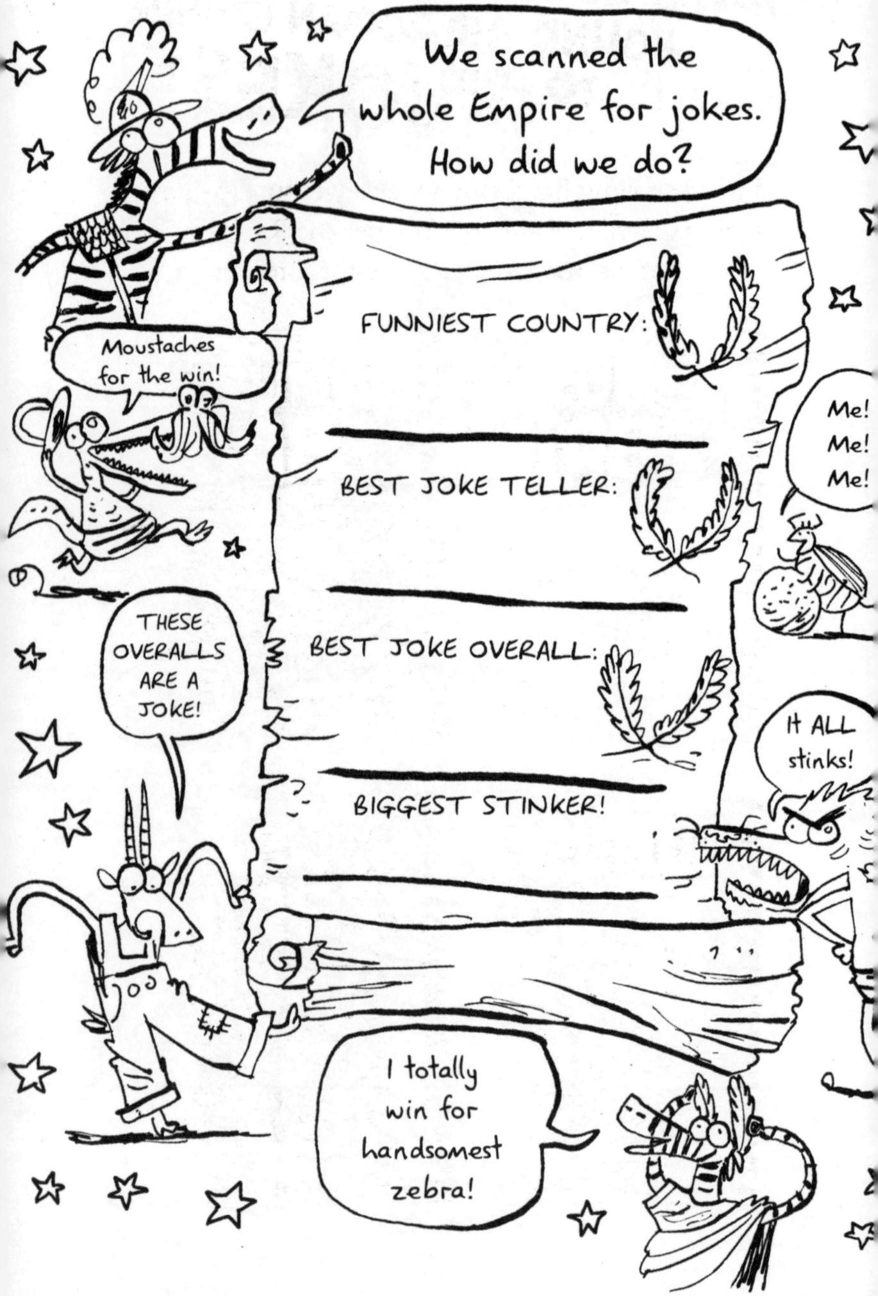
We scanned the whole Empire for jokes. How did we do?
Moustaches for the win!
FUNNIEST COUNTRY:
Me! Me! Me!
BEST JOKE TELLER:
THESE OVERALLS ARE A JOKE!
BEST JOKE OVERALL:
It ALL stinks!
BIGGEST STINKER!
I totally win for handsomest zebra!

ENJOYED TRAVELLING ROUND THE ROMAN EMPIRE TO FIND JOKES?

Why not follow Julius's previous adventures as he baffles, bewilders and bamboozles the Romans, the Britons, the Egyptians and the Greeks!

JULIUS ZEBRA
RUMBLE WITH THE ROMANS!
GARY NORTHFIELD

JULIUS ZEBRA
BUNDLE WITH THE BRITONS!
GARY NORTHFIELD

"SIDE-SPLITTINGLY FUNNY"
JULIUS ZEBRA
ENTANGLED WITH THE EGYPTIANS!
GARY NORTHFIELD

JULIUS ZEBRA
GRAPPLE WITH THE GREEKS!
GARY NORTHFIELD

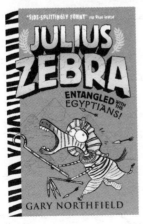

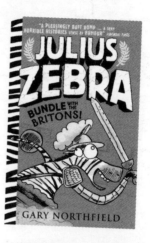

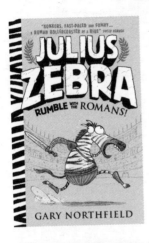

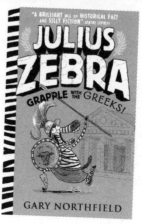

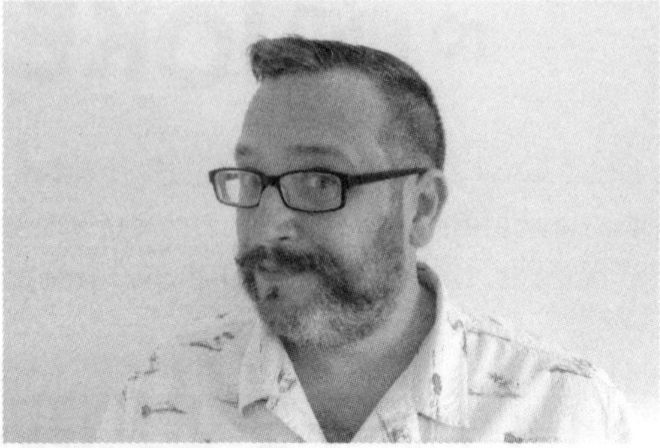

Gary Northfield is an award-winning and bestselling author and illustrator of children's books and comics. His bestselling Julius Zebra series has now been translated into fourteen languages worldwide and *Julius Zebra: Rumble with the Romans!* won the Spellbinding Book Award, voted for by children. Gary's other books include *The Terrible Tales of the Teenytinysaurs!* (Walker) and *Gary's Garden* (David Fickling), which was nominated for the British Comic Awards. Gary's work is also published in *The Beano*, *The Dandy* and *National Geographic Kids* among many other magazines. He lives with his dog Stan, partner Nicky and twins, Elsie and Arthur. Together they have launched Bog Eyed Books, a showcase for kids' comics. Find Gary online at www.garynorthfield.com, on Twitter as @gnorthfield and Instagram as @stupidmonster.

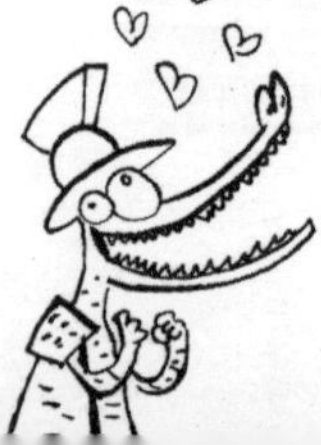

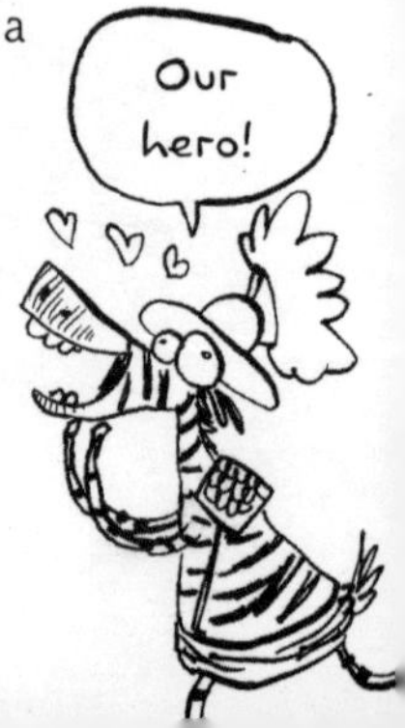
Our hero!